Vengeance on Tyneside

Vengeance on Tyneside

Agnes Lockwood Mysteries Book Three

Eileen Thornton

Copyright (C) 2019 Eileen Thornton
Layout design and Copyright (C) 2019 Creativia
Published 2019 by Creativia
Cover art by Cover Mint
Edited by Lorna Read
This book is a work of fiction. Names, characters, places, and incidents are the product of the author's imagination or are used fictitiously. Any resemblance to actual events, locales, or persons, living or dead, is purely coincidental.
All rights reserved. No part of this book may be reproduced or transmitted in any form or by any means, electronic or mechanical, including photocopying, recording, or by any information storage and retrieval system, without the author's permission.

Dedication

For my husband, Phil

Acknowlegements

With thanks to Creativia for their help in the publication of this novel.

Chapter One

Agnes Lockwood was in a good mood when she stepped off the train at Newcastle Central Station. She had spent the most delightful day at the coast, recalling the wonderful times she had spent there as a child, before her father had whisked his family abroad when he had been promoted to a new post. Now, all she wanted to do was get back to the hotel and relax in a warm bath and get dressed, before Alan – Detective Chief Inspector Alan Johnson, to give him his full title – picked her up for a dinner engagement.

Though her mind was still dwelling on the evening ahead, as she sauntered towards the station exit, she felt sure she heard a faint cry for help. She stopped and glanced around, but couldn't see anyone in any sort of distress. On the contrary, everyone seemed in good spirits; intent on getting to wherever it was they were going. However, as she continued towards the exit, where she hoped she would find a taxi, she heard the cry again, though it sounded weaker this time.

Perhaps she was allowing her over-active mind to take control. She had done that twice before in recent months and both times it had almost taken her to the point of being murdered. Maybe this time she should walk away. But when she heard the cry again, she knew she couldn't do that. Someone needed help. Looking around, she realised the sound had come from the row of rubbish bins lined up by a wall, not too far from where she was standing.

Agnes braced herself as she walked towards the bins. It could be that when she got there she would find nothing to worry about. Yet, at the same time, from past experience, she was well aware that she might find something horrifying.

Now, having reached the rubbish bins, she took a deep breath before peering behind them. For a moment, despite having prepared herself for the worst, Agnes was stunned at the sight of a young woman lying there. Her hands were clutched to her chest, desperately trying to stem the flow of blood streaming from her body and pooling on the concrete ground beneath her. Her blue eyes, wide open, were filled with terror. There were streaks of blood on her face and hair, probably from trying to brush her hair away from her eyes. One of her shoes was missing.

Lying to one side of her was a knife – but not the sort you might expect to find at the scene of a stabbing. This one looked like a penknife, though, admittedly, the blade was a little longer than any Agnes had ever seen before. Yet it still appeared to be a knife that could be folded and placed out of sight in someone's pocket.

Agnes stared down at the woman, too shocked to move. Not only because of the sheer horror of the situation, but also for another reason. She recognized this woman. She had seen her earlier in the day.

This was the woman in the red dress.

* * *

With the weather being so hot in the city, Agnes had decided to take a trip to the coast. It was likely to be much cooler there due to the breeze rolling in from the tide. She had been planning to visit the coastal area for some time, but for some reason, she hadn't yet got around to it.

Her first stopping off point had been Tynemouth. There, she had visited the remains of the Priory, which stood on the headland looking out over the North Sea. Then she had wandered along the coastline towards Cullercoats, a small village once known for its fishing community. How sad it was that the row of small white cottages facing the sea had disappeared.

Tracing her mind back down the years, she recalled the cottages had been occupied by local fishermen and their families. Usually, fish caught earlier in the day had been placed on tables set up outside the front doors of the cottages, waiting to be sold. Agnes reconciled herself with the knowledge that everything changed over the years. Nothing ever stayed the same.

Continuing on her walk, she finally reached Whitley Bay, another well-known holiday resort, only a mere ten miles from the city of Newcastle. She recalled how the beach used to be flooded with holidaymakers as far as the eye could see. Hired deck chairs and small tents, used for changing in and out of bathing costumes, had filled the scene.

Today, despite the glorious warm sunny weather, there was barely half that number of people sitting on the golden sands, which stretched from below where she was standing, right along the water's edge to St. Mary's Island in the distance. Some were playing around on the beach, while others were relaxing in the sun, topping up the tan they had probably picked up in another part of the world.

Her eyes misted, as she gazed at the long stretch of golden sands and thought back to the happy times she and her parents had spent there. If only Alan had been with her today. They could each have shared their own childhood memories of building sandcastles, darting in and out of the cold North Sea and enjoying the wonderful ice cream… and fluffy candy floss. Agnes was about to continue walking along the promenade, when two people suddenly popped into view. She recollected seeing them earlier, laughing and enjoying the day together. But they had disappeared when an overhanging rock had obstructed her view.

It had been the woman's bright red dress which had first drawn Agnes's attention to the couple, and now it had done so again. How could she miss it when it stood out so vividly against the golden sands? But what really concerned her was that the atmosphere between the couple seemed to have taken a change for the worse.

Agnes raised her binoculars to take a closer look. She had tucked them into her bag before setting out from the hotel, thinking they would be useful when looking at distant landmarks – not for invading someone's privacy. But surely one tiny peek wouldn't hurt.

No sooner had Agnes focused the lens on the couple than she saw the man grab the woman's arm. For one moment, she thought he was going to drag her off somewhere. But then the woman appeared to say something to him. Agnes was certainly too far away to hear what was said. Nor was she near enough to read the woman's lips. However, whatever she said seemed to calm him, as he released his grip and pulled his hand away.

What on earth could have happened in so short a time to cause such an upset in their relationship?

With the glasses still firmly fixed to her eyes, Agnes could tell that the woman looked younger than her male companion – maybe she was in her late teens or early twenties? It was hard to judge these days. But one thing was clear, she looked quite distressed. Maybe it was because of the way the man had grabbed at her.

But then, who wouldn't be upset about something like that, Agnes thought, as she continued to watch the couple. As far as she was concerned striking out at anyone in any shape or form was against the law. Though, on reflection, there had been a few times, just a few months ago, when she would have happily given Richard Harrison a strong punch on the nose. But he was now in prison, together with his accomplice Joe Barnes, where they were destined to spend a great number of years.

Still watching the couple, Agnes couldn't help wondering what could have happened to cause such an upset. They had looked so happy when she saw them earlier. She was still puzzling it over in her mind when the man suddenly reached out to take the woman's hand. However, it appeared she wanted nothing more to do with him as she pulled her hand away and, throwing her navy blue jacket over her shoulder, she strode off, her long, blonde hair billowing gently in the sea breeze.

Focusing her attention on the man now, Agnes saw he was wearing a jacket or a jersey with the hood pulled up over his head, which meant she was unable to see his face. She was surprised that he didn't follow his girlfriend and try to make it up with her. Instead, he stood watching her as she stomped off towards the promenade.

He waited until she was almost out of sight, before he decided to move away. Maybe he was hoping she would turn around and come back to him. If that was the case, then he must have been disappointed. Agnes was still watching him when he suddenly swung around and walked towards the steps leading to the promenade.

It was at that moment that she was able to see his face clearly for the first time. At a guess, she thought him to be in his late twenties – wasn't that a little old to be wearing a hoodie? But then, what did she know? She was from a totally different generation.

Agnes felt thoughtful as she lowered her binoculars. Hopefully, all would be well with the couple. The man had certainly looked shocked about something. Perhaps he hadn't expected her to storm off and leave him standing there. With a bit of luck, the argument would have been about something trivial and would be resolved over a coffee or a glass of wine. Though, she reminded herself, the man had grabbed the woman's arm rather sharply.

Agnes recalled how, only a few short months ago, she and Alan had had a small disagreement – well, to her mind, it had been quite a large one. But at least he hadn't struck out at her. Nevertheless, she had felt so hurt at his sudden outburst that she had almost packed her bags and left. But, for one reason or another, she had changed her mind.

Putting the whole incident from her mind, she continued to walk along the promenade. Now she could see the large white dome of the building once known as the Empress Ballroom. Even today, though it probably hadn't been used as a ballroom for many years, the name sounded very impressive. When she had mentioned her plan to visit the coast to Alan, he had warned her that she would see many changes – especially in Whitley Bay.

"The Empress Ballroom has gone," he had said. "Or, at least, that's what I heard. I gather a new restaurant and also a rather nice teashop have been installed." Though he had admitted he hadn't been there to see it for himself. She decided to take a quick peek inside and was fascinated at how, standing on the ground floor, she was able to look right up to the dome.

Back outside, she turned up Marine Avenue and onto Park Road. The smell of freshly brewed coffee wafting from a nearby café reminded her that she hadn't stopped for any refreshment since arriving on the coast. Perhaps it would be a good idea to have a coffee and something to eat, before making her way up to the Metro station, where she could catch a train back to Newcastle.

It was while Agnes was in the café, gazing through the large windows that she saw the young woman again. She was alone. It would appear the couple hadn't made it up – not yet, anyway. Perhaps the man hadn't been able to catch up with her.

Agnes was about to look away when she saw the woman glance towards the café. A moment later, she was outside the door. But, just as she was about to enter the café, the woman looked back down the road and changed her mind. In what seemed like a flash, she was gone.

Agnes scratched her head as she thought it through. Why hadn't the woman entered the café? What had she seen to put her off? However, a couple of seconds later, she knew the answer. The man she had seen arguing with the woman earlier in the day, wandered along the path outside the café.

Oh dear, she thought. *It seems the argument was pretty serious after all.*

Agnes had thought they had simply had a lover's tiff and would make it up very soon. However, that didn't appear to be the case. Nevertheless, the day was still young. Perhaps the young woman would allow him to catch up with her after she had left him to stew for a little while longer.

Finishing her coffee, Agnes left the café and headed up the road to the Metro station. By now, she had put the young couple out of her mind. Instead, she was focusing on what to wear that evening. Alan was taking her to a dinner dance at a rather fine hotel. The event was to celebrate the long service of a senior officer at the police station.

The officer, Chief Superintendent Lowes, had already been to London to receive a commendation from the powers-that-be, but the Newcastle and Northumberland Police felt they should also put on a show of their own. After all, the man was from the Northumberland area and had spent forty years in the police force.

Agnes spent the thirty minute journey to Newcastle reflecting on her day at the coast. She had enjoyed seeing everything again, even though so much had changed. At first, she had been upset at the changes, but now she had got over it. For goodness' sake, even the City of Newcastle had changed over the years and she had managed to accept it.

As the train pulled into Newcastle, Agnes turned her attention to the evening ahead.

Chapter Two

The morning had run quite smoothly for DCI Alan Johnson, allowing him and his sergeant to catch up with some paperwork. Superintendent Blake was a stickler for having all paperwork up-to-date and filed away. The superintendent had only been at the Newcastle Police Station for a few months, but already he had upset several officers due to his fixed ideas on how things ought to be done.

"Okay, that's sorted," Alan said, throwing a bunch of papers in the out-tray. "Shall we pop out for a bite to eat? It's on me."

"Aren't we supposed to file everything?" Sergeant Andrews asked.

"I just did." Alan nodded towards the tray on his desk. "It's all on the computer, anyway. If the superintendent wants it placed somewhere else, then he can pick it up and do it himself."

The sergeant looked back down at the papers on his desk and hid a broad smile.

Andrews was well aware that the DCI and Superintendent Blake didn't get on well together. Well, to be accurate, they didn't get on at all. If it had been down to Blake, Alan would have been out on his ear a couple of months ago, when they'd had words in the incident room. However, on that occasion, Chief Superintendent Lowes had sided with the DCI. Therefore there was nothing Blake could do about it. Nevertheless, they continued to look daggers at each other whenever they met.

"Well, are you coming, or are you happy to sit there and fill in more forms?" By now, Alan was pulling on his jacket.

"Yes, of course I'm coming," Andrews replied, jumping to his feet. "I'm almost done, anyway. So, boss, where are you taking me?"

He smiled as he began to list the names of a few high class restaurants in the area. However, he was sharply interrupted by the DCI.

"The pub, Andrews! Don't push your luck."

* * *

"So, are you looking forward to the dinner this evening?" Andrews asked, once their meal had been served.

They had both opted for a bowl of soup and a sandwich, mainly because of the event that evening; neither wanted to spoil their appetite.

"Yes, I am and so is Agnes. It should be an excellent evening and Lowes deserves nothing less. He's a fine officer and he's a gentleman. I'm just thankful this isn't his retirement party. I understand he plans to stay on for another couple of years."

"I suppose Superintendent Blake will take over, when the time comes," Andrews said, before taking a bite from his rather large cheese and pickle sandwich.

"I hope not," Alan replied. "Or, at least, I hope I've retired before he does."

Andrews was silent for a long moment. "Come to think of it, I don't think I would like to be at the station either, if Blakey were to take over."

"Blakey? Where did that come from?" Alan asked. But then he grinned when he recalled the old TV show, *On the Buses*. "Well, if it does work out that way, perhaps we could open our own detective agency."

"That's not a bad idea, sir," Andrews smiled. "I'm sure Mrs Lockwood would also be interested in joining the agency."

"Indeed she would. In fact, it would be difficult to keep her away," Alan replied. He paused. "Talking of Mrs Lockwood, I wonder how she's getting on? She went to the coast today to see how it looked these days."

"I think she's in for a surprise."

"A shock, more like," said Alan, downing his pint.

* * *

Back at the station, Alan had just sat down at his desk when his mobile phone rang.

"Alan, you must come quickly," Agnes said, before he had a chance to say a word.

"I don't believe it!" DCI Alan Johnson was already on his feet before Agnes had finished speaking. "That was Agnes on the phone. She's found a woman lying in a pool of blood. An ambulance is already on the way."

"Where is she? Where did she find the woman?" Sergeant Andrews asked, grabbing his jacket.

"The Central Station," Alan paused. "Get some uniformed officers over there. Once the press gets hold of this, they'll be swarming around looking for a story."

The paramedics were already attending to the victim when the DCI and his sergeant arrived at the scene. Agnes was standing nearby, wringing her hands in despair. After a quick word with the paramedics, Alan left his sergeant with them while he made his way across to Agnes.

"Are you okay?" he asked, wrapping his arm around her.

"Yes – I think so," she replied, slowly. "I..." Agnes broke off.

"I understand. It must have been a terrible shock for you to find her lying there."

"Yes, it was. But that's not the only reason." She glanced across towards the woman. "You see, I saw her earlier today – while I was at the coast."

"Did you speak to her?"

Agnes shook her head. "No, I simply saw her. She was with a man, who I took to be her boyfriend. They were walking along the beach at the time."

"How can you be sure it's the same woman?"

"Because of her red dress," said Agnes. "It stood out against the golden sands. Actually, I've seen her three times in all today, if you include my finding her here."

"Do you see the boyfriend now?" Alan waved his hand in the direction of the gathering crowd.

"No," she replied, after glancing at the faces nearby. "I don't see him, though he could still be lurking around somewhere. They'd had a bit of an argument – well, perhaps it was a big argument," she added, thoughtfully. "Because she stomped off and left him standing on the beach. When he did decide to move, he walked off in a different direction. Though, on reflection, the last time I saw him, I got the impression he could be following her."

"So you saw them both after the episode on the beach?"

"Yes."

"Where was that?"

"It was outside a café. I was inside having a coffee, when I saw the woman. She was alone. I thought she was going to come in, as there were a couple of empty tables. But she must have changed her mind as she hurried away. A few moments later, I saw the man. My guess was that he was following her."

Agnes fell silent as she thought through her last sentence. Was it possible that this man killed her?

"Is there a chance that this man might have spotted you while you were watching them?" Alan asked.

"No, I was up on the promenade looking down at them. I doubt he even knew I was there."

It was at that point that Andrews joined them. "The paramedics are ready to take her to hospital."

"Will she be alright?" Agnes asked.

"They don't know." Andrews glanced towards the ambulance crew as he spoke. By now they were lifting the stretcher into the ambulance. "It seems she's lost a lot of blood. But they won't know the full extent of her injuries until they get her to hospital. They did manage to get her name, address and her parents' address." He looked down at his notebook. "Wendy Hamilton – she rents a flat in Byker. Her parents live in Wallsend. She isn't wearing a wedding ring, so we can assume she isn't married."

"If only I had left the café earlier, I might have caught the train she was on and seen whoever did this to her," Agnes said, wistfully. She glanced at the ambulance crew. "Do you think I should go with her to the hospital?"

"Agnes, I think you have done everything you can for Miss Hamilton," Alan replied, quietly, but firmly.

"All I did was call for an ambulance. Surely, anyone who found her would have done that."

"But no one else found her. No one heard her call out for help except you – or if they did, they didn't respond." Alan paused. "Besides, I need you to make a statement about what you saw this afternoon. Perhaps you could even help one of our officers create a picture of the man you saw on the beach."

Alan wanted to keep Agnes from going anywhere near the hospital. His main concern was that the man who had tried to kill Wendy Hamilton might go there to try again. He was planning to have a uniformed officer outside her room for that very reason. But there was more to it than that. He wasn't totally convinced that Wendy's boyfriend hadn't already spotted Agnes watching them earlier in the day.

If she had recognised the young woman simply because of her red dress, it was possible the man might have noticed the rather striking blue skirt Agnes was wearing. If he *was* responsible for trying to murder the young woman, he might also believe it necessary to kill Agnes. Now, he needed to get her away from here before the press arrived. The last thing he wanted was her picture to be spread all over the newspapers.

"Yes, I suppose you're right," Agnes replied. "It's just that I feel I could have done more for her."

Chapter Three

The evening was in full swing. The meal was over and the formal speeches had been made. Now, it was time to relax and enjoy the second half of the evening. At one end of the room, a band was setting up their instruments on the small stage. Very shortly, they would be ready to play the first waltz.

Agnes took the opportunity of a lull in the conversation, to glance around at the other guests. Everyone had made the effort to look their best for the occasion. Even Detective Constable Smithers, who usually wore extremely well-worn outfits, was very smartly attired in a dark grey suit and a bow tie. Perhaps he had hired them. She had heard that it wasn't in his nature to rush out and buy something special for a function. Before his divorce, his wife almost had to drag him by his ear to the shops when he needed a new suit.

Agnes turned her attention back to the other four people seated around their table. It had been a foregone conclusion that Detective Sergeant Michael Andrews and his rather attractive fiancée, Sandra, would be joining them. Agnes had met Sandra a few times now. They had even been shopping together in the Eldon Square Shopping Mall. However, she had been a little surprised when Alan suggested Detective Constable John Morris and his latest girlfriend, Laura, should also sit with them.

Though Alan had never actually told her the full story, Agnes was aware he hadn't got on too well with the young man, due to something that had happened in the incident room a few months ago. However, it seemed all that had been swept under the carpet since Morris's fine job of undercover work at the hotel.

Agnes looked at Laura and smiled to herself. According to Alan, Morris seemed to have a new woman on his arm almost every week. How long would this one last?

"Would you like to dance?"

Alan interrupted her thoughts. The band had begun to play and already some of the guests had taken to the floor.

"Yes, thank you, Alan."

"So what were you thinking?" Alan asked, once they were on the floor. "You looked so deep in thought, I was a little reluctant to disturb you."

Agnes smiled. "I was wondering why you'd invited Morris to join us at our table – and before you start apologizing, I don't have a problem with it. In fact, I quite like him. It's simply because I understand the two of you got off to a bad start."

Alan glanced across to Morris before he spoke. "Yes, we did. But, looking back, I wondered whether I was a little hard on him at the time, so I thought I would ask him to join us this evening. You know – lighten the mood a little."

Agnes giggled.

"What's so funny?"

"You thought that inviting the young man and his latest girlfriend to join his superior officer at this function, when he could be with his friends at another table – would lighten the mood?" Agnes shook her head. "Oh Alan, you are priceless."

Alan didn't reply immediately. Instead, he glanced around the large room. The tables, which had been neatly set for six persons when they arrived for the dinner, had been pulled together now that the formalities were over. Friends wanted to join each other for the rest of the evening and, judging from the laughter, it seemed everyone was in good spirits.

Morris, on the other hand, was looking a little subdued.

Vengeance on Tyneside

"I wasn't thinking straight," Alan muttered, looking back at Agnes. "I thought I was doing the right thing."

Alan and Agnes were returning to their table just as Morris and Laura were taking to the floor.

"John," Alan said. "I've just noticed that the rest of the crew is grouped together over there." He pointed across the room. "Perhaps you might like to introduce them to Laura."

"Yes, thank you, I will," Morris replied.

"That was very neatly done," Agnes said, once they were seated.

"Thank you." Alan grinned. "You see, I *can* get it right sometimes." He looked at his sergeant. "What about you? Would you like to join the fun crowd?"

"I think we'll pass," Andrews laughed. "We're into the more sedate crowd at the moment."

"Thank you, Andrews – I think."

* * *

It was nearing the end of the evening, when Alan felt a tap on his shoulder. He looked around to find Superintendent Blake standing behind him.

"Can we have a word?"

Alan nodded and followed the superintendent across the room towards the door.

"I've just heard that the woman found in the Central Station earlier today died a short while ago," Blake said, once they were on their own. "They did everything they could to help her and, for a while, they thought she might pull through. But it wasn't to be." He paused. "This is now a murder investigation."

After a brief discussion, the superintendent went to rejoin his wife.

"What was that all about?" Agnes asked, the moment Alan reappeared.

Alan beckoned for Andrews to lean forward so he could also hear what he had to say. He quickly told them what had happened. "I gather the young woman wasn't able give any information as to who had stabbed her." He glanced at Agnes briefly before he continued. "All we have to go on at the moment is what Agnes has told us."

"If only I had found her earlier," Agnes said, quietly. "She looked so young – she had her whole life ahead of her."

"We went through all that earlier. You did all you could."

"I know, but, what if…"

"No buts or what ifs, Agnes. We are now looking at a case of murder." Alan looked at the dance floor; they were playing a waltz. "In the meantime, let's dance before they start playing all that pop music again."

Chapter Four

The following morning, the newspapers all led with the story of how a young woman by the name of Wendy Hamilton had been found with a stab wound at Newcastle Central Station. However, the news of her death had come too late for the national papers. Only the local daily newspaper carried the update.

Agnes bought a selection of newspapers from the small shop in the hotel reception to read while having breakfast. She was relieved to find that none of them contained a photograph of her. When she had called Alan after finding the victim at the Central Station, he had told her to stand well back until he arrived. She had understood his concern; on two occasions in the last eight months, she had been in the wrong place at the wrong time.

Nevertheless, she hadn't been too far away. She had stayed close by Wendy until the ambulance arrived. There was no way she was going to leave the young woman on her own. Even then, she had felt bad about stepping out of her line of sight. For heaven's sake, hers had been the only friendly face the poor woman had seen since someone had thrust a knife into her. But now, looking back, maybe Alan had been right to be cautious. What if the person who wielded the knife had still been loitering around somewhere in the crowd? And, what if the killer *had* been the man she had seen with Wendy earlier in the day?

Despite her earlier thoughts that the man on the beach couldn't have seen her, Agnes had to admit that it *was* possible he might have glanced up towards the promenade and spotted her looking down at them. She now understood Alan's concern that the man could have noticed her in much the same way she had spotted Wendy Hamilton; by what she was wearing. Agnes clutched her throat, recalling the vivid blue skirt she had chosen to wear that day. At the time, it was because it had almost matched the cloudless sky, but now it seemed it might not have been such a good idea.

It was while these thoughts were mulling through her mind that her eyes were suddenly drawn to someone in one of the photographs. Unfortunately, the face was partly hidden as the person had a hood pulled up over his head. Also, to make matters worse, he was tucked behind others in the group. Either he was unable to get any closer to the camera, or he didn't want to be identified. Nevertheless, Agnes couldn't help thinking it was the same man she had seen with the woman on the beach. She leaned forward to take a closer look, but the picture was too small to make out much detail. However, there was one thing about him that she was certain about; the hoodie was the same colour as the one worn by the man on the beach.

* * *

The morning hadn't gone well for DCI Alan Johnson. Though, having been a detective for several years and a member of the Military Police before that, he should already have been well aware that everything doesn't simply fall into place during a murder inquiry. Nevertheless, he had hoped the victim's parents might have been able to give the detectives a lead as to where to begin the investigation.

Who she had been meeting that day would have been a start. Yet, they had no idea as to who she was seeing or where she had been going. It had been news to them that she had been seen on the beach with a man at Whitley Bay prior to her death.

"Don't kids talk to their parents anymore?" Alan said, as he paced up and down the floor of his office. "For goodness' sake, my father wanted to know where I was going, who I'd be with and what time I would be home, before I was allowed out of the house!"

"Times have changed, sir." Andrews shrugged. "You need to keep up." The sergeant moved his face closer to his computer screen to hide a grin.

"Don't I know it?" Alan retorted. He stopped pacing and looked across towards Andrews. "And you can wipe that smile off your face!"

"Sorry, sir."

Alan moved over to his desk and slumped down into his chair. He sat quietly for a few minutes before he spoke.

"Do I seem old to you?" He pulled a face and shook his head. "Forget it," Alan said, before his sergeant had a chance to reply.

He picked up his pen and looked down at his diary.

"It's just that I've been running a few things through my mind lately," he mumbled.

But, after a moment, Alan heaved a sigh and threw down the pen.

"What I mean is – do I behave like someone older than my years?"

Andrews sat back in his chair and thought for a moment or two. He was aware that whatever he said would be the wrong answer.

"Well," he said, after a long moment, "maybe it's just that you're a little too set in your ways." He paused. "Anyway, what brought all this on?"

"Set in my ways?" Alan stroked his chin, thoughtfully. "Yes, I suppose I am... a *little* set in my ways." He looked across at Andrews. "But not too much. I do have an open mind!"

"Yes, of course you do, sir. But like I said, what's brought all this on?"

Alan sighed. "It's some of the things Mrs Lockwood says. Oh, she's probably fooling me around, but sometimes I wonder whether she might see me as..." He broke off, seeking the right words.

"A bit of a stick-in-the-mud?" The words tumbled from the sergeant's mouth before he could stop them.

"I wouldn't have put it quite like that, Sergeant," Alan retorted.

"Sorry, sir," Andrews apologized, for the second time.

Not knowing what to say next, the sergeant was thankful to see Morris stick his head around the door.

"Sir, the front desk has just phoned up to say that Mrs Lockwood is downstairs," he said, looking at the DCI. "She says she needs to have a word."

Chapter Five

After she finished her breakfast, Agnes made her way out of the dining room and across to the receptionist to enquire whether there was a magnifying glass she could borrow. She hoped that if the photograph in the paper was magnified, she might get a better view of the man's face. However, though a glass was found, it didn't help much. All it did was make the photo look rather grainy; most likely due to it already having been reproduced in the newspaper.

She looked at the picture again. The only other option was to see the original picture. But would the newspaper take her seriously? Perhaps if Alan were to request a copy to be sent to the police station, they would oblige. For a moment, Agnes debated whether to phone him with the news or simply turn up at his office. Once she had made up her mind, she grabbed her jacket and set off to the taxi rank.

* * *

Now, upstairs in the DCI's office, Agnes showed Alan the photo in the newspaper and explained the reason for her visit.

"So that's why I really need to see the original photo. It's the only way I can be absolutely certain that this is the man I saw with the young woman." She paused for a moment. "I was useless when I was trying to describe the man to your officer, but now, maybe I can make up for it. However, I thought if I were to approach the newspaper they might refuse, but surely they wouldn't refuse a DCI."

"Agnes, if you had gone to the local newspaper with this information, they would have welcomed you with open arms," Alan replied, his eyes still fixed on the photo. "It would have been a great scoop for them." He looked across towards her. "I can almost see the headlines – 'Woman sees a suspect in the murder of Wendy Hamilton in local paper'. No doubt they would have wanted to emblazon the front page with the story."

He glanced up at Andrews who was still staring down at the picture.

"However," he continued, "and I think Andrews will agree with me, I don't believe that would have been a good idea. It might well have put you in a dangerous position – especially if the man in the photo is guilty of the young woman's murder."

Andrews nodded. "If this is our killer and he's still in the area, then he'll be watching his back – reading all the newspapers to make sure no one will point him out."

"But you can still request the photo, can't you?" Agnes said, looking back at Alan. "I'm sure you could come up with some reasonable explanation for wanting to see it."

"Yes, we can and we will. I was simply trying to make you aware of the danger you might have put yourself in, if you'd gone to the newspaper."

"Okay, Alan, I get it." She gave them both a broad smile. "Now, when do I get to see the photo?"

* * *

"Does Mrs Lockwood really get it?" Andrews asked the DCI, once Agnes had left the building.

Alan had called a taxi and escorted her downstairs, leaving his sergeant to phone the newspaper office requesting copies of all photographs taken at the Central Station the previous day. Now he was back in his office.

"Yes, she does," Alan replied, lowering himself into his chair. "But she tends to make light of anything that involves her safety. Nevertheless, I can assure you, she'll be thinking through everything we said while on her way back to the hotel." He paused. "You got through to the newspaper okay?"

"Yes, we should have the photos within the hour. Whoever it was I spoke to sounded very keen."

"I bet they were!"

* * *

In the taxi on the way back to the hotel, Agnes considered what had been said at the police station. Alan and his sergeant were right; the newspaper would have shown a picture of her in several editions over the next few days. It would make great news for them, but at what cost to her? Her life?

She was beginning to wonder whether she was seeking out cases of murder – or were they lining up for her? Either way, there was one thing she was sure of; she would never look the other way.

Before she left the station, Alan had told her that he, or one of his officers, would bring the photo to the hotel the moment they received it. He had even promised to include a blown-up copy of the photo to make it easier to view. Now, all she had to do was to wait for it to arrive.

But waiting, for whatever reason, had never been a strong point with Agnes. She sighed as the taxi pulled to a halt outside the hotel. However, with so little to go on, what else was there for her to do?

Chapter Six

Agnes hung around the hotel, waiting for the photographs to arrive. As it turned out, it was Alan himself who brought them.

"I can't stay long," he told her. "As you can imagine, everyone is a little on edge at the moment. The body of Wendy Hamilton and the clothes she was wearing are with Doctor Nichols and his team and we are hoping to hear from him very soon. With a bit of luck, they'll find traces of DNA from her killer."

Agnes nodded.

"Anyway, here are the photographs," Alan said, handing her the pictures. "Take a look and tell me whether you think this is the man you saw with the victim."

Agnes took a long look at the copy of the photo she had first seen in the newspaper. The picture was much clearer than the reproduction in the paper and she instantly recognised the man she had seen on the beach. A swift glance at the enlarged version merely confirmed it. But there was something about the man, which disturbed her, though she couldn't put her finger on what it was.

"It's him," she said at last. "That's definitely the man I saw on the beach with Wendy Hamilton." She looked back up at Alan. "So, where do we go from here?"

"*We?*" Alan grinned.

"Let's not go through all that again," Agnes smiled. "But, if you insist, may I remind you that you wouldn't even have that face to go on if…"

"Okay, okay." Alan held up his hands. "I'll keep you in the loop."

"Is that a promise?" She gave him a sideways glance as she spoke.

"Yes, it's a promise."

He rose to his feet. "But now I must go. I really need to pass on the information you've given me."

"Can I keep these," Agnes held up the photographs.

She wanted time to think about what it was about the man that had caught her attention.

"I don't see why not," Alan replied. "We still have the originals at the station and now that you've confirmed this is the man you saw, we'll be printing off more copies. Why do you want them, anyway?"

"Oh. No particular reason." She shrugged and swiftly changed the subject. "With this new case, do you think you'll be able to get away in time for the concert at the Sage this evening?"

"I should damn well hope so," he replied. "I'm also planning to be here in time for dinner, too, just as we arranged."

* * *

Once Alan had left, Agnes hurried upstairs to her room. She needed time to look closely at the photographs and find out what it was that had troubled her. She poured herself a glass of wine and sat down at the table by the window and spent a few minutes staring down at the river. There was something about watching the water flowing gently beneath the window that seemed to help to clear her head.

Turning her attention back to the photographs, she stared closely at them. What was it about the pictures that had disturbed and alerted her? Then it suddenly came to her. All the people in the photo were looking towards where the paramedics were attending to the young woman; all, that is, except the suspect. His eyes appeared to be focused on something else. What had grabbed his attention? Surely, if he was innocent of the crime, he would have pushed his way through to reach his girlfriend, rather than standing at the back of the crowd?

But perhaps he didn't realise the person needing medical attention was his girlfriend? Agnes recalled that the last time she saw them both, Wendy Hamilton appeared to be trying to avoid him. Therefore, if he had wandered around the streets of Whitley Bay for a while, he could have arrived on a much later train. That would mean he had no idea who the medics were attending to. But, and it was a big but, if this man knew it was Wendy, because it was he who had stabbed her, then why on earth was he still hovering around the scene? Surely he would have scarpered as far away as possible?

She heaved a sigh. It certainly was food for thought. But, it still didn't answer her first question – what or who was this man looking at when the photo was taken? Still puzzling it over in her mind, she stood up and moved across to the window. The sun was shining down onto the Millennium Bridge, where a group of tourists were making their way towards the Baltic Art Gallery. No doubt, they would also be visiting the Sage before they left. Perhaps some of them had even booked for the concert that evening.

Turning back to the table to pick up her glass of wine, her eyes fell on the enlarged photograph. Now, seeing the man's face from this angle, she got the strange impression that he was looking at her. For a moment, she thought it was a trick of the light. But as she leant in closer from the same angle, the man's eyes still appeared to be resting on her.

She sat down and picked up the two photographs to study them once again. This time, she tried to focus her attention on where the picture had been taken. However, she found it difficult as she was unable to see much of the background, due to the group taking up most of the shot.

Nevertheless, after staring at the small space above the people's heads for a few minutes, Agnes was able to make out the sign of a coffee bar which she recalled seeing while standing near to where she had found the woman. It was just after the ambulance arrived and she was waiting for Alan. At least that was a start. Maybe if she looked hard enough, she would find something else to determine what the man was looking at. She stared down at the photo for a few more minutes and, just as she was about to give up, something on the left edge of the picture caught her eye. She picked up the photo and moved over to the window to take a closer look.

Despite there only being a small part of the person visible, she realised it was the man who had been selling the early edition of the local newspaper. She remembered seeing him holding up the newspapers to attract the attention of the commuters. Realizing that was all the information she was going to achieve from the photo, she began to re-run the events at the scene through her mind.

Once the ambulance men arrived, she recalled several groups of people hovering around the scene. Therefore, why had the photographer chosen this particular group to focus his camera on? But then, Agnes quickly dismissed that question. The photographer had probably taken several shots of the people gathered around the scene. It was probably the editor of the newspaper who had chosen which picture would go on the front page. So that was a dead end.

Agnes turned her thoughts to the other things she could see in the photograph and moved her hands around in the air as she played out the scene in her mind. The coffee bar was directly behind the group and the newspaper seller was to the left of the picture – almost out of shot, but not quite! He had been a short distance to her left, which meant...

Agnes swung around and grabbed the photograph from the table, hoping to prove that her last thought was out of the question. But all it did was confirm she was right. The man in the photo had been looking at her when the picture was taken. She suddenly felt the need to sit down.

She was on the verge of calling Alan to inform him of what she had discovered from the photographs, but then dismissed the idea. He would only start worrying about her and suggest she move away from the area until the police were able to talk to this man. They had gone through all that palaver on another case she had got herself involved in, only a few months previously. There was no way she wanted to start it all off again.

Anyway, just because the man happened to be looking at her, it didn't mean he recognized her from earlier in the day. It was possible he had simply seen someone standing nearby out of the corner of his eye and glanced across just as the cameraman took the shot.

She shook her head. Even to her, that sounded like a longshot. But it was one she was going to go along with – at least as far as Alan was concerned.

* * *

The DCI had given a briefing in the incident room and was now on his way back to the office he shared with his sergeant. He had instructed that more copies of the photographs should be printed and handed out to all the detectives.

"It is imperative that we find this man as quickly as possible and talk to him about his relationship with Wendy Hamilton," he had told them.

He had gone on to inform them of how the man had been seen by a reliable witness arguing with the victim in Whitley Bay only a few hours before she was found stabbed in the Central Station.

"The man might be totally innocent of the crime," he had continued. "He could simply have arrived back in Newcastle on a later train and had no idea who was being attended to. However, at this stage, we can't rule him out of our inquiries."

Alan had almost reached the office when Sergeant Andrews caught up with him. Andrews had stayed behind to hand out the photographs and answer any further questions. "At least we have somewhere to start, thanks to Mrs Lockwood," he said, holding up the photograph. "This man might hold some answers."

Alan entered the office and sat down. "Yes," he said thoughtfully.

The sergeant glanced at the photo. "Are you having second thoughts? Do you think she might have made a mistake?"

"No, no, it's nothing like that. Agnes is absolutely certain this is the same man she saw on the beach." Alan paused. "No, it's just that when she asked whether she could keep the photos, I had a feeling there was something she wasn't telling me."

Andrews glanced at the pictures again. "There's not much else to see," he said. "The group takes up most of the picture. There isn't anyone else visible. So what else could she have seen?" He looked up. "Didn't you ask her about it at the time?"

"Yes, I did, but by then the subject had changed to the concert this evening. It was only after I left the hotel that I really began to think about it." He shook his head. "Maybe it's just me. Perhaps I worry about her too much."

"You never know, she might mention it this evening. If not, you could possibly broach the subject again – in a firm tone."

Alan shifted uneasily in his chair. To him, that didn't sound a good idea. The last time he had been firm with Agnes, he had gone way over the top. Even his sergeant had commented on his brusque tone. Obviously, Andrews had forgotten about that.

At the time, Agnes had been so hurt by his outburst that she'd been on the verge of packing her bags and leaving Tyneside. That was the last thing Alan wanted. She was the love of his life, for heaven's sake. All he had wanted to do was protect her from the two scheming men the police were investigating at the time. But he had been way out of line by ordering her to go to her room as though she were a child. Agnes was a grown woman, with a mind of her own. He had apologized and their relationship had recovered. Only recently, they had talked about buying a house together. But with Agnes not keen on the idea of moving too far away from the quayside, they were still looking out for something to suit them both. Though, truthfully, he would be happy to settle for whatever she wanted. In the meantime, he was spending a great deal of time sharing her room at the hotel. Therefore, the last thing he wanted to do now was to upset everything by taking a firm tone.

Alan's thoughts were interrupted when the phone on his desk rang.

"That was the lab. Doctor Nichols is on his way over," Alan said, as he replaced the receiver. "He has some news about Wendy Hamilton."

Chapter Seven

"What do you have for us, Keith?" Alan asked, the moment Doctor Nichols stepped into the office.

"Give me a chance to sit down," Keith said.

"Sorry." Alan gestured towards the chair in front of his desk. "It's just that one of your staff gave me the impression you had learned something really important to the case."

Keith closed his eyes and shook his head, as he lowered himself into the chair.

"That would be Janice, the latest member of our team. She's a lovely lady and very keen about her new position. However, she does tend to over-dramatize things a little."

"So, you don't have any further information?" Alan glanced at his sergeant.

His disappointment was clear to Andrews. Before Doctor Nichols arrived, they had both believed the pathologist must have found something really fundamental to their case, otherwise why would he have taken the trouble to come here in person?

"Then why have you rushed over here?" Alan added, returning his attention to the pathologist.

"I didn't *rush* over here, as you put it," Doctor Nichols replied, emphasizing the word 'rush'. "It just so happens that I'm due at a meeting in this area shortly, so I thought I would stop by and drop off my preliminary report on the way." He pulled a folder out of his briefcase.

"But by the way, nor did I say I didn't have any information. It's just that what I do have won't solve your case."

"Did you say *preliminary* report?" Alan raised his eyebrows.

"Yes, there are one or two things I really need to go over again."

Alan waited impatiently, while the pathologist sat back in his chair and stretched out his legs before opening the folder.

Keith Nichols was not a man to be rushed.

"I discovered that Wendy Hamilton was pregnant at the time of her death. About three months, I would say." Doctor Nichols placed the report on the DCI's desk. "You can go through the whole report once I've left. But…"

"Pregnant!" Alan interrupted. He sat up in his chair and stared at the pathologist. "Her parents told us she had just turned seventeen. Though I suppose in my job and in this day and age, I shouldn't really be surprised," he added after a moment's thought. "It's just that…" He gestured towards Doctor Nichols. "I'm sorry, please continue. I feel you have something more to tell us."

"Yes. She was pregnant."

Keith heaved himself up in his chair and shuffled around uneasily. Even after all the years as a pathologist, picking away at bodies in his lab, he had never got to grips with this part of his job.

"The baby was a girl," he said at last. "However, the thing that puzzles me the most is, the post-mortem showed the victim had never had intercourse."

"She was expecting a baby, yet you're telling us she was still a virgin!" Andrews exclaimed.

"Didn't I just say that?" The pathologist glanced at Andrews and shook his head.

"The press is going to have a field day with this," the sergeant said.

"Therefore, unless we are able to come up with some other explanation," the pathologist continued, "she must have received IVF treatment."

"Are they allowed to do that?" Alan asked. "You know – give IVF treatment to a young virgin woman?"

Like Sergeant Andrews, he was amazed at the news.

The pathologist was thoughtful for a few seconds. "I recall the subject was brought up a few years ago. I gather there was a big thing about it at the time and there are probably still a number of people who don't agree with it. Nevertheless, it is happening, so it must be lawful." He hesitated. "I admit, I haven't kept abreast of all the details and this is the first time I have ever come across it in my laboratory."

He looked at his watch and rose to his feet. "I'm sorry, but I really must go. However, before I leave, I have one other piece of information for you to ponder on. If the knife had been a couple of centimetres lower, I believe the victim may have survived. Which means you'll need to give some thought as to whether the killer really meant to kill the young woman and succeeded, or merely wound her – give her a fright, so to speak – in which case he failed." He nodded towards the file he had placed on the desk. "It's all in my preliminary report. But, I'll be taking a further look at the victim tomorrow. Like I said, there are a couple of things I need to look at again before I say any more."

"Thank you for stopping by, Keith," Alan said, picking up the pathologist's report, "Oh, and by the way, you were right," he added.

Doctor Nichols, who had almost reached the door, stopped and swung around. "Always glad to help. But what was I right about?"

"Your information certainly hasn't helped solve our case," the DCI replied. "If anything, it's made it even more complicated."

* * *

Both Agnes and Alan enjoyed the concert. The artist, who had been impersonating Frank Sinatra, was really very good. Closing her eyes a couple of times during the performance, Agnes felt the great man himself was really up there on the stage.

Being such a pleasant evening, they had chosen to walk the short distance across the Millennium Bridge to the Sage. If the weather had suddenly changed during the performance, they could always have called a taxi to take them back to the hotel. But, as it turned out, it was still quite warm when they emerged from the concert. Therefore they decided to stroll back to the hotel. The bar was still open when they arrived, allowing them to enjoy a drink before retiring for the night.

"You didn't say much about the case over dinner," Agnes said, twisting the stem of her wine glass between her fingers. "Only that Wendy Hamilton was pregnant. Yet, I got the impression there was something you were keeping from me. I believed you when you said you would keep me up-to-date."

Alan took a long sip of his whisky, while he thought about his reply.

"That works both ways, Agnes," he said, slowly placing his glass back onto the table.

"What does that mean?"

"You told me the man in the photo was the man you saw on the beach."

"Yes – he was. He was definitely the man I saw in Whitley Bay." Agnes looked puzzled. "Has someone said it couldn't have been him and given him an alibi?"

"No. No, nothing like that," Alan replied. "It's just that when I was about to leave, you quickly asked whether you could keep the pictures."

"So?" Agnes shook her head.

"So, when I enquired why you wanted them, you brushed over my question and hastily changed the subject." Alan grinned. "Now, did that mean you really didn't have a particular reason for wanting them? Or were you keeping something from *me*?"

He reached across the table and placed his hand over hers. "Talk to me, Agnes. I know you have something on your mind. You must tell me."

Agnes shook her head and smiled. "It seems I can't keep anything from you anymore." She hesitated for a moment before continuing. "When you first showed me the photos, I had a strange feeling that something wasn't quite right."

She went on to tell him how, after studying the pictures in depth she realized that, despite the drama unfolding in front of him, the man was looking in a different direction.

"Everyone else in the photograph was looking straight ahead at the paramedics."

"I guess we'll never know what he was looking at," said Alan. He thought about her comments for a moment. "But you think this is important – don't you."

It was more a statement than a question.

"It depends on how you look at it," Agnes replied. She took a sip of her wine, before carrying on. "I have to say, it took me a while before I figured it out. But, I finally came to a conclusion as to what he was looking at."

"So, what was it?"

"Me, Alan, I believe he was looking at me."

Alan had been about to take a drink from his glass, but instead, he hurriedly replaced it back on the table.

"When were you going to tell me this?"

His anxious look made Agnes feel a pang of guilt. "I don't know," she replied, slowly. "I knew you would only start worrying about me all over again. Maybe even try to bundle me out of the area for a while. So, I sort of decided to keep it to myself. Besides," she quickly added, "I could be wrong. He might not have been particularly looking at me at all. He could simply have given a sideways glance in my direction just as the photo was taken."

"Even so, you really believe he was watching you, don't you?"

Agnes nodded.

"I'm surprised you didn't see him at the time," Alan said, thoughtfully. "I mean, if he was right there in front you, how you could have missed him? Especially as you picked him out in the newspaper, even before we got copies of the original photograph."

"I was probably too busy watching the paramedics," she explained. "When they arrived, I told them to let me know if there was anything I could do for the poor woman. They said they would call me over if she needed extra support."

Alan looked thoughtful as he picked up his glass and took a sip of whisky.

"What're you thinking about now?" she asked him, hoping her revelation hadn't spoiled their evening.

"I was thinking about the newspaper photographer," Alan replied.

"Why? He was just doing his job, wasn't he?"

"Andrews and I set off the moment you called. I also asked for uniformed officers to attend the scene, to stop the press getting in the way when they began to arrive. Yet he was there, at the scene, taking pictures of the crowd and the ambulance crew. Did you see him arrive?"

"No, I didn't actually see him arrive, but I recall seeing a man taking pictures of various people at the scene. Though I must admit, I didn't take too much notice." She shrugged. "Anyway, it's possible he had just stepped off a train having been on another assignment and found the paramedics attending to someone in the Central Station."

She cocked her head on one side. "Now it's your turn. What were you keeping from me?"

Chapter Eight

That night, Agnes couldn't sleep. She tossed and turned as she thought about what Doctor Nichols had found during the post-mortem.

It was possible the answer was really quite simple. Wendy Hamilton could have wanted to have a baby and found a clinic willing to help her to get pregnant, though she would probably have had to lie about her age. But why hadn't she told her parents? Could there have been another explanation – something much more sinister – trafficking?

Even while Alan was telling her about Doctor Nichols's findings, the thought of people paying women to carry a child they could then sell to a childless couple, had immediately sprung to mind. Was it possible that Wendy had been paid to carry a baby, only to pass it over to some unscrupulous person, to be sold to the highest bidder?

Despite it being warm that night, Agnes shivered as that last thought ran through her mind. What kind of woman could do something like that? Thinking of her two sons, she knew she would never have given such an idea a moment's consideration – no matter who had proposed it, or how much money they had held out in front of her. How could anyone hand over their baby to someone they didn't even know?

Propping herself up on one arm, she punched her pillow in frustration. She would have got out of bed, made a cup of tea and looked down at the bright lights shining from the Millennium Bridge, if Alan hadn't been spending the night with her. However, she didn't want to wake him. He would only insist on sitting up with her to talk things through, even though he had to be up early for work the next day. Anyway, she liked to float ideas around in her head before discussing them with anyone.

She flopped back down onto the pillow, only to bounce back up again a few minutes later when a sudden thought popped into her mind. However, she was forced to pause for a few moments when Alan stirred. Fortunately, he turned over and went back to sleep.

But by now, Agnes was wide awake. Her brain was far too active to allow her to sleep. Perhaps she should slide out of bed and look out of the window, or even sit on the sofa while she thought everything through. Carefully pulling back the duvet, she slipped out of bed and crept across the room. Sinking heavily into the comfortable sofa, she recalled her last thoughts.

Maybe Wendy had agreed to such a deal in the beginning, but then backed out. Could that be what the young couple had been arguing about on the beach? If Wendy Hamilton had changed her mind and wanted to keep her baby, it would certainly have been enough to throw the cat among the pigeons. Yet, Agnes had a nagging doubt scratching away in her mind. Wendy hadn't struck her as the sort of person who would agree to such a deal in the first place.

Admittedly, she knew absolutely nothing about the young woman. Her entire assumptions were based on what little she had seen of Wendy almost forty-eight hours ago. Nevertheless, Agnes believed herself to be a good judge of character. There must be something else going on.

"But what?"

The words had slipped out of her mouth before she could stop them. For one brief moment, she had forgotten Alan was only a few feet away. She quickly glanced across to the bed. Thankfully, though he stirred and turned over, it appeared her outburst hadn't woken him.

She drew her knees up to her chest as she back-tracked over the previous two days. If only she had spotted the man standing in the crowd at the Central Station, maybe she would have been better able to judge what was going through his mind. The photograph hadn't really told her anything, other than the fact that he was at the Central Station and looking in her direction.

Had he recognised her from the coast and been shocked to see her there? Or was he simply wondering who she was and why she had been allowed to get so close to the injured woman? Certainly, seeing him in the flesh would have given her the opportunity to evaluate what he was thinking – especially if their eyes had locked.

And then there was the other piece of news the pathologist has passed on. Wendy might not have died, if the stab had been slightly lower. Was it possible the killer hadn't really meant to kill her, or had he misjudged where he was thrusting the knife? The knife! Agnes sat up on the sofa. That was another thing worth some consideration. It wasn't the usual sort of knife you would expect villains to carry – especially if they were setting out to kill someone. But then, she had already come to the conclusion that the murder hadn't been planned.

There was also Wendy's missing handbag. Perhaps she had been the victim of a robbery. She might have been stabbed while trying to fight off the thief. If that was the case, it could mean the man on the beach wasn't the killer after all.

The police had found her mobile phone partly hidden by her body, when the paramedics moved Wendy to the ambulance. She must have tried to call for help, but unfortunately the battery was flat. Agnes made a mental note to ask Alan whether the police had found anything helpful on the phone. She thought it strange he hadn't brought up the subject when they had been discussing the case last evening.

She yawned. At last, she was beginning to feel sleepy. Maybe it was time she went back to bed and switched off her brain for the night. She could restart it again in the morning and hopefully come up with something new.

Though, at this rate, she wouldn't put money on it.

* * *

By the time Agnes awoke, Alan had already showered and dressed.

"Gosh, what time is it?" she asked, swinging her head around to look at the clock. "Have I overslept? Why didn't you waken me?"

She relaxed a little when she saw it was only seven o'clock.

"I thought I would make an early start. I tried not to wake you," Alan replied. "I know you couldn't sleep last night. I heard you shifting around, so I thought you might like to lie a while longer this morning."

Agnes sat up in bed. "I just couldn't seem to settle last night. I kept thinking about what you told me – you know, about Wendy Hamilton being pregnant and whether the man I saw her with might have had some connection with it."

"Did you come to any conclusions?" Alan raised eyebrows.

He recalled that, in the past, Agnes had often come up with something positive after mulling things around in her head. Without much else to go on at the moment, he would be more than willing to listen to anything she had to offer.

She shook her head. "No. I'm afraid not." She paused. "Whenever something new popped into my mind, it always led me back to square one after giving it more thought. But then, I suppose you must be used to that. I expect it happens to you and your officers all the time."

She looked back at the clock.

"Are you having breakfast before you leave? If so, I'll join you. That is, if you have time to wait until I take a quick shower and get dressed. I'll only be a minute."

* * *

It was almost an hour later, when Agnes and Alan left the room and headed down to the dining room.

Though Alan had planned to get an early start at the station, he had since gone off the boil regarding that idea. Quite honestly, there was no real need to rush into the office at the crack of dawn. For heaven's sake, he had absolutely nothing to get 'an early start' on. There were no fingerprints on the knife, no DNA on the victim's clothes and even her own parents hadn't been any help. They had no idea at all as to how their seventeen-year-old daughter was living her life. Goodness only knew how they had reacted when they heard the news of their daughter's pregnancy from the bereavement officer he had sent to inform them. He would only hear about that later this morning, when he spoke to the WPO who had accompanied the officer.

If only Wendy Hamilton had been able to give the police a few clues. But, once the paramedics arrived, she had closed her eyes after telling them her name and address. Andrews had had to gently coax the address of her parents out of her, otherwise they would have been left to hear it via the news bulletins.

Even at the hospital, despite the surgeon's desperate attempts to save her life, she had died without giving any further information to help the police find her killer. Therefore, at the moment, Alan was relying on the national press to help identify the man Agnes had picked out in the photograph.

Unfortunately, so far, the updated story showing the main suspect had only been printed in the local paper. Alan had hoped he could persuade the local paper to highlight the picture of the man they wished to make contact with and pass the photographs and information on to the national press. However, the editor had refused, his argument being that it was their photographer who took the photograph in the first place, therefore, it was their scoop.

Alan had tried to reason with him. "For goodness' sake, this is a murder inquiry! Surely you understand that we need to get the information out there as soon as possible, in case the man leaves the area – or even the country? I'll make it abundantly clear to TV stations and all newspapers who carry the story, that your newspaper should be given the full credit for taking the picture in the first place. Isn't that enough?"

But apparently it wasn't enough. The story had appeared on the front page of the local paper the previous evening. The photographer was applauded and a photograph of him was printed next to the various pictures he had taken at the scene. However, so far, no one had come forward to identify their suspect.

Though he was frustrated about the arrangement, Alan was aware the newspaper industry was a tough business; each paper fighting the others to be the first to break the news. Yet it meant that the photograph showing the suspect's face would only hit the national press and TV News headlines this morning.

"I'm going to have the full English breakfast," Agnes said, once they were seated. "What about you?"

Alan didn't reply. His mind was still elsewhere.

"Alan!"

"Sorry, I was miles away." He looked at her. "Yes, I'll have the same."

"You're still dwelling on the wretched newspaper report, aren't you?" Agnes sighed. "You know as well as I do that no editor is going to pass an exclusive story over to a rival. For goodness' sake, get over it!"

The waiter appeared before Alan could say anything further. Besides, what could he say? She was absolutely right.

"So, what are you going to do with yourself today?" Alan asked, once the waiter had taken their order.

"I haven't decided. I might take another trip over to Low Fell – I didn't see much of it the last time I was there."

Agnes's thoughts drifted back a few months to when she had visited Low Fell, the area where she had been born. The idea had been to take a peek at the house where her family had lived and the school she went to, along with other places from her past. However, after seeing the street where she had lived and walking down to Kells Lane School, her visit to the area had ended rather abruptly, when she thought she was being followed. As it turned out, she had been mistaken. But, by then, the trip had turned a little sour, so she had made her way back to the city centre.

"Or, I might just laze around here on the quayside," she continued. "They say it's going to be another really hot day – not the sort of day for trundling around. More like a time for catching up with some reading."

"Sounds like a really good plan," Alan replied, as the waiter appeared with their breakfast.

Chapter Nine

The next two days passed quite smoothly for Agnes. It was too hot to venture far from the air-conditioned hotel. Even the gentle breeze, which wafted along the quay as the river flowed past, offered no relief. It seemed more like a fan heater than a cooler. Therefore she was thankful she had found a rather interesting book in which she could get involved.

It was a pity the same couldn't be said for Alan and his team, who were stuck in the police station. The station, having been built quite a number of years ago, didn't have the luxury of air-conditioning. Instead, the DCI, his officers and other members of his team had to make do with the more old-fashioned electric fans, which, to their mind, simply moved the hot air from one part of the room to another. To make matters worse, Alan was no further forward with the inquiry. The man they were looking for seemed to have vanished completely. Even after his face was splashed all over the newspapers, not one person had come forward with any information.

The people listed on Wendy Hamilton's phone hadn't been much help, either. Once the phone had been recharged, the officers had contacted and visited each one of them in turn. Yet no one had been able to shed any light on why she had been murdered. Moreover, none of the men questioned had matched the man shown in the photograph. Everything had led to a dead end.

"This is bloody ridiculous," Alan muttered, throwing himself into his chair. He placed his hand on the back of his neck. "How can it be possible that no one in the city has seen this man?"

Sergeant Andrews shrugged. "Perhaps the people who do know him haven't yet seen the newspapers or the television," he suggested. "They might be on holiday or something."

"What, all of them? For heaven's sake, Andrews, he must have friends, relatives and work colleagues! Surely they can't all be on holiday? Someone must have seen the headlines. Why haven't they come forward? It's almost as though the man never existed."

"Unless he's paid them all to stay silent," Andrews said, quietly.

"What was that?"

"Sorry, sir, I was thinking aloud. I was wondering whether he might have paid people to keep quiet."

"That would take an awful lot of money…"

"Yes, I agree – that was a stupid idea," the sergeant interrupted. "But, I've just had another thought. Maybe he isn't from this country. That could be the reason why no one has recognized him."

"Now, that's a thought." Alan pointed at the sergeant. "But then he would have to be staying somewhere. Surely one of the staff at a hotel or a guest house would have seen the news headlines and picked him out?"

"Yes, I suppose so." Andrews sighed.

"Nevertheless, it's something worth thinking about. It's not as though we have anything else to go on," Alan replied.

Andrews watched the DCI tap his fingers on his desk, as he thought it through.

"If you're right, and he is a foreigner," Alan said, "he could be in the country illegally. In which case, he'll be keeping his head down. Sleeping rough – staying well out of sight – that sort of thing."

Andrews glanced down at the photograph lying on his desk. "From what little we can see of him, he doesn't look as though he's sleeping rough." He pointed to the hoodie covering the man's head. "That looks a little too clean for a man sleeping in some shop doorway."

Alan picked up the picture and took a closer look.

"Then maybe he's staying with a friend or relative," he replied, handing the photo back to Andrews. "But if that's the case, and he *is* here illegally, then I can't see them coming forward to help our inquiry. They could find themselves in as much trouble as he is."

Alan paced up and down the office, as he thought it through.

"Well, at least it's a start," Andrews said.

"Is it?" Alan stopped pacing and faced his sergeant. "How do you propose we start looking for friends or relatives of a man, when we don't know a single thing about the man himself?"

He sank back down in his chair. "To my mind, Andrews, we still haven't reached the starting blocks!"

Chapter Ten

Agnes awoke and glanced at the clock. She was just about to reach across to wake Alan when she saw that his side of the bed was empty. She raised herself up and looked around the room, expecting to see him making coffee, but then flopped back down onto the bed, when she recalled he had spent the night in his own home.

Alan still owned a semi-detached house in a quiet part of Heaton, a short distance from the city centre. He had planned to put it on the market, when they had talked of buying something together. But, so far, he hadn't got around to it, which meant he needed to go back every now and again to make sure everything was as it should be.

Agnes heaved a sigh as she got out of bed. She had spent the last couple of days within easy reach of the hotel as it had been too hot to venture far. But today, she felt the need to go out somewhere – anywhere.

Reading the newspaper over breakfast, she noticed that a penthouse, quite close to the quayside, was up for sale. There were also a couple of photographs showing the inside of the apartment. They were too small for her to make out much detail. Yet, from what she could see, the main room looked quite spacious. The apartment might be just what she and Alan were looking for.

She grinned to herself at that last thought. She was well aware that Alan wasn't really too bothered about where they lived. He had even suggested they move into his house, but she had declined.

"I think we should start our new life together afresh," she had told him. "Besides, I really would like to live close to the quayside or, at the very least, be able to see it."

Perhaps she should ask Alan's opinion before she did anything. But, on the other hand, surely just taking a peek at the property wouldn't hurt? Looking back down at the photographs, she made up her mind. The estate agent would be her first port of call today.

* * *

"Where are you off to today?" Ben asked, as Agnes stepped into his taxi. "The park or the shopping centre?"

Agnes had met Ben when she first arrived on Tyneside and, as they got on so well, she had used his cab ever since.

She laughed. "Oh, Ben, you know me so well. But it's neither of those places today. I'd like you to drop me off at the estate agent on Clayton Street. I'm interested in a property I saw advertised in the newspaper this morning."

"You mean you're thinking about moving out of the hotel?" Ben sounded surprised. "I thought you liked staying there."

"Yes, I do. But there are times when I feel I would like to have a place of my own. Somewhere I could kick off my shoes and put my feet up."

"Can't you do that at the hotel?"

"Not without going upstairs to my bedroom," Agnes laughed. "It would be unseemly to do something like that downstairs in the drawing room."

"I suppose so," he agreed.

The quayside seemed busier than usual. Ben was forced to slow down several times, even though he wasn't really going very fast to begin with.

"I'm not sure what's going on today," he said, as he was forced to pull to a halt due to the hold-up in front of him. "Maybe I should have taken the route up to City Road."

"Not to worry, Ben, I'm not in any hurry."

Glancing out of the window, Agnes's eyes were drawn to a group of people on the pavement. Most of them were women and they all appeared to be trying to speak to a man at the centre of the throng. Some were even taking selfies. Maybe he was a film or television star on location. That would explain why the quayside was so busy today. However, it only took her a few seconds to realise that the man wasn't an international star. Far from it. In fact, he was Harold Armstrong, the newspaper photographer who had taken the pictures at the Central Station on the day of the murder.

Since Agnes had identified a man in his photograph as one of the last people person to see Wendy Hamilton alive, his photographs had appeared all over the national news. For a time, the local newspaper had also included a picture of the photographer who had captured the shot. Now, it seemed he had been recognised by a group of his new-found fans and was enjoying every moment.

Indeed, the photographs had certainly brought his name to the fore. A case of being in the right place at the right time; had he been a little earlier or later, he would have missed what had probably turned out to be the scoop of his life.

"But think about it," Ben continued, interrupting her thoughts. "At the hotel, everything is done for you. Your meals are put in front of you without the bother of cooking or clearing and washing up afterwards. Not only that, your room is cleaned, the bed is made and most likely your washing and ironing is done without you even having to raise a finger. Good grief, Mrs Lockwood. Living in a luxury hotel, with everything done for you, or a house which needs to be kept clean and tidy, as well as the other chores I've mentioned? I know which of the two my wife would prefer!"

He fell silent, reflecting on his rather sharp remarks to the best customer he had ever had. Mrs Lockwood always used his taxi, she gave him generous tips and had even handed him her winnings when she had visited the races at Gosforth Park earlier in the year.

"I'm sorry," he said, swinging around to face her. "It's really none of my business. Please forget what I said."

Agnes reached across and placed her hand on Ben's shoulder. "Don't worry. I know you mean well. It's just that there are times when I feel I would like to have a place of my own." She laughed. "But, you know something? You're right. I'll give it a great deal of thought before making a final decision." She lifted her eyes and looked through the windscreen. "I think the traffic is moving again."

For the rest of the journey, Agnes considered what Ben had said. Not whether she should refrain from moving out of the hotel; at the end of the day, that was her decision to make. But what had really troubled her was when he had mentioned his wife and how she would love a break from her daily chores.

Agnes knew their son, Alec, had several health issues and she was aware of how difficult it must be for them both, as his parents. Ben worked his socks off to bring in money to keep them above water. Since learning of his situation, she had tried to help by frequently calling for his taxi, even when there wasn't any need. But surely there was something else she could do – something that would give his wife, Maria, a break from the drudgery of her everyday life?

A holiday, somewhere far away from here, would be the best option. However, Agnes knew that wasn't possible at the moment. Alec was on a new course of treatment and needed to be monitored regularly. By all accounts, he was responding well, so there was no way they could take a holiday abroad, even if one was handed to them on a plate.

"We're here," Ben said, interrupting her thoughts.

"Thank you, Ben." Agnes paid the fare and stepped out of the taxi. "I'll give you a call if I need a lift back to the hotel."

Inside the office, she told the agent which apartment she was interested in viewing.

"Ah, yes," he said. "It only came on the market a couple of days ago, but I'm sure it will be snapped up very quickly."

Mr Holmes, the agent, went to explain that the owners had really loved living there. But, due to work commitments, they'd had to move abroad.

"If you are interested, Mrs Lockwood, I'd be happy to escort you to the property and show you around."

Agnes agreed and a short while later, she found herself stepping inside the apartment.

She wasn't disappointed. The layout was most impressive. There was a large sitting room and dining room. The kitchen was well equipped. There were three large bedrooms, each with their own shower room. There was also a small separate bathroom. It was perfect.

Stepping out onto the balcony, which ran around the whole apartment, she was able to see the River Tyne and three of the bridges, while the other three sides showed two different views of the city and one of Gateshead, on the other side of the Tyne Bridge.

Agnes was so delighted with the property that she would like to have bought it on the spot. But, at the same time, she felt she ought to speak to Alan first.

"What about parking, Mr Holmes?" she asked, suddenly remembering that Alan would need somewhere to park his car. The city centre was not the best place to find a parking spot.

"Each apartment has its own garage," he replied. "Plus there are extra spaces for visitors."

Agnes wandered around the three-bedroom apartment again, wondering whether she should call Alan and ask him to join her now. But then she decided against it. Perhaps it would be better if she mentioned it casually over dinner, rather than jump in head-first.

"I really do like the property, but my partner will need to see it before a decision is made," she said. "Maybe I could speak to him and arrange a time tomorrow. We could meet you here."

"No problem. But be aware that any property of this calibre gets snapped up very quickly," Mr Holmes said.

He gave her one of his cards, before dropping her off on the quayside.

As she was strolling back towards the hotel, she saw the newspaper photographer again. By now, most of his fans had deserted him, though there were still a few people watching as he focused his camera on the Millennium Bridge. It was being raised to allow a vessel to float upstream.

It is a wonderful sight, she thought, as she looked at the bridge, *but I doubt these photographs will bring you the same acclaim as your last ones.*

As Agnes was about to move away, she saw him turn back to face the group of people standing behind him. At first, his smile appeared to be for them all. However, she couldn't help noticing that his attention seemed to linger on one person in particular.

Following his eyes, she picked out the person concerned. It was a woman. Okay, it was a woman. Most of the people standing around were women. But, why choose that particular woman? Did he already know her? Or had she just caught his eye?

Agnes had to admit, the woman in question was very attractive. Young, blonde and slim – a woman likely to catch a man's eye, whatever she was wearing. Nevertheless, her outfit today, a white vest and extremely short, bright orange shorts, certainly made her stand out from anyone near her.

The young woman smiled at Armstrong and, raising her hand, she wiggled her fingers at him.

Agnes couldn't watch any more. What was the woman thinking? Armstrong was old enough to be her father! But maybe she was looking for a career in the newspaper business or modeling industry and saw him as a way of reaching her goal. Agnes shook her head, as she continued walking towards the hotel. What young people got up to these days was unbelievable.

By now, she had almost reached the entrance of the hotel. However, after a moment's thought, she decided to change direction and head for her favourite café near the Millennium Bridge. There were two or three tables vacant outside, so she pulled out a chair and sat down and ordered a glass of wine. Once she was settled, she took out her mobile phone and found the photographs she had taken during her time in the apartment. She had thought she could show them to Alan before making another appointment with the estate agent. But, gazing at the photos now, she could already see them both living there.

First off, she would need to put her house in Essex on the market as soon as possible and have her furniture moved to Newcastle. Though she had never seriously thought about going back to Essex, for some reason she hadn't even considered selling her former home – until now. Maybe it was because she and her husband had lived there until he died. Or perhaps she had kept it on as a bolt-hole; somewhere she could escape to if she suddenly felt the need to get away. Like, for instance, when she had almost left the area a few months ago, due to Alan's abruptness towards her in front of his officers. If he could do it once, who was to say he wouldn't do it again?

Agnes sighed. But, would she really have left Tyneside back then? Thinking it through, she realised she hadn't really wanted to leave the place she loved so much. If push had come to shove, she would have simply moved hotels and not told him where she had gone. Since coming back last year, she had made Tyneside her home.

Putting those thoughts aside, she turned her attention back to the property photographs. The more she thought about it, the more she believed it was the right place for her to begin her new life here on Tyneside. It had everything she could wish for. She really hoped Alan would like it as much as she did…

A shadow appeared across her table, interrupting her thoughts. Glancing up, she found a man staring down at her. Raising her hand to block out the sun, she recognised him as the newspaper photographer she had seen earlier. Now, seeing him up close, she believed he was in his middle fifties, about her age. However, he seemed to be trying to fight off his age, by wearing a black, crumpled T-shirt and jean with holes around the knees.

"Do you mind if I join you?" he asked.

Without waiting for her reply, he swiftly pulled out a chair and sat down.

Casting her eyes over his shoulder, Agnes noticed that there were two empty tables behind him. He must have seen them. He had walked past each of them to reach her. Therefore, there had to be a reason why had he chosen to sit with her.

"And, if I did?" She raised her eyebrows.

"I think we've met somewhere before," he said, ignoring her question.

Agnes rolled her eyes. That was a chat-up line if ever she had heard one.

She shook her head. "No – I can honestly say I've never met you."

"How can you be so sure?"

"Because I'm pretty good at recalling people I've spoken to. So I'm sure I would have remembered you." She smiled. "But, I tend to come to this café quite often. Maybe you've caught a glimpse of me here?"

"No, I don't think so," he said, cocking his head to one side. "You see, I don't come to the quayside very often – unless my job brings me here, of course. By the way, my name is Harold Armstrong – but you can call me Harry." He winked. "I'm a photographer-stroke-reporter with the local newspaper. My photographs have been plastered all over the national and international news lately. You've probably seen them."

He paused and looked at her for a long moment.

It was on the tip of her tongue to say, *yes, I know who you are,* but Agnes held back. That was probably just what he was expecting to hear. Instead, she simply shrugged one shoulder.

"In that case, allow me to explain," he continued. "I just happened to be at the Central Station the day the murder took place." He sounded very proud of himself. "I was able to take lots of photographs at the scene of the crime." He took a deep breath. "And, as it turns out, one of my pictures showed the man the police want to speak to as part of their enquiries. I guess someone must have recognized him, as the police requested copies to be sent to help with their investigation." He paused. "I only wish I could have delivered the photograph to the police station myself. Just think – I could have taken photographs of the witness!"

He leaned across the table. "You must have seen the pictures? They've been broadcast on all the national television channels. I have a few copies with me, if you would like to have one. I'll even sign it for you. You never know, it could be worth a lot of money one day."

He placed his camera on the table and began to fumble around in his pockets.

"So – Mr Armstrong, is your job the reason you're here today?" Agnes asked slowly, ignoring his last statement.

"Sorry?" he queried, as he pulled out a handful of photographs.

"You said you only ever came to the quayside if your job brought you here. I just wondered if you were here for a special reason."

"No, not exactly," he replied, holding up one of the pictures.

He appeared to be disappointed when she didn't even glance at it.

"I guess you don't want this then."

His subdued tone gave away his frustration at her lack of interest in his prize photograph.

"Not really," she said. "In that case, why are you here on the quayside?"

"I had some time to spare, so I wondered whether there might be something going on around here," he said, impatiently.

"And did you find something which would keep your name on the front page?"

"No! Not a damn thing! Nothing newsworthy, anyway," he said, sharply.

Agnes leaned across the table and spoke slowly and deliberately. "I think what you really mean is that you haven't come up with another case of murder. Tell me, Mr Armstrong, does someone else have to die so that you can stay in the limelight?"

He narrowed his eyes and glared across the table at her.

"No! Of course not," he said after a long moment.

Agnes was slightly alarmed by his cold stare. Maybe she had gone too far. But then, she hadn't asked him to join her. Nor did she want to sit here, listening to him going on about how famous he was. She picked up her glass of wine and sat back in her chair.

"I'm relieved to hear it," she said, trying to sound calmer than she felt, as his eyes continued to bore into hers. "So, if there isn't anything else, I think we're done here."

"Yes, I believe we are – for the time being. But, you never know, we could meet again. I think you're simply playing hard to get."

Without another word, he rose to his feet and walked away.

Watching him as he made his way towards the Millennium Bridge, Agnes considered his parting words. Surely he didn't think she was interested in him! What on earth could have given him that idea? Her eyes were still fixed on him, when, quite suddenly, he stopped in his tracks. Fortunately, there wasn't anyone immediately behind otherwise they would have walked straight into him. She hastily looked away, hoping he hadn't felt her eyes following him. However, due to the large windows of the café, she was still able to see his reflection.

Agnes watched him, as he turned his head and glanced back in her direction. For a few seconds, she wondered whether he was going to come back and insist she look at his wretched photograph. Despite the heat, she felt a cold shiver run down her spine at the thought. But instead, he smiled broadly and blew her a kiss before turning back towards the bridge.

Agnes was still thinking about it, when she heard someone call out his name. Following the direction of the voice, she saw a woman making her way across to him. The woman, who looked to be in her early fifties, appeared to be carrying too much weight. Either that or she had squeezed herself into a matching top and skirt a couple of sizes too small for her. She seemed to be very angry about something as she was waving her arms around as she spoke.

Glancing at the passers-by, Harold tried to calm her down. However, it appeared she didn't want to be pacified, as she continued to rant on – her voice growing louder with each passing word. Then, quite suddenly, she stabbed a finger in Agnes's direction.

"Is that another of your floozies?" she bellowed. "I leave you for five minutes, only to find you flirting with another bit of skirt that's shown you her leg. How could you? After everything I've done for you!"

Agnes looked around at the people nearby. By now, most of them had turned to look in her direction. She was horrified at being dragged into something so sordid. After all, she hadn't wanted the wretched man to sit with her in the first place.

Her first instinct was to rush across and put the woman straight. But that would only cause more fuss and drag her further into the pantomime being played out only a few yards away. Therefore, the only other alternative was to sit here and sweat it out.

After what seemed like an age, Harold finally managed to persuade the woman that it was time they moved on. But, before they left, she gave Agnes a long, icy stare.

Agnes could feel her face flushing with embarrassment as she tried to turn her attention back to the photos on her phone. But her thoughts were elsewhere. Was the woman Harold Armstrong's wife, or his latest girlfriend? The reporter hadn't been wearing a wedding ring, but that didn't mean he wasn't married. Looking down at her own wedding ring, she twirled it around her finger. She and Jim had ordered two gold bands for their wedding – one for each of them. But did men wear wedding rings these days?

She shook her head, and tried to turn her attention back the photos. Thankfully, she and Harold would never meet again – well, certainly not if she saw him first.

Chapter Eleven

"That was a complete waste of time." Sergeant Andrews flung his jacket over the back of his chair. "I really thought we had our first lead."

Earlier in the day, the desk sergeant had received a call from a member of the public saying that he had spotted a man resembling the suspect the police were looking for. The caller had gone on to say that the man in question was sitting in a café on Shields Road in Byker. As that was the same area the murder victim had been living in at the time of her death, the police had taken the call seriously.

Andrews, together with Detective Constables Smithers and Jones, had hurried across town, hoping to apprehend the suspect. However, when they arrived, there was no one in the café even resembling the description of the man in the photograph. Fair enough, he could have left before they arrived. Yet, when Smithers showed the photo of the man they were looking for to the lady behind the counter, she had been adamant that she had never laid eyes on the man.

"I've been here every day this week," she had said, stabbing her finger on the photograph, "and, I can assure you, that man has not been here today, yesterday or the day before. If I had seen him, I would have rung the police – I watch the news!"

"Someone was having a joke at our expense," Andrews added, flopping down into his chair. "Looking back, I reckon it was too good to be true."

"I agree," said Alan. "However, we can't afford not to take any call seriously."

"I understand all that," Andrews retorted. "But, in this heat, I'd rather not have to rush out on some wild goose chase because some idiot feels like having a lark!"

The DCI looked up sharply, but didn't say anything.

The sergeant bit his lip. He shouldn't have spoken to his superior officer in that manner.

"I'm sorry, sir. But the damn air conditioning in my car is playing up and even with all the windows down, it was still stifling. And if that wasn't bad enough, there was so much traffic on Shields Road, we had to stop and start all the way there. I couldn't use the sirens or flashing lights as it would have warned the suspect. Though, as it turned out, it wouldn't have mattered if we had dropped in from a low-flying helicopter."

Andrews should have stopped talking after his apology, but he had continued to ramble on. Therefore, he was more than relieved when the phone on the DCI's desk rang, stopping him in full flow.

He mopped his forehead as the DCI answered his phone – saved by the bell!

* * *

The call had been about another stabbing in the area. Though Alan had listened to the call until the end, most of it had gone over his head the moment he learned that the victim, a woman, had been found in a narrow road just off the quayside.

Alan had only one thought on his mind as he and Andrews hurried out of the station and clambered into his car. Was the woman Agnes? Knowing her the way he did, it was possible she had spotted the police suspect and he had lashed out at her to stop her from raising the alarm. With that thought in mind, he wanted to get to the scene as quickly as possible.

Once they arrived, Alan leapt from his car and hurried towards the ambulance. The woman lying in the road was of slim build. Her brown hair matched the colour of her eyes, which were wide open and staring up at him. Her arms were spread out on each side of her bloodstained body. There was no sign of a knife.

Though he was shocked at the sight and felt so sorry for the victim, Alan was relieved to find that the woman lying there wasn't Agnes. One of the paramedics quickly informed him that the victim had died only a few minutes earlier.

"She managed to tell us her name," he said, looking down at the body. "It's Janet Cunningham. She also told us that she worked in a café here on the quayside. But that was all."

"Who found her?"

"A man and his wife," the paramedic replied. He pointed across to where the couple was standing. "That's them over there. I suggest you tread carefully, they're a bit shocked."

The DCI nodded to his sergeant, indicating he should take a statement from the couple.

"I'm sure they are," Alan said, turning back to the paramedic. "It's not the sort of thing you usually find while out for a stroll."

A few minutes later, the pathologist and his team arrived at the scene.

"Okay, thanks. We'll take it from here," Doctor Nichols said, once the paramedics had given him the details.

Alan walked across to meet up with his sergeant, who was still talking to the couple who had found the young woman. At a guess, he would put them in their early seventies.

"Mr and Mrs Bramston tell me that the victim works there." As he spoke, Andrews pointed towards a large café on the corner at the bottom of the road. "They go there for coffee most mornings and have seen her several times."

"Yes – she's a lovely young woman. Who would want to do something like this to her?" Mrs Bramston said. "They ought to be hanged!"

"Rest assured, we'll do everything we can to make sure that we apprehend the murderer," Alan replied.

He turned to his sergeant. "Have you got everything you need?"

When Andrews nodded, Alan turned back to the couple. "Would you like an officer to take you home?"

"Yes, thank you," Mr Bramston replied.

Once an officer had shepherded the couple towards a police car, Alan and his sergeant made their way down to the café, leaving Detectives Smithers and Jones with the forensics team. Meanwhile, uniformed officers kept the gathering crowds behind the tape cordoning off the area.

However, as Alan moved off, he caught a swift glimpse of a face he recognised. Harold Armstrong, the newspaper photographer who had been at the Central Station, after the stabbing of Wendy Hamilton. Now he was here, taking photographs of not only where the woman was found, but also shots of everyone looking on.

The café was very busy when the detectives arrived. Looking around, they found it to be quite large, with tables both inside and outside the café. Yet they were all filled. It appeared to be very popular place.

Alan managed to stop one of the assistants as she rushed past him on her way to the kitchen with a tray full of used crockery. He told her he would like to speak to the person in charge. She nodded and, a few minutes later, a woman appeared through a door marked *Staff Only*.

"I'm Mrs Bolton, the manageress. I understand you wanted to see me?" she enquired.

"Yes." Alan looked around. "Is there somewhere we might talk?" he added, showing her his warrant card.

She took one look at the card and led the way to her office.

"We want to talk to you about Janet Cunningham," Alan said, the moment the door closed behind them.

"Oh, Janet." The manageress smiled. "I'm afraid you've just missed her. She went off to lunch about fifteen minutes ago."

"I'm sorry, but I'm afraid we have some bad news. Miss Cunningham was found lying in the road a short distance away. She had been stabbed in the chest."

"Oh, my goodness!" the manageress replied, her face going pale with shock. She slowly lowered herself into her chair. "Is she going to be alright?"

"No, I'm afraid she died of her injuries." Alan glanced at his sergeant for a moment. "Do you know whether Miss Cunningham had any enemies – anyone who might have held a grudge against her?"

"No. She seemed to get along with everyone," Mrs Bolton said quietly, tears welling in her eyes. "I can't think of anyone who would want to harm her."

"Can you tell us anything about her friends? Did she have a boyfriend?"

"I know she was very friendly with Pauline Mintoff, another member of the staff. They were around the same age and often worked the same shifts. I believe they enjoyed going to night clubs together. She might be able to tell you more about her social life. But I'm afraid Pauline is off-duty today, though I could give you her home address."

"Thank you, that would help. I would also be grateful if you could give us the address of Janet Cunningham. I'm afraid she had no identity on her when she was found. We only know her name because she was able to give it to the paramedics before she passed away."

"Yes, of course."

Mrs Bolton was about to open a drawer in her desk when she looked up sharply.

"What do you mean – no identity? Janet was never without her large handbag. She always carried it with her wherever she went. Her colleagues often joked about it, saying she had everything in there except the kitchen sink."

"I'm afraid whoever stabbed her must have taken it. There was no sign of it at the scene," Alan replied.

Mrs Bolton shook her head as she pulled out a file and slid it across the desk towards the detectives.

"Thank you," Alan said, as his sergeant made a note of the two addresses. "Now, before we leave, perhaps we could have a brief word with your staff?"

***

Mrs Bolton had agreed wholeheartedly. Yet, despite speaking to everyone on duty, no one had been able to supply any further information. Most were several years older than Janet Cunningham, which meant they had never really mixed with her socially.

By the time the two detectives arrived back at the crime scene, the pathologist had moved the body into his van and the forensic team were pulling off their coveralls.

"We're just about ready to leave," Doctor Nichols told them. "But I'm afraid the team hasn't found any leads. Whoever did this didn't leave a single clue." He glanced towards his large van. "Hopefully, I'll be able to tell you more when I get her back to the lab. But don't get your hopes up. If it's the same person who killed Wendy Hamilton, then I doubt I'll be able to give you much more information. Whoever is doing this seems to know how to cover their tracks."

"Thank you, Keith. Get back to me the moment you have finished the post-mortem," Alan said, before heading towards his car.

"We need to see Miss Cunningham's parents before we speak to Pauline Mintoff," the DCI mumbled, as he started his car.

Andrews nodded. Informing the victim's relatives of the death of a family member was the one part of the job that he disliked. Nevertheless, it had to be done.

When they reached the house, a large, detached residence in Jesmond, they found both Janet's parents at home. Very often, at this time of the day, everyone was at work.

"Who is it, Ann?" James Cunningham called out from somewhere upstairs, when his wife asked him to come down. "I'm a bit tied up at the moment."

"It's the police," she replied, as she led the detectives through to the neat and tidy sitting room.

"Your husband is here?" Alan asked.

"Yes. James runs his own business. He's usually at his office in Wideopen at this time of the day. But today, he's working from home.

He does that occasionally." She peered at the DCI. "But that's not why you're here, is it?"

Before Alan could reply, Mr Cunningham strode into the room.

"I think you had both better sit down," Alan said.

"What is it?" Mr Cunningham asked. He paused and then shook his head. "Okay, what's my son been up to now?"

Robert, their twelve-year-old son had been getting up to mischief lately, though, so far, nothing that had required police intervention. But there was always a first time.

"We're not here about your son. Please sit down."

Alan went on to explain what had happened to their daughter, Janet.

Mrs Cunningham broke down into floods of tears when she heard the news and clung to her husband for support.

"I understand how difficult this is for you both. But I'm sure you know that, in order to catch the person who did this as soon as possible, we need to ask you a few questions."

James Cunningham swallowed hard and blinked back the tears rolling down his cheeks, before he spoke.

"We'll do everything we can to help you catch the bastard. What do you need to know?"

Alan went on to ask whether he knew of any issues Janet might have had with anyone. However, neither of the parents could think of anyone.

"Did your daughter have a computer?"

"Yes, a laptop. It's upstairs in her room."

"Would you mind if my sergeant took a look at the room and the laptop?"

"Go ahead," Mr Cunningham replied. "Do whatever you need to do." He glanced towards Sergeant Andrews, "Top of the stairs – first door on the right."

"Thank you."

Andrews pulled on a pair of latex gloves as he climbed the stairs. He stood in the doorway for a few seconds, taking in the scene before him. The bed had been made and the room looked rather tidy – unlike some he had seen in the past. He spotted the laptop sitting on the bedside table and decided took a look at that first.

Switching it on, the sergeant quickly found that Janet was into social media. She appeared to have accounts with Facebook, Twitter and Instagram, though, on the face of it, there didn't seem to be anything to worry about. Yet even he, who was not particularly at home using the internet, was aware that there were many hidden areas. He would need to take the laptop back to the station where it could be scrutinized by the IT division. It was possible someone might find something buried beneath the surface.

He smiled to himself as he began to check out the wardrobe. Where was Timothy McGee of *NCIS* fame, when you needed him most?

Chapter Twelve

The DCI was in the incident room going through the case with his team.

"After speaking to Janet Cunningham's parents and also to one of her closest friends, Pauline Mintoff, I'm afraid we were unable to learn anything helpful," he told them.

Though Pauline had been at home when he and Sergeant Andrews called, the interview had been fruitless. After giving her some time to get over the shock of hearing the news about her friend, they had asked a few questions about Janet's boyfriends. However, she hadn't given been able to give them the information they had hoped for.

"We didn't talk about boyfriends," Pauline had told them. "Yes, we'd say if we were asked out on a date. But we'd never go into details about who the guy was, or where we were going."

"Don't you think that's a little strange?" Andrews had enquired. "I thought you all liked to talk about it, whenever a new boyfriend or girlfriend appeared on the scene."

"Where did you dig up that from? The film, *Grease*?" Pauline had rolled her eyes. "No – that doesn't happen these days."

"Hopefully," Alan continued, "someone downstairs will be able to pick up something from her laptop, which we brought back from her room. In the meantime, it is more important than ever that we find this man," he stabbed his finger on the photograph taken at the Central Station, "even if just to eliminate him from our enquiries. At the moment, he is our only suspect."

Alan ended the discussion with his detectives, by instructing them to go back out onto the streets and show the photo to every passer-by.

"That photo has been all over the news for the last few days, sir," Andrews said, as they walked back to the office. "What makes you think someone is going to suddenly remember it because a detective holds it up in front of them?"

"I know all that, but what if someone had been on holiday abroad and hadn't seen the news? They might remember seeing him somewhere before they went away," Alan replied. "Or what if…"

"What if, what if… you're beginning to sound like Mrs Lockwood!" Andrews laughed.

Alan shook his head. "Yes, you're right, I am. It must be catching."

* * *

Alan was only halfway through writing up his report on the murder of Janet Cunningham, when the phone rang. He listened carefully to what was being said, hardly able to believe his ears.

"There's been another stabbing," he told Andrews, the moment he replaced the phone. "A young woman again, but I understand she's still alive."

"What!" the sergeant looked up from his computer. "Where did it happen?"

"St Ann's Street – just off the quayside," Alan replied. He was already at the door. "Get a team of officers down there to cordon off the area – we'll speak to the pathologist on the way."

Once Andrews had finished snapping out the orders, he slammed down the phone and hurried out of the room to catch up with the DCI.

By now, the roads were busy. Even the flashing blue lights fitted to Alan's car didn't help them to get to the scene more quickly. Though the traffic in front of him courteously stopped in an effort to let him through, the road was so packed with cars and delivery vans coming in the opposite direction, there was no way he could overtake the vehicles in front of him.

"I'd forgotten about the Friendly Football match at St James's Park this afternoon," Alan muttered, when his car was held up for the fourth time.

Finally reaching the scene, Alan pulled up sharply and leapt from his car. He rushed across to where a paramedic was attending to the victim. For the second time that day, he heaved a huge sigh of relief when he found it wasn't Agnes. But, at the same time, he felt a great deal of pity for the young woman lying in front of him.

Though there was blood oozing from the wound in her chest, thankfully, it didn't appear to be flowing quite so freely. Plus, there was no blood lying on the ground where she lay and, while she was staring up at him, there was life in her eyes; unlike the other victims who he had seen lying in the road. Hopefully, this meant there was a chance this young woman would live. If so, was it possible that the culprit had caught sight of someone watching and hurried off before the knife penetrated too deeply? Alan looked at the tall office block behind him. Perhaps someone had been at the window and seen the attack.

Meanwhile Andrews, who had been following closely behind, stopped suddenly, to hold back the people who were beginning to gather. St Ann's Street, a rather steep hill leading from the quayside to City Road, was usually quite quiet as it was closed to most traffic. Unless drivers were using the multi-storey car park, or had any other authority to use the road, it was a no-go area for transportation. Therefore, the people standing around must have been on foot, as there were no cars parked at the kerb.

He looked around the group, drawing his own conclusions. As far as he knew, no one had claimed to have been the one who found the woman and reported it to the police. Had they scarpered the moment they phoned it in, making sure they would not be involved any further? Or, could the stabbing have been reported by the person who had actually committed the crime? If that was the case, then it was possible the individual was still here – watching the drama unfold.

Andrews was still gazing at the crowd, trying to pick out a likely suspect, when the uniformed police officers arrived. He was rather surprised they had managed to get through the traffic so quickly. But then, a vehicle with wire netting stretched across the windscreen and filled with police officers was always going to get priority over a car – even one with flashing blue lights.

He told the police officer in charge to keep the public back from the scene. "Also, tell your men to keep a sharp lookout for anyone behaving suspiciously. The culprit could still be here."

"Is she going to be okay?" Andrews asked, as he approached the DCI.

"She's lost a lot of blood, but they believe the alarm was raised in time. They need to get her to the hospital as quickly as possible."

While Alan was speaking, Harold Armstrong suddenly popped into his line of sight. At that point, his camera was focused on the victim. However, a moment later, he turned his attention to the people gathered behind the police tapes and began taking photographs of them.

Until a few days ago, Alan had never even heard of the man. Maybe it was simply because he never took much notice of the names of the reporters or photographers shown under the headlines. His main interest had always lain with the story, not the writer.

Yet, since Armstrong's photographs taken in the Central Station, Alan hadn't failed to notice that the man had made quite a name for himself. Instead of his name appearing in small letters somewhere at the foot of the page, they were now highlighted below the photograph in question.

"Do you want me to move him on?" Andrews asked. He had noticed the DCI looking across towards the photographer. "The man's a bloody menace."

"No, leave him." Alan replied. "Yes, he *is* a bloody menace, but he's only doing his job. Besides, with a bit of luck, his pictures will help us to find our killer." He paused. "Nevertheless, I'd be interested to know how he always manages to appear at the scene of a crime so quickly."

Andrews nodded. "You have a point there, sir. We should look into that."

Alan agreed. "But keep it between ourselves for the moment," he added before turning back to face the victim.

"She told the crew her name is Susan Matthews. She also said that she lived in Walker. They didn't press her for any further information."

Andrews nodded. He could understand that. But before he could reply, Doctor Nichols and his team arrived on the scene.

When Andrews had been on the phone to forensics, while they were making their way to the quayside, Alan had suggested the pathologist should accompany them – despite the victim still being alive.

"So what's all this about?" Keith asked, as he joined the two detectives. "Why am I here, Alan?" he added. "I thought the victim had survived the attack." He paused. "Oh, I'm sorry. Didn't she make it after all?"

"So far, she is doing okay." Alan hesitated. "Look, Keith, I know this isn't the norm, but, in this instance, could you make one tiny exception and accompany the young woman to the hospital in the ambulance? Is that possible?"

"Yes, it's possible – if the person in question agrees. Normally, a police officer accompanies the patient in a case like this." Keith cocked his head on one side and scratched behind his ear. "So, what's the reasoning behind your sudden request?"

"I feel sure she'll agree to it," Alan replied, quickly. "The young woman has been stabbed and probably fears for her life. Therefore I think she'll be relieved to have a fully qualified doctor accompanying her to the hospital."

Alan glanced at the paramedics, who were now lifting the stretcher bearing Sue Matthews into the ambulance.

"But we're wasting time, Keith," he added. "While you are with her, find out whether the knife penetrated her body from the same angle as our last two victims – you know what I mean."

"Hang on a minute, Alan. I can't really say from what angle the knife penetrated the last victim. I haven't had a chance to examine her yet."

Alan looked over Keith's shoulder. The stretcher was now onboard.

"Okay then, the first victim. No time for any more questions. The ambulance is ready. Go, before it moves without you."

"But I can't just start examining her for no reason! You know that!"

"Yes, I understand, Keith. But if something should happen on the way and you get the chance…" Alan broke off. "Look, we need a heads-up on this one. We can't afford to waste any more time."

Keith closed his eyes and shook his head.

"Okay. But you owe me a drink," he said, before hurrying over to the ambulance.

"You'd better make that a large one," he called out, after a quick word with the patient and crew.

A moment later, Keith had hauled himself into the ambulance.

Chapter Thirteen

In the ambulance, Doctor Keith Nichols strapped himself into the chair near Susan. He watched carefully as the paramedic continued with the usual tests to make sure the patient's temperature, blood pressure and heartbeat had not worsened since being lifted into the ambulance. Though, at the same time, he was well aware that readings taken in an ambulance could be distorted due to both the sirens and engine noise. However, when there was a sudden drop in all three readings, the paramedic didn't hesitate before asking for his help.

Keith was on his feet in seconds. Having seen the results on the small screen, he had already undone the safety strap on his chair. A moment later, he was at the young woman's side. It seemed that the bleeding from the stab wound had restarted; it could have happened when the ambulance had gone over a large pot-hole in the road.

"When are they going to get this damn road repaired?" Keith muttered, as he attended to the patient.

Thankfully, he and the paramedic were able to stop the bleeding. But he knew it was imperative that she should arrive at the hospital quickly. He didn't like to think of the outcome if this were to happen again. Yet, even with the sirens blaring and lights flashing, the driver was still finding it difficult to get up any speed, due to the heavy traffic.

Now that the crisis was over, Keith took a closer look at the wound. It appeared the knife had been thrust into her body in very much the same way as the first victim, Wendy Hamilton. He'd had very little time to examine the second victim thoroughly, having being called out again so quickly, but he had picked up signs that she had been stabbed in pretty much the same way. To his mind, this meant it was most likely that all three attacks had been carried out by the same person.

Doctor Nichols was still mulling it over in his mind, when the young woman opened her eyes and looked up at him.

"Am I at the hospital yet?"

"No," Keith answered. "But, hopefully we're nearly there."

He looked at the paramedic for confirmation, but none was forthcoming. The ambulance was stuck in a traffic jam.

"I'm going to die, aren't I?" she whispered.

"No! Not if we have anything to do with it." Keith glanced at the paramedic, before turning back to the patient. "Susan," he said, softening his tone. "Did you see the person who did this to you?"

"No, someone grabbed me from behind." She closed her eyes.

"If this is too much for you, it can wait," Keith said. He began to move away, feeling a little guilty at asking these questions. It wasn't really his job. Usually, his patients were already stone cold by the time he saw them.

No." She lifted herself slightly and reached out to grab his arm. "I need to tell someone before it's too late."

She flopped back down onto the bed and gripped Keith's hand before telling him what she knew about her attack.

"I had just come off duty from the hotel where I work, when someone crept up behind me and swept their arm around my waist. At first, I wasn't too concerned. I thought it was the lovely guy I work with – he has a habit of doing that. It's all in fun, you understand," she added, quickly. "He doesn't mean any harm – everyone knows that."

Keith nodded.

"Our shifts were due to end at the same time today," she continued, "and we had planned to meet up with another couple of friends and have coffee together at the Italian Coffee Shop at the top of the lane leading from the quayside. However, when his relief phoned in to say he would be an hour or so late, Larry told the supervisor he would stay on until Brian arrived. So, when I felt the arm around my waist, I immediately thought that Brian had turned up earlier than expected, and Larry was able to join us for coffee after all."

She closed her eyes for a few seconds. "But then, when I saw his other arm sweep around me with a knife poised in his hand, I realised it wasn't Larry."

"You say 'his' other arm with a knife in 'his' hand. That implies you believe it was a man who man attacked you."

"I really can't say for certain," Sue confessed. "But whoever it was had me totally locked in their grip." She paused for a moment to gather a little more strength. "I've had few lessons in self-defense. I should have been able to do something to help myself. Yet I couldn't, because his grip on me was so strong. That's why I believe the attacker was a man."

"Did the man say anything while this was happening?"

"No, not a word."

"And you're certain it wasn't this Larry character?"

"Yes, I'm absolutely sure it wasn't Larry. He wouldn't do this to anyone – he's a nice guy. He gave me this for my birthday."

As she spoke, Wendy raised her free hand and began to feel around her neck. But both Keith and the paramedic could see there was nothing there.

"Where is it?" she cried out. "My pendant – it's gone!"

"May I?" Keith said. He gently raised her head and looked at the back of her neck. There was a red mark where the pendant had been ripped away from her.

"Whoever stabbed you must have taken it," he said, carefully lowering her head back onto the pillow. "I think you'd better rest now. We should be at the hospital shortly."

Sue nodded and closed her eyes.

Keith was thoughtful as he watched her lying there. Her hand was still grasping his and he made no attempt to remove it. He wasn't used to his patients clutching his hand for support anymore. That sort of thing had ended years ago. Yet, if it gave this young woman comfort, then he was more than happy to accommodate.

His thoughts then turned to what Susan had told him about the attack. No doubt DCI Johnson would be waiting to hear what he had learned. Therefore, he needed to be in a position to answer all the questions. Though, thinking it through, he didn't have a great deal to tell him. Susan hadn't actually seen her attacker, as whoever it was had struck from behind. Yet, she had given him a name to go on. The chances were that this Larry character would turn out to be innocent. Susan certainly didn't believe he was the man who attacked her. But who knows?

Just then, Keith heard the driver call out to say that they had entered the grounds of the hospital.

From that moment on, everything happened fast. Once the ambulance pulled up outside the Accident and Emergency Department, the doors were swung open and the patient was swept away into the hospital. Doctor Nichols and the ambulance crew accompanied the trolley carrying Sue through corridors towards the Operating Theatre, while answering questions thrown at them by the hospital staff. Once their patient disappeared into the theatre, the ambulance crew left the hospital. No doubt their services were needed elsewhere.

Keith was thoughtful as he sat in a waiting room near the theatre. There wasn't really any need for him to stay here, either. He had done his job and the young woman was in good hands. Yet, at the same time, he felt reluctant to leave. There was something about this woman that appealed to him.

However, he had yet to decide whether it was due to her inner strength and determination to tell him what little she knew of her attack, despite her serious injuries, or because he was attracted to her for more personal reasons.

Maybe it was a little of both.

Chapter Fourteen

About twenty minutes after the ambulance crew left the hospital, Alan and his sergeant arrived there. They were accompanied by a woman police officer.

"Damn traffic," Alan grumbled, as he sat down next to Keith. "We should have been here ten minutes ago." He looked at the pathologist. "I didn't expect to see you here. I thought you would have gone, once you had dropped off the patient."

"I thought I would hang on for a while – you know, just to see how she got on in there." He gestured towards the Operating Theatre. "Besides, they might need to ask me something about her relapse on the way here."

"What happened?" Alan asked.

"I'm not sure," Keith admitted. "But suddenly her BP and heart-rate dropped. It could have been caused by the noise going on around us. However, when the bleeding restarted, we knew something was amiss. We did everything we could."

"Do they think she'll be okay?" Andrews asked, nodding his head towards the doors of the Operating Theatre.

"I don't know – I haven't heard anything since she was wheeled in there. I can only hope so." Keith buried his head in his hands. "If only it hadn't taken so long to get here, she might have had a better chance. But we were stuck in a traffic jam."

"This is WPC Margaret Somers," Alan intervened, aware the pathologist was feeling uncomfortable. "She'll be staying close by the patient until another officer relieves her later this evening."

Keith looked up and smiled at the officer. But, after a moment's thought, he turned his attention back to the DCI.

"You believe whoever did this, will try again – don't you?"

"We can't be too careful," Alan replied, with a sigh. "We'd be failing in our duty if we didn't look out for her."

Keith nodded. "Yes, I understand." He took a deep breath. "Okay, you want to know whether I learned anything while we were on the way here."

Alan nodded. "Anything she told you, however insignificant it may seem, could give us somewhere to start looking for this killer."

* * *

The DCI and Sergeant Andrews discussed what the pathologist had told them, as they made their way to the Millennium Hotel.

"The fact that Susan Matthews stated she was attacked from behind, certainly confirms what Doctor Nichols found after rechecking the body of Wendy Hamilton," Andrews said.

The pathologist had rung the DCI to inform him that, after taking a further look at the wound on Wendy, he was of the opinion the attack could have come from behind.

"It's all to do with the way the knife penetrated the victim," Doctor Nichols had told them. "It was an upward thrust, which, to my mind, means it could have come from someone attacking from behind."

"Absolutely," Alan replied to Andrews's comment. He paused for a moment, as he negotiated his car around a parked lorry.

"But when I was talking to Keith earlier, he happened to mention that he believed Janet Cunningham had been stabbed in much the same way. He admitted he hadn't had time to do a full post-mortem. However, he did look at how the knife entered the body. Therefore, we really need to speak to this Larry character."

By now, they had reached the quayside.

"Don't forget, Susan Matthews doesn't believe it was Larry who attacked her," Andrews reminded him.

"Yes, I understand that. But, let's face it, she didn't see who it was, so it could well have been him – especially as she said he was known to creep up behind women and grab them around their waist. Besides, at the moment, his name is the only one we have."

By now, Alan had pulled up outside the hotel. "I'll go to speak to the manager," he added, as he stepped out of the car, "while you check out whether Larry is on duty."

Less than two minutes later, the two detectives had entered the hotel and were making their way towards reception.

"Is Mr Jenkins in his office?" Alan asked, as he neared the desk.

"Yes, I'll tell him you wish to speak with him," the receptionist replied, placing her hand on the telephone.

"No need, I'll tell him myself," he decided, walking towards the manager's office.

Andrews accompanied the DCI as far as the lift, where, after a brief word, they parted company. The sergeant pressed the button to call the lift to the ground floor and while he was waiting, he watched his superior officer enter the manager's office without even knocking on the door.

* * *

As he approached the manager's office, Alan could hear the phone ringing.

"You'd better answer that," the DCI said, as he swung open the door and stepped inside. "I think someone is trying to tell you that I'm here and I need to talk to you."

Mr Jenkins picked up the phone. "It's alright, I know. The DCI is here now," he said, replacing the receiver onto its cradle.

"What can I do for you?" The manager turned his attention back to the DCI. "Please don't tell me that someone's had their jewellery stolen again. We've had safes fitted in all the rooms since…"

"No, that's not why I'm here," Alan interrupted.

"Then why *are* you here?" Mr Jenkins asked. "Who found it necessary to call the police? You'd think they would have the decency to talk to me first."

"No one from the hotel called the police," Alan replied.

"Then, I repeat, why are you here?"

"If you give me half a chance, I'll tell you." By now, Alan was beginning to lose his patience.

"I'm sorry. It's just that after all the problems I've had…" He paused. "But, please carry on." He gestured towards the chair in front of his desk.

Lowering himself into the seat, Alan began to unfold the reason for his visit.

"I'm here because Susan Matthews, a member of your staff, was found lying in the road a short distance away from the hotel." Alan said quietly. "She'd been stabbed and it appeared that she had lost a great deal of blood. However, the doctor at the hospital believes she has a good chance of pulling through."

"I can't believe it!" Mr Jenkins choked. "Sue is a lovely young woman and a valued member of our staff. Why would anyone want to hurt her?"

"That's exactly what we're trying to find out."

* * *

After her encounter with Harold Armstrong, not to mention the woman who had screamed out at her, Agnes had kept her head down. Her eyes had been focused on the photographs she had taken of the penthouse apartment earlier that day. It was only the thought of moving into such a wonderful new home that had kept her afloat. At one point, she had considered calling Alan and asking him to join her, but then she had dismissed the idea. He could be out somewhere, making an arrest.

Fortunately, one by one, the people at the tables around her moved on and the spaces were quickly filled by new customers. Thankfully, she wasn't the centre of attention anymore. Perhaps now would be a good time to go back to the hotel.

She entered the hotel and had almost reached the lift, when someone called out to her.

"Madam, I think you've dropped something."

Agnes turned around to find a man standing by the reception desk. He was holding up a glove.

"Thank you, but that isn't mine," she replied. "Besides, why would I want to wear gloves in this heat?"

"You are right, of course." The man smiled. "What was I thinking?"

As Agnes turned back towards the lift, she noticed him sliding the glove into the overnight bag he was carrying, rather than handing it to the receptionist. Obviously, pretending to find a glove as a woman passed by was his chat-up line.

However, the man wasn't prepared to allow it to end there, as she discovered when she heard him creep up behind her.

"It seems I've arrived a little early," he said, as she swung around to face him. "They tell me my room isn't ready yet. Therefore I'm at a bit of a loss as to what to do. Would you care to join me for a beverage?" He looked around the reception area. "I'm sure there must be somewhere in the hotel where we can get something to drink. Or maybe we can go out somewhere."

"I..." Agnes was about to decline the offer, but she didn't get the chance.

"Please, madam. I'll feel so conspicuous sitting here alone," he continued. He looked at his watch. "Can't we just have one drink together?"

Agnes glanced at the clock above the reception desk. It showed the time as two-fifteen. Checking-in time was usually three o'clock. She looked back at the man. She had the impression he was slightly younger than her. He was quite smartly dressed in a dark blue suit, with a matching tie over a white shirt. His dark-brown hair was cut short with a parting at one side and he was clean-shaven. Perhaps he was a business man here in Newcastle for a meeting. If that was the case, then he would probably be gone in a couple of days.

"Very well, I don't see why not," she said. She pointed to the sitting room. "We can go in there and order something. Tea or coffee would be fine."

"Champagne, I think," he replied. "This is my first day in Newcastle and I have met a most wonderful woman. I think that's a good reason to have champagne."

Chapter Fifteen

Meanwhile, Alan was still discussing the stabbing of Susan Matthews with the hotel manager.

"I understand you have a young man by the name of Larry working here at the hotel," the DCI continued.

"Yes, Larry Parker, he's one of our lift attendants." Mr Jenkins thought for a moment. "Why do you mention him?"

"You don't have any other member of staff called Larry?" Alan persisted. "Not even someone who might prefer to be called Laurence?"

"No. I assure you, we only have one person named Larry, Laurence or any other variation of the name, on our staff – Larry Parker." Mr Jenkins looked puzzled. "Look, where is this going? What on earth has our lift attendant got to do with the attack on Miss Matthews?"

* * *

Sergeant Andrews had waited impatiently, while the lift slowly descended to the ground floor. It had stopped at every floor on the way down, which meant that there might be several guests pouring out once the doors slid open. He had been tempted to hold his finger on the button, hoping the attendant would pay heed and by-pass the other floors. However, he was aware that discretion was required. The last thing he wanted was to draw attention to himself. Also, if the attendant on duty was Larry, it could mean that he hadn't left the hotel at the time of the incident and he would be in the clear with regards to the attack on his co-worker.

At last, the lift stopped on the ground floor and Andrews waited for the doors to slide open. He had met Larry while working on another case at the hotel, therefore he would recognize him instantly. The doors slid open, but it wasn't Larry who ushered the guests out of the lift.

"Going up?" the attendant asked, beckoning Andrews into the lift.

"No and neither are you," the sergeant replied. Holding up his ID card, he stepped into the lift.

"What's all this about?" The young man looked troubled and took a step backwards.

"It's okay," Andrews replied. "No need for concern. I just want to have a few words with you." He nodded towards the lift doors. "Are you able to disable the lift so that we can talk privately?"

For one brief moment, the sergeant imagined himself in the role of Special Agent Gibbs. The *NCIS* agent would often flick a switch to pull the lift to a halt when he wanted to talk privately with someone onboard.

The attendant pointed to one of the buttons. "If I were to press that, it would give the impression the lift is out of service. Though I don't know what the manager will say. We have some guests here who can't manage the stairs."

"Do it," Andrews instructed. "This won't take long – providing you answer my questions."

The attendant nodded and pressed the button.

"Okay, what's your name and at what time today did you come on duty?"

"Have I done something wrong?"

"That depends. Just answer the questions."

"My name is Brian Hockley and," he glanced at his watch, "I think I came on duty about two hours ago." He paused. "My shift was due to start earlier, but I was a little late because of personal problems. However, I phoned in to let the staff supervisor know, so she could arrange cover. If you need the exact time of my arrival, you'll find it on my timesheet. We all sign in when we arrive and sign out when we leave."

"I see." Andrews looked up from his notepad. "Where will I find the timesheets?"

"Mrs Telford's office. She keeps all the paperwork in there."

"Thank you, Brian, you've been most helpful," Sergeant Andrews said, as he finished scribbling in his notebook. "I think that's all for the moment."

He didn't see the need to keep the young man any longer. As far as he could tell, Brian Parker had answered his questions promptly and without any fuss.

"You can put the lift back into operation and go about your duties." The sergeant gestured towards the buttons.

"Is that it?" Brian asked. "I thought you were about to ask me a hell of a load of questions."

"Yes, that's it – for the moment." Andrews replied. "But, should I need to talk to you again, I know where to find you," he added.

When the doors slid open, they found Agnes in the throes of moving away from the lift towards the stairs.

"I take it the lift is working again?" she said, cheerfully.

"Yes," the sergeant replied. "I think there was a minor problem. But it seems to be sorted now." He glanced at Brian "Right?"

"Yes, that's right," Brian replied. "I think pressed the wrong button, because we ground to a halt and the emergency lights came on."

"I see," Agnes replied, with a shrug. "It's easily done," she added, the smile never leaving her face.

She looked at each of the men in turn. Neither of them had made a move.

"So, Sergeant, are you about to go up? Or had you just come down?"

"Sorry, I've come down," Andrews said, swiftly stepping out of the lift.

Once the sergeant was clear of the doors, Agnes stepped into the lift and gave Brian her floor number.

"Nice meeting you again, Sergeant," she called after him.

The sergeant closed his eyes, as the doors closed and the lift soared upwards, taking Agnes Lockwood with it. At least she hadn't asked him any pertinent questions; such as, why was he here. Andrews had hoped he and the chief inspector wouldn't bump into her while they were at the hotel. But that hadn't worked out.

It wasn't as though he had anything against Agnes – except the fact that she had a habit of poking her nose into their investigations. But, on reflection, maybe he was a little jealous because she always came up with the right answers.

* * *

Agnes's mind was racing as the lift travelled up to the fourth floor. Her encounter with the hotel's latest guest, John Alton, was driven from her mind as she mulled over various reasons why Sergeant Andrews was at the hotel.

Yes, for a few minutes, John had been amusing, telling her about his job and why he was here in the north-east. It was exactly as she had first thought; the man was here on a business meeting and would go back to London in a couple of days. At first, Agnes had declined the offer of champagne, not wanting to give him the wrong impression. But he had been insistent – telling her he was entitled to the odd bottle of champagne now and again to impress his clients.

"But, I'm not one of your clients," she had stated, realizing she was being drawn into his web.

"Maybe not yet, but you might be, when you see what I have to offer a woman such as yourself."

"And what would that be – John?"

"A woman on her own, lonely, in need of a man to guide her…"

At that point, Agnes wished she had never agreed to join him. She had been about to stand up and walk away, but, when the waiter appeared with the champagne, she decided to wait and hear what else he had to say.

Nevertheless, to be on the safe side, she had signalled to the waiter to add the champagne to her account and not Mr Alton's. That way, she would not be beholden to this dreadful man. Once she had taken a few sips from the glass, she had made her excuses and left him sitting there.

Now, her thoughts were on Sergeant Andrews. It wasn't normal for him to show up here. Therefore, had there been some sort of an incident – another robbery, perhaps? If that was the case, then might he have been upstairs to interview the people concerned in the theft?

She glanced at the lift attendant. It was a pity Larry hadn't been on duty. He would have been bursting at the seams to tell her anything he could, regarding the visit from the police. Though, on reflection, even Brian was usually a little more talkative than he was today, though he was never as forthcoming as Larry. Yet today, Brian didn't have very much to say at all. Maybe he'd had a tiff with his girlfriend last evening and was still stewing over it.

By now, the lift had reached the fourth floor.

"This is your floor," he said, as the doors opened.

"Thank you, Brian." Agnes stepped out of the lift.

By the time she reached her room, Agnes had dismissed Brian from her mind. She didn't have time to ponder on his feelings at the moment. She was more interested in why the police were at the hotel. Closing the door behind her, she removed her jacket and threw it onto the bed before sinking down into the comfortable chair by the window.

It had been such a strange day.

It had started out well enough. Agnes had viewed the penthouse apartment near the quayside and had adored everything about it. It was exactly what she was looking for and she could hardly wait for Alan to see it.

However, later in the day, things turned had rather sour. First, Harold Armstrong had suddenly decided to join her at the café under the pretext that he had met her before. Even when he left, he'd had the nerve to turn around and blow kisses at her, just as his wife or lady friend turned up. The woman had been furious – if looks could have killed, Agnes felt she would be dead now.

Since then, Agnes had spent her time kicking her heels around the quayside, making sure she wasn't being followed. The last thing she wanted was for either Armstrong, or his woman friend, to learn she was staying locally. But then, after finally arriving back at the hotel, intending to go up to her room and freshen up before relaxing in the drawing room with her book and a glass of wine until Alan arrived, she had bumped into John Alton.

She glanced across to her bed where she had tossed her bag, along with her jacket and the room keycard. For a moment, she was tempted retrieve her phone and call Alan to ask if there *was* anything going on at the hotel. But then she had another thought. What if the chief inspector was already downstairs?

Of course! Why on earth hadn't she thought of that earlier? What was wrong with her?

At that point, Agnes leapt to her feet and grabbed her bag. If Alan was down there, what the hell was she still doing up here?

Chapter Sixteen

Agnes decided to take the stairs to the ground floor, rather than the lift. She didn't feel like meeting Brian again at the moment; not if he was in the same dismal mood. She spotted Alan just as she rounded the last bend in the staircase. Though he was alone at that point, she knew Sergeant Andrews would still be around somewhere.

"I guessed it wouldn't be long before you joined us," he laughed.

"I expect your sergeant told you that he'd seen me. So what has brought you here? Is something going on?" She raised her eyebrows.

"Yes, Andrews mentioned he'd bumped into you. So, what have you been up to today?" he asked, avoiding her questions.

"Quite a lot, actually," she replied. "I have something we really need to discuss, but…"

She didn't get the chance to say any more, as John Alton stepped out of the lift and interrupted her.

"Hello, Agnes," he said, when he saw her. "How nice to catch up with you again. I thought you told me you had a date." He glanced at Alan. "Oops, sorry, sir, I had no idea she was referring to her father. Well, enjoy some time with your daughter."

He waved as he strolled towards the entrance. "See you tomorrow, Agnes. More champagne – methinks."

"Who the hell was that?" Alan erupted, once the man had left the hotel. "So I'm your father, am I?"

"His name is John Alton," Agnes replied. "For goodness' sake, get a grip. He arrived at the hotel this afternoon and just happened to see me when I came back into the hotel."

She explained how the man had arrived early and what had transpired.

"But I really want to talk to you about something else. Something…"

"Can't it wait, Agnes?" Alan snapped.

He was feeling a little hurt that Agnes had been sharing champagne with another man.

"Andrews will be back in a minute or two, so I haven't got time for idle chit-chat." He glanced over her shoulder as he spoke.

"I see," she replied slowly, ignoring his rude tone. "So there *is* something going on here at the hotel."

Alan closed his eyes. He had been caught out again. But what the heck; the incident would be all over the local news later this evening, if Harold Armstrong had anything to do with it.

"No, not *at* the hotel," he said, lowering his voice. "But there have been two stabbings *near* the hotel. The latest one was a member of the staff. She was attacked in the street leading up to City Road."

"Oh, my goodness!" Agnes exclaimed. "Is she going to be alright?"

"We hope so. She's at the hospital now. They think they caught her in time, but it's touch and go. Her name is Susan Matthews."

Agnes gasped at the news.

"Are you okay?" Alan asked, forgetting his hurt feelings for the moment. "Do you need to sit down?"

He guided her over towards the drawing room. Thankfully, it was empty. Obviously, everyone was outside, taking advantage of the warm weather.

"Yes, I know Sue," Agnes said, once she had lowered herself onto a sofa.

She was silent for a moment as she thought back to her last encounter with the hotel's liaison officer. They had shared a joke when they had bumped into each other in the corridor only that morning.

"She's a lovely young woman. Why on earth would anyone want to hurt her?"

"That's why we're here." Alan hesitated. "We need to find out whether anyone had a grudge against her."

"I can't imagine anyone having a bad word to say against Sue. She is liked by..." Agnes paused and looked straight at Alan, narrowing her eyes. "Yet you believe someone here at the hotel tried to kill her, don't you? That's the real reason you're here."

"We don't know," Alan protested. "But we have to start somewhere."

"Nevertheless, something must have brought you here."

"It was just something she said."

"So, what did she say?"

Alan found himself repeating what Sue had told the pathologist.

"And now you think Larry Parker crept up behind her and pushed a knife into her chest," Agnes retorted.

If it was a question, she didn't give him time to answer.

"I don't believe it," she continued. "Larry wouldn't do something like that. Besides, he was still on duty, wasn't he? Didn't you just tell me that he agreed to stay on because Brian was going to be late?"

"As it turns out, Brian arrived earlier than expected," Alan explained. "At the moment, Andrews is checking out the timesheets."

"I still don't believe it," Agnes choked. "It's just not possible."

"It *is* possible, Agnes," Alan said.

His voice was firmer than necessary. He was still stinging over John Alton's proposed meeting with Agnes the following day, even though she hadn't said yes.

"Anything is possible in this day and age. We read about things happening every day – things we never thought would happen."

"But... Larry!" she insisted. "He's so friendly – so helpful. No! It's *not* possible."

"You only know the Larry you've met here at the hotel," said Alan. "You have no idea what the real Larry is like, once he is outside these four walls. He could be a totally different person." He took a deep breath. "How many people do you know who creep up from behind and grab someone around their waist?"

"Not many," Agnes admitted. "Yet I can think of one."

"And who was that – your husband?"

"No, Alan. It was you," she replied. "You used to do that at school all the time."

"I never did – did I?" Alan grimaced, as he recollected his schooldays. "Okay, maybe I did, once or twice. But it was all in fun – and don't forget, it was a long time ago, and I was young."

"So can't Larry be doing it 'in fun'?" Agnes made quotation marks in the air as she spoke. "He's young, too."

"I know all that, Agnes. But perhaps, in his case, the fun part changed into something more sinister."

"So – you're saying that Larry killed Wendy Hamilton and Janet Cunningham, too?" Agnes retorted. "But what about the man I saw with Wendy in Whitley Bay? Is he now out of the equation?"

"Agnes, you know we've had every officer available out looking for this man, ever since you pointed him out. The photograph of him, taken by the local paper's photographer, Harry Armstrong, has been all over the news. Yet still no one has come forward with a positive ID. Don't you understand, Agnes? We haven't any other alternative – we must to look into this latest information."

Alan was relieved when his sergeant appeared in front of them. He didn't want any more arguments here in the drawing room.

"You've seen the log-in book, Sergeant?"

"Yes, sir and it appears that Brian Hockley's statement checks out." Andrews replied. "He signed in just before Susan Matthews signed out."

"And Parker, when did he sign out?"

"It seems Larry Parker signed out at the same time Brian Hockley signed in." Andrews held up a sheet of paper. "I thought that was a little strange, so I acquired a copy for our records."

The chief inspector rose to his feet. "This means we need to speak to Larry Parker ASAP. Were you able to get his address from the staff supervisor?"

The sergeant nodded. "Mrs Telford is a formidable lady. However, I got the impression that she is protective of her staff. She appeared to be very sorry to hear the news regarding Miss Matthews, but assured me that no one at the hotel was capable of doing such a terrible thing. She reckons everyone gets on well together. Therefore, not wanting to put any one person in the frame, I took the precaution of asking her for the addresses of everyone who left the hotel today at around the same time as the victim. I told her that one of them might have seen something without realizing what was happening."

"Good thinking," the chief inspector replied. "Well done."

Alan looked at Agnes. "I'm sorry, but I'll have to go." He began to move away, but then paused. "You said you had something to tell me."

"Forget it." She shook her head. After his brusque tone earlier, there was no way she was going to tell him about the apartment. "I'll sort it myself."

Agnes watched the two detectives stride out of the drawing room. Due to the angled mirrors in both the drawing room and the reception, she was able to see them both as they headed towards the entrance. At one point, Alan paused and glanced back towards the drawing room. Was he going to come back? However, if it had crossed his mind to return, he appeared to dismiss the thought. Instead, he swiftly carried on walking towards the entrance.

Disappointed, Agnes drew her attention back to Larry. There were a couple of questions that needed answering. There were probably a lot more, but, for the moment, she was focusing on two.

First, was it possible that, because the police hadn't found their first suspect – the man she had seen with Wendy Hamilton on the beach and later at the Central Station – they were now set on pinning the murders on Larry Parker? And secondly, had Sergeant Andrews even bothered to check whether Larry was on duty at the times when Wendy Hamilton and Janet Cunningham were murdered?

She would like to believe the sergeant had looked into her second thought. But, as both he and his boss seemed to have their minds fixed on Larry being the new suspect, who knows? Perhaps she should have a word with Mrs Telford.

Agnes rose to her feet and brushed down her skirt. The staff supervisor would be her first port of call.

Chapter Seventeen

Though Agnes had never actually spoken to the staff supervisor, she had been pointed out to her some time ago. Since then, she had seen Mrs Telford striding around the hotel on several occasions, carrying out random checks to make sure everything was up to standard. Apparently, she was a stickler for detail.

"Please sit down." Mrs Telford smiled as she gestured toward the large, comfortable chair in front of her desk.

"Thank you," Agnes replied.

As she lowered herself into the chair, Agnes couldn't help noticing how neat and tidy the supervisor's desk was. Everything appeared to be in place – unlike the one she had sat behind when she worked in an office all those years ago. Back then, anyone looking on would have thought her desk was a shambles. Nevertheless, she had always been able to put her hand on exactly what she wanted, just when she needed it.

"What can I do for you, today?" Mrs Telford asked, once Agnes was seated. Her smile suddenly changed to a frown. "Are you here to make a complaint against a member of my staff?"

"No, not at all," Agnes quickly replied. "I have nothing to complain about. I think everyone does a wonderful job."

"Thank you," said Mrs Telford, the smile quickly returning. "We all do our very best to make sure the guests have a wonderful stay." She paused. "In that case, what *can* I do for you?"

Agnes recalled Larry mentioning how, despite her brusque exterior, she had rather soft spot for her staff and always stood up for them.

Agnes took a deep breath. "It's about Susan Matthews. I was so very sorry to learn she had been attacked shortly after leaving the hotel earlier today. I gather she is undergoing surgery at this very moment."

"Yes, it's terrible news. I was absolutely horrified when the police told me. She is such a lovely young woman." She paused. "But how do you know about it? I only heard it myself a short while ago. It certainly can't have reached the news yet."

"Does it matter how or where I heard it?" Agnes said, staring across at the woman sitting opposite her.

"I don't suppose so. But I would like to know why you want to discuss it with me, Mrs Lockwood."

"You know who I am?" Agnes was surprised. She hadn't given her name or room number, yet the staff supervisor knew who she was without even looking at a file or computer.

"Of course I do. I know exactly when every guest registers into the hotel, how long they are staying, and what room they are given. But that's part of the job. However, I tend go the extra mile. I like to make a point of fitting a face to a room."

Agnes wasn't sure whether she was impressed, or a little spooked. How could the supervisor possibly know so many details… unless she was peering over the shoulder of the receptionists when they handed out the keycards?

Agnes decided to be open with this woman, at least for the moment. After all, she needed her help.

"As it happens, I heard the news from the same source as you – the police. Yes, I agree, it *is* dreadful news about Sue and I do hope she will recover." She hesitated. "But the reason I'm here is because I want to talk to you about Larry Parker."

"Larry is one of our two lift attendants," Mrs Telford replied. She paused for second. "What can I tell you? He's a lovely young man who treats the guests with respect – I thought he would go far. But now…" She paused.

"But now the police believe he tried to kill Susan Matthews." Agnes finished the sentence.

"Yes, they do. But I don't want to believe it." Mrs Telford shook her head vigorously. "Larry wouldn't do that. He couldn't. It's not in his nature to hurt anyone, let alone attack them with a knife."

"I totally agree with you," Agnes said. "In this instance, I believe the police have got it all wrong. But, if I'm to prove his innocence, I need to see everything you showed to Sergeant Andrews."

"So, Mrs Lockwood, how do you know it was Sergeant Andrews who questioned me about Larry?"

"Because I just happened to be with the chief inspector when the sergeant passed on the information you gave him." Agnes took a deep breath. "Look, Mrs Telford, you really need to trust me. Like I said, I don't believe Larry did this. But, if I am to help him, I need to know exactly what you told the sergeant."

The staff supervisor and Agnes sat with their eyes fixed on each other for a long moment. It was almost as though both were trying to work out what the other was thinking.

"I think what you *really* mean is, if *we* are going to help him." Mrs Telford was the first to speak. Without diverting her eyes, she opened one of the drawers in her desk and pulled out a large file. "I will give you the information you ask. However, in return, I would like you to keep me in the loop about whatever you find. Also, if there is anything I can do, no matter what, I want you to feel able to call on me – day or night."

"Agreed," Agnes replied. "I'd like to believe we're on the same side and we both want to clear Larry of any blame."

Mrs Telford didn't reply. She quickly scribbled her home address and phone number on a piece of paper and slid it across the desk.

Picking up the note, Agnes glanced at it, before looking back across the desk.

"Flo?" she questioned.

"Short for Florence," Mrs Telford replied. "I was named after a maiden aunt. Normally, I insist on people using my full name. 'Flo' always make me sound a bit like the tide coming in on the coast. However, as we're working together, you can call me Flo. Florence or Mrs Telford can be a bit longwinded."

"Then, you must call me Agnes." She laughed. "I, too, was named after a relative – my grandmother. But when I kept getting called Aggie at school, I made up my mind I would change it to something with a nicer ring, once I was old enough. But when my mother and father moved abroad, the people over there learned to speak my name as it was spelled out to them. To each and every one of them, I was known as Agnes."

"Okay, Agnes it is. Now, let's get back to the case." Florence tapped her finger at the list of signatures on the top sheet in the file. "Sergeant Andrews took the names and addresses of all the staff who had signed in and out on the recent shift change. He told me they would all need to be questioned before being eliminated from their enquiries. However, I didn't fail to notice that he really only focused on the details of one person – Larry Parker. I casually enquired why the police thought one of the staff might be responsible, but he fobbed me off by telling me he couldn't divulge that sort of information."

"Then let me tell you why they've picked on Larry," Agnes said.

She went on to inform Florence about what Susan had told Dr Nichols while on her way to the hospital.

"I see," Florence replied, slowly. "Yes, now I can understand where the police are coming from."

She looked up sharply, as though suddenly realizing Agnes was still there.

"Sorry, I'm mumbling. But it crossed my mind that if, as Sue said, she didn't see his face, they can't really be sure it wasn't Larry who attacked her, can they?" Flo shrugged. "All I'm saying is, Larry is their only suspect, so what else can they do other than look into it?" she added.

"Surely that's why we must work together to find something to prove Larry's innocence," Agnes insisted.

"Yes, of course. You're right," Florence faltered. "So, tell me what I can do to help. Where do we go from here?"

"You've given me Larry's home address, but I think the police will have made that their first port of call, the moment they left the hotel."

Agnes paused. Was she missing something? Flo appeared to be a little hesitant at times. But, on the other hand, they had only just met. Maybe Flo was simply being as cautious as she was about their new friendship.

"However," Agnes continued, "assuming Larry doesn't always go straight home after signing out, do you know of anywhere else he might go at the end of a shift? I appreciate the staff won't tell you what they do away from work, but…"

"A café," Florence quickly interrupted. "I've heard that sometimes, after an early shift, a few of the staff go to an Italian coffee shop at the top of the narrow road immediately behind the hotel. I believe they like to meet up and talk about everything and nothing." She shook her head. "I'm sorry, but I just can't think of the name of the café."

"No problem, Flo. Rest assured, I'll find it," Agnes leapt to her feet. "Or I know someone who will. Hopefully, Larry will still be there and I can at least make him aware of what is going on. Thank you, Flo. You're a star. I'll let you know what happens if I get to meet up with him."

"But he will *still* be wanted by the police, won't he?" Florence said.

"I'll think of something," Agnes replied, as she hurried out of the door. She popped her head back for a second. "By the way, did the sergeant enquire whether Larry was on duty when Wendy Hamilton and Janet Cunningham were murdered?"

"No, he didn't."

"Then can you check back to when those murders took place, and look at Larry's worksheets?"

"Will do," Florence replied.

"Also, try to remember anything else the sergeant asked while he was here."

"Such as?"

"I don't know, Flo. Just anything the police might try to use to prove their case against Larry."

Agnes was thoughtful as she rushed up the stairs. First, she needed to call Ben, the taxi driver, and ask him to pick her up. She hoped he would be free because, with the festival going on in the city, there were more tourists than usual. Once he had told her he could be with her in about fifteen minutes, she gathered her things together and set off.

"Going down?" Brian grinned, as the doors slid open.

Apparently he was in a better mood now.

"Yes," Agnes replied. She gave him a broad smile as she stepped into the lift. "Ground floor, please, I have some shopping to do."

Shopping was the last thing on her mind, but why let anyone know where her real destination was?

Brian touched his cap as he pressed the button. "Absolutely, Mrs Lockwood. Where would you ladies be without your shopping?"

Agnes faked a smile at the lift attendant as the lift reached the ground floor. "Indeed," she said. "I guess you have us women sussed."

"Enjoy your shopping!" Brian called out, as she strode across towards the hotel entrance. She didn't reply, giving the impression she hadn't heard his last remark.

Agnes walked out of the hotel to find Ben waiting for her.

He jumped out of the taxi and held the passenger door open for her. "Okay, where to?"

"Good question," Agnes replied, as she stepped into the taxi.

Chapter Eighteen

"Yes, I know the café you mean," Ben said, once Agnes had passed on what little information she had. "It's on New Bridge Street."

"Great, take me there." Agnes sat back in the seat.

"But I understand that particular café is frequented by the more – er – younger set."

"Are you trying to tell me something, Ben?" Agnes grinned.

"No – no, not at all," he blabbed. "I was just…"

"Ben, have you anything else lined up for the rest of the afternoon?" Agnes interrupted.

"I have to pick up someone at the Vermont Hotel in ten minutes and drop them at the Central Station. After that, I'm free until the next call."

"Okay, then mark me in as your next call," Agnes replied. "I want to hire you and your taxi for the rest of the afternoon – if that's okay with you."

"That's fine by me," Ben said, pulling up outside the café. "I'll be back here ASAP."

"Thank you," Agnes said, as she stepped out of the taxi.

She stood by the kerb and watched Ben pull away before turning her attention to the café. Even from here, it was obvious that the place was filled with young people, due to the loud chatter and laughter emitting from the open door. Now and again, she picked up the sound of some music, but most of it was drowned by the babble of voices.

Ben was right. This wasn't her scene.

It used to be. But that was many years ago, at a time when she had been part of a crowd meeting up for coffee after work. She and her friends would talk for what seemed like hours, about how their day had gone and what they would be wearing for the disco that evening. However, those days had long gone. Now she had two sons, both older than some of those inside the café. Agnes swallowed hard before walking across the pavement towards the entrance.

The chatter stopped when she stepped inside and everyone's eyes turned in her direction. It was only when a middle-aged woman emerged from behind the counter and pulled out a seat for her, that they all start talking again.

"I seem to have interrupted something," Agnes said, as she sat down. "Maybe I shouldn't be here. But I felt like a coffee and I had heard that this place was good."

"Not at all, pet," the woman said. She had a broad Tyneside accent. Obviously she wasn't the Italian proprietor. "Why, everybody's welcome here." She gestured towards the group of young people. "Don't let that lot bother you. They think they own the place because they stop in after work every day for coffee or tea. I have no idea why Mr and Mrs Loreto put up with it. Now, what can I get you?" she added, without pausing for breath. "We have some of the most delicious cakes you'll find anywhere around here."

Agnes could have told her why the Loretos put up with it. It was all to do with money. But she let it pass.

"I'd like a latte," Agnes replied. Though she wasn't hungry, she realised that she needed to spend some money if she was going to get any information from either this woman, or the man tending the coffee machine, who she took to be Mr Loreto. "And perhaps I could have one of those," she added, pointing towards one of the most expensive cakes in the display cabinet. "They look really delicious."

"Of course, right away," the woman said, before bustling off.

Once she was alone again, Agnes took a few minutes to look around the café. Despite the number of people in here, there were only three or four faces she recognised from the hotel, though she doubted that they would know her. She had just seen them on the odd occasion when they popped into the drawing room to make sure the cushions were plumped up and that any newspapers left lying on the sofas were removed.

However, Larry didn't appear to be here and he was the guy she really wanted to talk to. Perhaps he had been here earlier and had already left to go home. If that was the case, then Alan and his sergeant were probably talking to him right now, or trundling him to the police station in handcuffs.

"There you go, pet." The woman setting her coffee and cake down onto the table broke into her thoughts. "If there's anything else you need, then please let me know."

"Yes, actually there is something you could help me with," Agnes said, before the woman had a chance to move away.

She quickly glanced around at the other customers, but no one appeared to be taking any notice. They all seemed to have got used to having an older woman in their midst.

"Please, can you spare a moment?" She nodded towards a chair next to her.

The woman glanced towards the counter and, seeing that no one was waiting to be served, she sat down.

"Do you know Larry Parker? Agnes asked.

"Yes, he's here..." The woman broke off and looked across the café, only to find he wasn't where she had last seen him. "Well, he was here a few minutes ago. Perhaps he's visiting the men's room." She frowned. "But, why are you asking me about Larry? Are you his mother?"

"No!" Agnes shook her head, with a laugh. "No, I'm not his mother."

The woman narrowed her eyes. "Then what the hell's goin' on? Don't tell me you've got your eyes set on him? For goodness' sake, you're old enough to be his mother."

"Can you please keep your voice down?" Agnes asked firmly.

She glanced around at the other tables, but, as the chatting continued, it appeared no one had heard anything.

"As I said, I'm not his mother." Agnes kept her voice low, despite feeling angry at this woman's insinuations. "Nor have I got my eyes set on him, as you so delicately put it," she continued. "I simply needed to speak to him urgently."

"Then why didn't you just damn well say so?" the woman snorted.

"I just did."

"I meant earlier – instead of all this pussyfooting around?" the woman retorted. "I thought you were..."

"Okay, say no more." Agnes held up her hand to stop the woman from saying anything further. "I can guess what you thought. Look, we got off on the wrong foot," she admitted. "Please, can we start again?"

"Yes," the woman bristled. "I think that would be a good idea." She pointed to her name-badge pinned to her blouse. "My name's Margaret. You can call me by that name."

"Thank you. Then you must call me Agnes."

"Are you from around these parts?" Margaret enquired. "You don't quite have the Geordie accent. Yet, at the same time, I can pick it out now and again."

"Yes, actually, I am," Agnes replied, slowly. "But I have been away from the area for quite a while. I only returned last year."

She didn't quite know where to go from here. At first, she had thought that Margaret looked friendly, but after her outburst... Agnes was relieved when she saw Larry suddenly appear through the door leading in from the street. Obviously, he had popped out to buy something.

"Mrs Lockwood," he said, the moment he laid eyes on her. "What're you doing here?"

He glanced at Margaret, whose eyes were darting back and forth between him and Mrs Lockwood.

"I guess she must have heard about the wonderful coffee you serve here, Maggie," he added.

"It's Margaret. How many times do I have to tell you?" She wagged her finger at him, before rising to her feet. She glanced down at Agnes. "There's no respect these days. At one time, you could give kids a clip around the ear if they were rude, but nowadays, you'd have the law on you."

"I'm not a kid," Larry replied.

"Then why do you act like one?" she retorted. "Anyway, Agnes here wants to talk to you."

"You're here to talk to me? What's going on?" Larry barely waited until he was seated before asking the question.

Agnes waited until he had sat down properly before she replied. "Larry, there's been an attack on Susan Matthews."

"Susan Matthews?" His face looked blank for a moment, but then his eyes shot open. "You don't mean, Sue?" he uttered. "Sue from the hotel?"

Agnes nodded. "Yes. Someone stabbed her after she left the hotel earlier today."

She hesitated. She would like to have given him more time to absorb the news, but the police could turn up any minute. Once they didn't find him at home, they would make further enquiries and no doubt someone would tell them about the café he frequented after work.

"I'm surprised you didn't see the police working at the scene in the lane leading up here from the hotel. I understand that's the route you normally take – isn't it?"

"Yes, it is. But that's when Sue, me and a few others leave the hotel together, with the plan to come here. However, I was a little late leaving work today, so I decided to enjoy the sunshine. I strolled along the quayside and took another road up to New Bridge Street. I hoped I would catch up with Sue and the rest of the gang here in the café. When she wasn't here, I just thought I'd missed her. But," he gestured towards the group who were chatting like there was no tomorrow, "when they told me they hadn't seen her, I assumed she had decided to give it a miss today."

"I believe you, Larry."

"What do you mean, you believe me? That's what happened."

"Keep your voice down." Agnes glanced around the café, but no one appeared to be taking any notice. "Look, Larry, the police are anxious to talk you about the attempt on Sue's life."

"Are you telling me I'm the suspect?" Larry looked stunned. "*Me?*" he added in an incredulous tone, pointing towards himself.

"Yes, you," Agnes swiftly replied. This was not the time to beat around the bush. Enough time had been wasted already. "It's due to something Sue said on the way to the hospital in the ambulance. I think the police have blown it up out of all proportion."

"What could she have said? I haven't seen her since…"

"Larry," Agnes interrupted, "we don't have time to go into the ins and outs of what Sue said. Take my word for it – the police are paying a visit to your home address. They could be there right now."

Larry looked at his watch. "Then they'll be disappointed. They won't find anyone in. My mother will still be at work. She has a part-time job in one of the department stores in the city."

"What about your father? Is there a chance he might be at home?"

"No. He'll be at work, too."

Agnes breathed a sigh of relief. At least she could stop peering at the door. The police wouldn't have a clue where he was at this moment. Had his mother been at home, she might have felt inclined to answer their questions as to his whereabouts.

Larry swallowed hard. "Mrs Lockwood, do you think I should go to the police station? What I mean is – if I go there of my own accord to tell them that I'm not the person they are looking for, do you think they will believe me?"

"They might. But I honestly don't know."

Agnes would like to have been in the position of assuring Larry that the police would take him at his word. Yet, she was well aware that, at this point, they had no other suspects. The man she had seen with Wendy Hamilton at the coast still hadn't been found. Therefore, it was possible they might try to pin her murder on him, also. In other words – case closed.

"Larry," she continued, "I want you to know that if you feel you need someone with you, then please count on me. I would be more than happy to accompany you – I have a taxi waiting somewhere outside. But I understand if you would rather have your mother or your father with you at this time. Just tell me how to get in touch with them and I'll get straight onto it."

"I would rather they didn't know that I'm suspected of attempted murder." He paused. "Maybe I could clear up this mess before they need to be told. Please, Mrs Lockwood, would you come with me? I don't think I could face this alone."

"Of course I will, Larry. We'll go there right now."

A moment later, they both headed out of the door.

Chapter Nineteen

"Well, that was a waste of time," Alan grumbled, as he and his sergeant climbed into his car.

They had called at Larry Parker's address only to find there was no one home. A couple of neighbours had told them that both Larry's parents were at work at this time of the day. One had tried to be helpful by informing them that Mr and Mrs Parker's son worked at the Millennium Hotel on the quayside, before she closed the door.

"Why didn't he come home? Do you think he's made a run for it?" Sergeant Andrews pulled his seat belt around him as he spoke. "Maybe we should get some men to the Central Station and Newcastle Airport, just in case."

"Andrews! You need to get a grip." Alan said, as he started the engine. "The lad is only about eighteen or nineteen years old. Would you have gone straight home at the end of your shift at that age – especially if your shift happened to end in the middle of the afternoon?"

"No, I suppose not," Andrews said. He stroked his chin as he reflected on his youth; not that it was too far behind him. "So, what do you suggest?"

"I suggest we go back to the station and have a rethink," Alan replied, as he shifted the gear into first and slid away from the kerb. "There're too many prying eyes here."

The sergeant glanced out of his window and saw what the DCI meant. There were a few blinds being pulled to one side, in the nearby houses.

Back at the station, Alan was surprised to learn that there were two people waiting to see him. Looking through a one-way window, he saw Agnes sitting alongside the young man they wanted to talk to.

"Good thing we didn't start a nationwide search this afternoon, Sergeant," he joked, pointing towards the window. "Otherwise we'd have been laughed out of the force."

Alan decided to use his office to speak to the suspect, rather than the interrogation room. After all, the lad had come in of his own free will.

"So, you claim you took a different route to the café today, because you were late leaving the hotel?" the chief inspector questioned, once Larry had explained what had happened.

Larry nodded.

"Yet, you still believed that you would meet up with Susan Matthews," Andrews mused. "I'd have thought you'd take the shortest route possible, if you wanted to make sure that she and the others would still be there."

"I know. But when I left the hotel, I thought it was later than it actually was. It was only when I heard a clock chiming that I looked at my watch and realised the time. Brian had said he would be at least forty-five minutes late. But, as it happened, he turned up earlier than he thought. I just didn't realise it at the time."

"Yet you added the time on the sheet when you logged out," Andrews persisted. He sat back in his chair and shook his head.

"I know all that. But I wasn't really thinking. I just wrote down the same time that Brian used when he signed in. I've done that before. Do a couple of minutes really matter? My mind was elsewhere."

"Where was it – your mind, I mean?" Alan pounced into the conversation at that point. "What *were* you thinking about? Could it be that you were considering who your next victim would be?"

Even Agnes had to admit Larry's answers sounded a little cagey. Had she got it all wrong? Could Alan be right in assuming the young man had tried to kill Susan? On the other hand, she understood from past experience how confused people can become when under pressure. She was about to intervene when there was a knock at the door.

"Sir, you need to see this," Detective Jones said, as he strode into the room. He was holding up a sheet of paper.

Alan reached out and took it from the detective. After reading it through, he handed it back to the detective with a nod. "We'll be with you in a moment."

There was a determined look on his face when he turned back to Larry.

"We need to go out for a while. However, I would like you to remain at the station until we return. I have to say, things are not looking good for you. I'll instruct an officer to take you to an interrogation room – you can wait there."

He took a deep breath. "Mrs Lockwood, you may leave. I really don't see the point of you staying here. Go back to the hotel." He stood up and threw on his jacket, which had been hanging over the back of his chair.

"What are you talking about – Larry is to remain here?" Agnes retorted. "Can you do that? Doesn't he have to be under arrest before you retain him? *Is* he under arrest?" She paused. "What's happened to cause this? What was written on that paper?"

Agnes closed her eyes for a second when a terrible thought flashed through mind.

"Sue Matthews – has she…"

"No," Alan interrupted. "It wasn't about Miss Matthews." He paused. "And no, I can't just keep him here without charging him and reading him his rights, which is why I said I would *like* him to remain here."

Agnes turned back to face the young man. "What do you want to do?"

"It's okay. I'll wait here," Larry murmured.

Alan nodded before he and Andrews hurried over towards the door.

Once the two detectives were outside the room, Agnes grasped Larry by his shoulders and peered at him. "Before we go any further,

I need to know whether you tried to kill Sue Matthews. Look at me, Larry, and tell me honestly – was it you?"

"No. No, I swear, it wasn't me. I didn't do it."

"Okay, I believe you," she replied, softly. "Now, I need to leave for a little while. But I want to know if you'll be okay on your own."

Larry nodded. "I'll be fine."

"Great, then I'll be back the minute they return," said Agnes. "In the meantime, don't answer any questions without a solicitor being present. Is that clear?"

"Yes. But where are you going?" Larry asked.

"At this moment, I have absolutely no idea. The only thing I can tell you is that I'm going to wherever they're going," she replied with a wink, before slipping out of the door.

* * *

Agnes found Ben waiting patiently in his taxi when she emerged from the police station.

"Where to?" he asked, when she stepped inside the cab.

"You're the second person to ask me that in the last five minutes," Agnes replied.

"So, what did you tell this other person?"

"I told him that I didn't know."

"I assume you were speaking to the chief inspector."

"No, Ben. I was speaking to the suspect in a case of attempted murder. I told him I'd be going to exactly the same place Alan and his sergeant were heading for."

"*What?*" Ben exclaimed, as he swung around to face her. "You mean you want me to follow a police car?"

"Ben, I believe the young man in custody is innocent. But to prove it, I need to know everything the police know." She pointed towards a car heading out of the police car park. "That's it. Follow that car."

"Okay," Ben replied, as he swerved away from the kerb. "I just hope you're right."

You and I, both, Agnes thought, as the taxi glided down the road.

* * *

The chief inspector pulled up on the quayside, a short distance from the Millennium Bridge. By now, a crowd had gathered around the small area cordoned off by the police. An officer moved a few people to one side to allow the two detectives to make their way through.

Now that they were closer, they could see that the pathologist was already at the scene and bending over a body.

"You talk to whoever found the body, while I have a word with Keith," Alan said to his sergeant.

Andrews nodded and walked across to where the ambulance was parked.

"What can you tell me, Keith?" Alan asked.

"Not a lot at this stage," he replied. "However, what I *can* tell you is that the man has been in the water for a few days."

Alan looked down at the dead man lying at his feet. For a moment, he was taken aback when he saw who it was. He leaned in closer to make sure.

"You say he's been in the water a few days?" Alan said, without taking his eyes off the man's face.

"Yes, definitely a few days," Keith replied. He frowned. "Alan, are you alright?"

"Yes, yes, I'm fine." Alan waved off the question. "I missed lunch, that's all. So, at this point, you can't tell me whether he was dead before he hit the water?" he added, getting back to the case in hand.

"No. I need to get him back to the lab before I can be sure. However, I can tell you that he's been hit over the head with something rather hefty." Keith moved the man's head slightly and pointed to a large wound. "I can't say whether that's what killed him, though – at least, not until I do the post-mortem."

"Okay, thank you, Keith. But I need to hear from you the moment you learn anything."

Alan was glancing around looking for his sergeant when his eyes happened to fall on Agnes. Somehow, she had managed to get through the crowd and was standing just behind the police barrier.

"What're you doing here?" he asked, as he approached her. "I told you that you could leave the station and go back to the hotel."

The words, and his tone, sounded sharper than he had meant. But he was still smarting over Agnes having met that damn Alton man. But that wasn't the real reason. Men checked into the hotel every day. It was obvious that she was going to bump into one or two during the course of the week.

What he was really peeved about was the way this man had cozied up to Agnes in the drawing room with a bottle of champagne.

"Well then, what are you griping about? I've done exactly what you wanted. I left the station and here I am – right outside my hotel," she retorted, gesturing towards the hotel in the background.

Agnes was aware she had been a little economical with the truth, but she felt angry. Alan had sounded so aggressive that she wanted to hit back. She glanced across towards the pathologist and gave him a friendly wave, before continuing.

"So Alan, what's your problem?"

The chief inspector couldn't argue. That's what he'd said. But he hadn't believed she would take him at his word. He had thought she would have gone shopping in the city centre.

"Well, I might need you to identify the body at some point," he said, shifting from one foot to the other.

"So, you *do* need me, after all. What are we waiting for, then?" She reached out to lift up the police tape cordoning off the area.

"Not now, Agnes. It's too harrowing." Alan stepped in front of her. "Wait until Doctor Nichols has him back at the laboratory. You know – cleaned him up a little."

But Agnes wasn't having any of that. At this moment, she was fed up with Alan Johnson. Ever since he had heard about her having a drink with John Alton, his whole attitude towards her had changed. After his interview with Larry had ended rather abruptly, he had cut her short when she attempted to reason with him. Maybe Alan wasn't the right man for her, after all. Perhaps she had misjudged him. She was thankful she hadn't yet told him about her visit to the estate agent. Perhaps asking him to move in with her hadn't been such a good idea.

"Surely, the sooner the man is identified the better?" Agnes retorted. "You, of all people, should know that." She peered at him. "But you already know who it is, don't you?"

"I think I do."

"Okay, then let me see him."

Alan nodded to the officer to allow her through. She was right. They couldn't afford to waste any more time.

Agnes looked down at the body. She recognised him instantly as the man she had seen at the coast earlier in the week.

"Doctor Nichols believes he's been in the water for a few days, which means he can't have been responsible for the attack on Miss Matthews earlier today," Alan explained.

"That's why you haven't been able to find him," Agnes said. "You were looking in the wrong place."

Alan looked relieved when Sergeant Andrews joined them.

"It was a woman who spotted him in the water. She's in a bit of a state. It took me a while to get her to talk about how she had discovered the body. Anyway, it seems she was here on her lunchbreak. She bought something from the bakery across the road and intended to sit here on one of the benches and eat it. But she didn't get the chance because, just as she was approaching the bench, she thought she saw something bobbing around on the water. At first, she dismissed it, believing it was an old piece of rag someone had tossed away. But then a small boat floated past, causing the water to swirl a little. What she thought was a rag, moved and she saw a face staring up at her."

He paused and looked back towards the woman. "I have to say, she's pretty broken up about it. It was quite a shock for her."

"Yes, it must have been," Agnes said, recalling how she herself had seen a body in the Tyne only a few months ago.

Alan walked across to the side of the river and looked down at the gently flowing water. Agnes and the sergeant followed closely behind.

"The current isn't strong," Alan said. "But then, it hasn't been for quite some time now. This heatwave has slowed it down."

He turned back to look at his sergeant. "At the moment, Keith can't tell us for certain whether or not the man was already dead when he entered the river. That will have to wait until he does the post-mortem. But either way, with the slow current, the body must have taken some time to reach this point. Therefore, I suggest he first entered the water some miles upstream."

Andrews leaned over the railings and looked down at the river. "I think you're right, sir. This could mean that the murder, suicide, whatever it was, took place away well from the quayside. Maybe we need to start looking for clues further upstream."

Agnes stepped forward and peered down at the water, before turning her head to look upstream. She was thinking back to the time she saw the body in the river.

"What do you think, Agnes?" Alan asked.

Agnes looked back at him and shrugged. "You and Sergeant Andrews seem to have it all worked out between you, so why bother to ask me?"

"For heaven's sake, Agnes, I just meant, do you agree."

"Then, no, Alan – I don't agree with you. Certainly not until I learn more from Doctor Nichols."

Alan threw his arms up in the air despair. "So, what is there not to agree about?"

"Are you asking me? You're actually asking me for my opinion?"

"Yes, Agnes, I'm bloody asking you for your opinion. What the hell is there to disagree about?"

"Well, Alan, as you are asking so politely, I'll tell you," Agnes seethed. "As I see it, there are a couple of other possibilities. For a start, the body could have been weighted down and thrown in the river only a *little* further upstream, in the hope it would never be found, or, at the very least, the weights would hold out for a few days to put the police totally off-track. And secondly, his body might have got trapped on something, which stopped it from floating downstream."

"Such as?" Alan raised his eyebrows.

"I don't know – you're the detective!"

"Don't you think you're letting your imagination run away with you, Mrs Lockwood?" the sergeant asked, quietly.

He didn't know what had happened between his boss and Mrs Lockwood but, whatever it was, it appeared to be getting in the way of the investigation.

"No, she isn't. Mrs Lockwood has a very valid point, sergeant."

They all swung round to find the pathologist standing behind them. They had been so engrossed in their rather heated discussion, they hadn't heard him approach.

Keith winked at Agnes before turning his attention to the chief inspector.

"I thought you ought to know, Alan, I've just found some marks on the victim's legs, which makes it possible that something was fastened to him before he entered the water. Or," he glanced at Agnes for a moment, "it could be that he was stuck on something while he was in the river."

Keith looked at each of the three people in turn. Agnes was smiling at him, but the two detectives didn't look quite so happy.

He frowned and pointed across to where the body was being lifted into the forensics van. "You know something? I think I should be going now."

"Thank you, Keith," Alan called out, as the pathologist walked away. "I'll be at the lab shortly."

He turned back to speak to Agnes, but she had gone.

She was already making her way across towards the hotel.

* * *

Ben, who was waiting in the pick-up and drop-off area alongside the hotel, eyed Mrs Lockwood as she headed towards him. It was unusual to see her looking so angry.

"Is everything alright?" he asked, when she pulled open the door and stepped into his taxi.

"No, Ben. Everything isn't alright." She gave him a watery smile. "But it's nothing for you to worry about. How much do I owe you so far?"

Ben looked at the meter and quoted a price.

She opened her wallet and pulled out the amount he said, but then added another twenty pounds.

"No!" Ben started to protest, but she held up her hand.

"Take it," she said, thrusting the money at him. "Besides, I need you to take me back up the road." She sighed. "Ben, do you like being a taxi driver – at everyone's beck and call?"

"Some of the time," he replied. "It depends who I have in the car at the time. Some people are really nice, while others seem to go out of their way to be very nasty – especially those who've been out drinking on a Saturday or Sunday night." He hesitated. "Why do you ask?"

"I was just curious. I get these notions once in a while." She laughed. "Forget it."

It had occurred to her earlier in the day that if she decided to buy the apartment, she might like to have a car and driver at her disposal. But maybe it was a little premature to be thinking down those lines.

"Now, could you please drop me off at the police station? I have a little unfinished business."

Chapter Twenty

"I think that's all for the time being, Ben," Agnes said, when they reached the police station. "If I need you later, I'll give you a call."

She was just about to close the car door, but then something else popped into her mind.

"Ben, if Alan should decide to question you as to where you took me today, promise you won't say where I went earlier this morning."

Ben pondered for a moment. "You mean the estate agent?"

"Yes, the estate agent."

"Then my lips are sealed," Ben replied.

"Thank you."

Inside the police station, Agnes asked to speak with Larry Parker. There was a great deal of mumbling between the officers on duty before they allowed her to see him.

"Larry, I wanted to make sure that you won't say a word to anyone without a solicitor present," she told him, the moment they were alone.

"Why, what on earth has happened now?"

"I think you're about to be charged with the attack on Susan Matthews." Agnes paused. "And there is no easy way to say this, but I also believe the police will try to pin the murders of Wendy Hamilton and Janet Cunningham on you, too. Janet was the young woman who was stabbed earlier today."

"Bloody hell!" he exclaimed. But then, realizing who he was talking to, he quickly apologized. "Sorry, Mrs Lockwood, but I..." he shook his head, "I just can't believe this is happening to me. It's like I'm living through a nightmare."

"Don't worry, Larry. I've heard a lot worse than that in my time. Besides, I quite understand how you must be feeling at the moment."

Agnes's eldest son, Jason, had been held responsible for a crime he didn't commit. He had been accused of murder and it had taken both her and her husband, Jim, every ounce of their strength to keep going through that awful time. Everything had been against Jason. The police, believing they had found their murderer, wouldn't listen to anything else they were told. Yet, in the end, with an excellent solicitor, Mr Jarvis, plus the right private investigator, the real culprit had been found and proved guilty. Nevertheless, once it was over, Jason had decided to leave England and settle in another country.

"How can I stay here?" he had moaned, when his parents had tried to talk him out of it. "Even though the case never reached the courts, everyone in the town still points at me. I have no future here."

His father had suggested that they all move to another part of the city. But Jason had turned it down. He didn't believe it would make any difference.

"Another town, another city – I doubt that will help. My face was plastered all over the news for weeks on end. I need to get away from this country if I want to have a life."

His parents had both understood he meant it and, albeit slowly, they got used to the idea. But then, William, their youngest son, suddenly announced that he wanted to go with him. No amount of pleading would talk him out of it and now both were on the other side of the world. But it was only to be expected. He and Jason had been the best of friends all their lives.

"How can you possibly understand?" Larry mumbled, slumped in the chair.

"I'll tell you about it sometime. But, in the meantime, we need to work on getting your name cleared."

He looked up at her. "How can they charge me with the murder of those two women? I didn't even know Wendy Hamilton." He thought for a moment. "As for Janet, I had seen her. She worked at the café across from the hotel. But I didn't know her. Besides, I thought the police were already looking for a man in connection with the first murder. Hasn't his face been in the papers for the last few days?"

"They found the man today," Agnes whispered.

"Then why am I still here? Why haven't I been allowed to leave?"

"Because, Larry, he was dead when they found him." Her voice was barely above a whisper.

"What?" Larry uttered. He closed his eyes and shook his head. "Where did they find him?"

Agnes blinked back her tears. Maybe she should have left it to the police to inform Larry of what had happened in the last couple of hours; they were more used to dealing with this sort of thing. But then she recalled the interview Alan had held with the young man only a short while earlier and realised they would have delivered the news in a much colder and more direct manner.

"I'm sorry to have to tell you this, but he was found floating in the River Tyne earlier today. The pathologist said he would need to examine the body properly before he could give the police the exact cause of death."

Agnes placed her arm around the young man's shoulders.

"However," she went on, "he was able to inform them that the man had been in the water for several days, which means he couldn't have killed Janet Cunningham or attacked Susan Matthews."

There was a long silence.

"So that's it." Larry spoke first. "Now they have no one else, they're going to pin all this on me. But – why pick on me?"

At the moment, Agnes was reluctant to tell him of the conversation that had taken place between Susan and Doctor Nichols on the way to the hospital. Though she was aware the police wouldn't hesitate to inform him. After all, that was the reason they had sought him out.

However, Larry spoke again before she needed to say anything.

"Sue!" he uttered. "Oh, my goodness – how is Sue? Have you heard anything? Is she okay?"

"I think she's okay. Doctor Nichols, the pathologist, was in the ambulance with her on the way to the hospital, so…"

"Pathologist?" Larry gasped. "Don't they usually work on dead people?"

"Yes." Agnes shrugged. "But he was around at the time and, don't forget, pathologists are doctors." She paused. "I'll go to the hospital this evening and find out how Sue is progressing and I'll come back tomorrow and let you know."

Larry nodded. "Okay, thank you Mrs L."

Agnes hid a smile. That brought back memories. One of Jason's friends used to call her Mrs L, whenever he was at the house – it was good to hear it again.

"Now, Larry, you must start thinking about yourself. To begin with, you're going to need a good solicitor."

"I can't afford a solicitor," he replied. "Nor can my parents."

But then he had a thought.

"Don't the courts offer the services of a solicitor to a suspect when they can't afford one?"

"Yes, they do," Agnes agreed.

However, Agnes hadn't been very impressed with the solicitor her son had been offered. He had seemed to be more concerned about getting to the golf course, than helping his client. Jim had quickly dismissed him and happily paid for another to take his place; someone more interested in doing the job.

"But I sometimes wonder whose side they're really on." She took a deep breath. "Larry, you've done me a couple of favours over the last few months, both of which could have saved my life, so I'd like to something for you. I'd like to hire a solicitor for you."

Larry opened his mouth to protest, but Agnes held up her hand.

"Please, Larry, let me help you." She paused, as another thought sprung into her mind. "Have you been in touch with your parents?"

"No." Larry slumped back down in his chair. "I really thought the police would realise they'd made a mistake and my parents wouldn't even have to know I'd been here."

Before Agnes could reply, the door to the interrogation room swung open and the chief inspector walked in. He looked at each of them in turn before turning his attention to Agnes.

"I heard you were here."

Agnes stared back at him. "Then seeing me won't have come as a surprise, will it?" She shrugged. "I thought someone should be with Larry. I was just about to ask him if he would like me to get in touch with his parents."

As she spoke, she looked beyond Alan, expecting to see his sergeant hovering around in the background. However, there was no sign of him.

"We can do that, Agnes."

"That means you intend to keep him here, Chief Inspector?"

Alan winced at her knife-edge tone.

"I don't have any other choice."

"Very well," she replied.

She looked back at Larry. "Remember what I said. Don't say a word until I find a solicitor for you."

Larry swallowed hard and nodded.

"Then I'll be back tomorrow." Agnes gave the young man a bright smile. "I know it's difficult, but please try not to worry. It's going to be alright."

She rose from the chair and walked out of the room.

Alan followed her out into the corridor, closing the door behind him.

"Agnes, I think we got off on the wrong foot earlier..."

"You think?" Agnes swung around to face him. "You *think*, Chief Inspector? After your outburst earlier this year, you swore you would never speak to me like that ever again, especially in front of your detectives. Yet, this afternoon on the quayside..." She broke off and shook her head. "Just forget it. I have things to do. And by the way, my name is Mrs Lockwood," she added, before storming off down the corridor.

Alan watched as she disappeared around the corner. Very soon she would be at the front entrance. Maybe he should have warned her she would be stopped by the sergeant on duty and instructed to sign out, after speaking to a suspect. But no doubt she would find that out for herself in a minute or two. On the other hand, there was the possibility that the duty sergeant was the one who had met up with her earlier. Therefore, he would already know better than to upset Mrs Lockwood.

However, at the moment none of that was his main concern. Alan was well aware that he had lost his temper too many times that day. First off, there had been his outburst at the hotel, then his rudeness in the interrogation room, earlier that afternoon and again on the quayside. The quayside... He cringed when he recalled how he had spoken to her on that occasion. What the hell had got into him? What had he been trying to prove?

He began walking down the corridor to the corner where he had lost sight of Agnes. But then, aware he desperately needed to catch up with her before she left the building, he lengthened his pace. A few moments later, he broke into a run and caught up with her just after she had signed out.

"Was there something else?" Agnes snapped. She pointed towards the large glass sliding doors leading to the street outside. "I'm just about to leave."

"Give us a minute," Alan said, glancing at the duty sergeant.

The sergeant nodded and disappeared into the office behind him.

"Agnes... Mrs Lockwood, I think we need to talk." Alan took hold of her arm as he spoke.

"We do? What do we need to talk about?" She looked down at Alan's hand fixed firmly around her arm. "And is that really necessary? You're hurting me."

Alan released his grip. "I'm sorry," he said. "It's just that I don't want you to leave – not like this. We really need to talk about *us*." He glanced at the people entering the building. "But not here. Somewhere more quiet, just the two of us."

"You want to talk about us?" Agnes retorted. "What do you mean – *us*? There is no *us*."

"There was." Alan's voice was low.

"Yes, I agree. There was." Agnes blinked back the tears forming in her eyes. "But what we had between us has disappeared." She took a deep breath. "It's over, Alan."

She turned and walked away.

"Agnes!" Alan called desperately. "Wait a moment!"

But Agnes continued walking towards the entrance. As she drew nearer to the glass doors, they slid open, allowing her to step out of the building into the busy street and out of sight.

Chapter Twenty-One

Alan was thoughtful as he slowly made his way back to the interrogation room. His jealousy about the man at the hotel must have warped his brain. Since then, he had acted like an overgrown school boy. He winced when he thought back to the episode on the quayside.

Maybe he had been over-intimidating; though, to be honest, Agnes could be very trying at times. She was certainly a woman with a mind of her own. Even at school, she had always voiced her opinions strongly. But wasn't that why he had admired her? Meeting up again after all these years had been wonderful – for him, it was a dream come true. Everything had been going so well. They had even talked of buying a home together. But his dream had been shattered.

By now, Alan had reached the interrogation room. He peered through the tiny one-way mirror set in the thick, heavy door. Larry was still sitting exactly where he had left him, but now his elbows were perched on the table and his face was resting in his hands.

Alan stood outside the room for several minutes as thoughts of the day's events flooded his mind. Could it be possible that this young man wasn't the killer they were looking for? Was Larry really capable of killing two women, before trying to kill a third? And if so, for what reason?

At the moment, he and his team were working on what Susan Matthews had told Doctor Nichols on the way to the hospital. Yet, even when she thought she might die, Sue had stressed that Larry would never have stabbed her. Nevertheless, everything checked out: the time he signed off duty and the fact that he was known to creep up behind his friends and wrap his arms around them. His sergeant was convinced they had the right man in custody.

"Case closed," Andrews had said, as they drove away from the quayside.

And, at this point, despite what Agnes thought, or how innocent the young man looked, Alan felt he had to agree with his sergeant.

Larry looked up when the door opened and the chief inspector walked in.

"Larry Parker, I am arresting you on the charge of murder. Anything you say…"

* * *

Outside the police station, Agnes blinked back tears. She was sorry her relationship with Alan Johnson had ended. But she couldn't allow him to talk to her the way he did today. While she didn't want him to believe he had to agree with everything she said, there were other, more civil ways of questioning why she thought differently to his assumptions.

Crossing the road, she made her way towards the taxi rank. Normally, she would have called Ben, but she didn't want him to see her looking like this. Truthfully, she would prefer to go straight back to the hotel and sink into a warm bath. But she had promised Larry she would visit the hospital this evening and, checking her watch, it was getting very close to visiting time. Where had the day gone?

She ran the day's events through her mind as she hurried down the street. The day had started so well. She had looked around a penthouse with a view to buying it and beginning a new life with Alan. Since then, everything had gone downhill.

Susan Matthews was in hospital after being attacked not far from the hotel. Larry, the young lift attendant at the hotel, was suspected of not only attacking Susan, but also of the murder of Janet Cunningham, who had been stabbed a short while earlier. Even Wendy Hamilton's name had been added to the list. And, if things weren't already bad enough, the man she had seen at Whitley Bay and again at the Central Station, who had been the main suspect, had been found floating in the River Tyne this afternoon. Could things get any worse for Larry?

By now, she had reached the first taxi in the rank.

"The RVI," she said.

The driver nodded and a moment later, she was on her way.

The Royal Victoria Infirmary was only a short distance from the police station. Therefore, it wasn't long before the taxi drew up outside the main entrance. Agnes paid the fare, stepped out of the cab and entered the building.

She went to the reception desk and told the man on duty that she would like to see Susan Matthews, the young woman who had been brought in earlier that day.

"Perhaps you would be so kind as to tell me which ward she's in. She had been attacked by someone – with a knife."

"Are you a relative?"

"No. But I'm staying at the hotel where she works," Agnes replied. "I simply thought I would call to see how she was getting on. I'm sure all her friends at the hotel are anxious to learn how she is."

The man kept his eyes focused on her as he picked up the phone on the desk and stabbed in a few numbers.

"There's a woman here in reception wishing to see Miss Susan Matthews," he said, when someone replied. "No, she's not a relative, but she says she is staying at the hotel where Miss Matthews works."

There was a pause.

"Very well, I'll tell her."

The man put down the phone.

"Someone is coming down to see you. Perhaps you would like to take a seat."

He pointed towards a group chairs in one corner.

"Thank you," Agnes replied, with a twinge of anxiety. Had something happened to Sue?

She walked across and took a seat near a small table with several magazines neatly lined up on top. Obviously, someone had been around recently to tidy them up. In waiting rooms, magazines were usually tossed back onto the table haphazardly when a visitor had finished with them.

She hadn't been seated long when a doctor walked into the reception area. The man behind the desk pointed over to where Agnes was waiting and the doctor came over to meet her.

She stood up as he approached her.

"My name is Doctor Walsh," he said. "But…"

"Is Susan going to be alright?" Agnes interrupted. All this cloak and dagger stuff was worrying. "Doctor Walsh, has she recovered from the stabbing?"

"Yes, she's doing well – under the circumstances." The doctor scratched his head. "Forgive me, but I'm rather puzzled as to why you're so interested in her wellbeing. I mean, if you're simply a guest at the hotel where she works, you can't know her *that* well. Yet here you are at the hospital, enquiring about her."

Agnes was relieved to hear that Susan was recovering. Nevertheless, she wasn't sure how to answer. She didn't want to mention Larry, as, until it was proved otherwise, he was suspected of trying to kill her. Yet the doctor was waiting for her to say something.

"I'm a friend of Doctor Nichols," she replied, saying the first thing that came into her mind. "I'd heard he'd accompanied Susan in the ambulance, so I thought they must be friends. I thought it only right that I should stop by and see how she was getting on."

Agnes had been about to add that she would also be able to pass on any news to Susan's colleagues at the hotel. But she decided to stop while she was ahead.

"I see."

Doctor Walsh cocked his head on one side as he thought through what Agnes had said. However, she didn't fail to notice that not once did he stop studying her face.

"Well," he said, after what had seemed like an eternity, "as Doctor Nichols is with Miss Matthews at this moment, why don't we go upstairs and see them both?"

* * *

Agnes heaved a huge sigh of relief as she stepped out of the hospital. Thankfully, it had all gone well and she had been allowed to see Susan – or Sue, as she wanted to be called.

Doctor Nichols had looked rather amused when he had been called upon confirm she was his friend. Nevertheless, despite them hardly knowing each other, he had obliged.

"Yes, Agnes is a friend of mine," he had said.

However, a couple of minutes later, Keith told those around him that she was also a friend of Chief Inspector Johnson. Although she understood that he had said that to get her past the sullen police officer guarding Sue's room, the words had stung little. But how was the pathologist to know about the row which had taken place between her and the DCI only a short while earlier?

Now, as she made her way down the steps outside the hospital, Agnes focused her thoughts on Sue. She recalled how well the young woman looked, considering what the poor girl had gone through a few hours earlier. At least she would be able to pass on some good news to her friends. But then another thought passed through her mind, causing her to stop in her tracks.

Would it be a good idea to inform everyone at the hotel of how well Sue had come out of her terrible ordeal? What if the person who had tried to kill her was someone at the hotel; a guest, or one of her so-called friends? If so, on learning of her recovery, they could assume she had seen who had attacked her and would be in a position to inform the police.

Agnes swung around and looked back towards the entrance. Should she try to have another word with Sue? There were so many questions that needed answers. But then she realised that was a stupid idea. She'd almost had to jump through hoops to see her earlier and even then, it had only been for a few minutes. There was no way she would be allowed back in to ask the sort of questions only a police officer could put to her.

Yet, if she was going to help Larry, then she needed answers to some questions and, as things stood between her and Alan right now, there was no way she could rely on him for any assistance. His mind seemed to be set on proving Larry Parker was the murderer.

So, who else was there? She sighed deeply as she ran through the alternatives.

Sergeant Andrews was her first thought, but she quickly dismissed him. He would simply agree with whatever his boss said. She only had to think back to earlier, when they were all on the quayside. When Alan had stated that the body had probably been thrown in the Tyne some miles upstream, Andrews had agreed without a second thought. The sergeant was usually a man who thought things through for himself. So why had he been so quick to accommodate his boss today? Could it be that he needed to keep on Alan's good side for some reason?

No, she needed someone who could talk to Sue, yet was totally unbiased with regard to the investigation. Maybe someone like Doctor Keith Nichols?

Agnes hadn't failed to notice the bond between Keith and Sue. That thought had struck her the moment she entered the room. It had even crossed her mind that they might have already known each other for some time before she was attacked. It was only something that had been said during her short visit which made Agnes realise they had met for the first time only a few short hours ago. Yes, perhaps Doctor Nichols could help her out by putting a few questions to Sue – but would he agree?

That settled – well, sort of – she pondered on what her next move should be. Should she go straight back to the hotel and have that long soak in the bath that had been so tempting earlier? Or find some tiny bar where she wouldn't be recognized and have a quiet glass of wine, while thinking through the day's events?

Chapter Twenty-Two

Meanwhile, on the other side of the town, Alan was in a sullen mood as he left the police station and headed towards to his car. It had been a really bad day. Nothing had gone right. Well, certainly not from the moment he had met John Alton. Now, even the thought of the man made him see red. But was that because he had cozied up to Agnes with champagne, or was it more about Alton's insinuation that he was her father?

But then, when he had found Agnes sitting alongside Larry Parker, the police suspect, he had been really taken aback, though he had tried to play it cool with Andrews. Nevertheless, even now he wondered how she had been able to find the young man, when he, his sergeant and another couple of detectives had not.

As if that hadn't been bad enough, she had then turned up on the quayside at almost the same time as himself and Andrews. It was then that he had really started to lose his cool with her. Alan paused for a second and shook his head at that last thought. *Lose his cool* – where did that come from? That was a phrase usually used by a totally different generation to his. What he meant was, lose his temper.

His sergeant hadn't said much on their ride back from the quayside to the station. But then, what could he say? Anything between Agnes and him had nothing to do with anyone, most especially his sergeant. However, Andrews was usually a little more talkative; tossing his thoughts around in the hope that one of them would help to bring something to light. Yet today, he had been rather silent – shuffling his feet around in the well beneath the passenger seat.

Now, approaching his car, Alan sighed as he pressed the button to unlock the doors. Normally, at this time of day, he would jump in his car and head for the Millennium Hotel to meet up with Agnes. However today, that seemed out of the equation.

The alternatives were to go back to his own home in Heaton and either switch on the television, or settle down with one of the books on his shelves, all of which were still waiting to be read. Yet neither idea appealed to him. All he could think about was Agnes. Where was she now? What was she doing?

Stepping into his car, Alan started the engine. His mind was made up. There was no way he could leave it like this. He needed to talk to her – and he needed to talk to her right now.

* * *

Agnes had been back in her room at the hotel for only ten minutes when the phone by the bed rang. After a great deal of thought, she had decided to go back to her room for a soak in the bath, while she mulled over the events of the day. However, when she picked up the phone, she began to wish she had found a quiet bar somewhere, after all.

"Mr Johnson is here in reception. He wishes to see you. Is it okay for him to come up?"

Alan had debated whether he should just go straight upstairs, as he normally did – after all, he did have a key – or have the receptionist announce him. In the end, he had chosen the second option.

"No, it's not!" Agnes replied. "Tell him I'm busy."

There was a pause while the receptionist conveyed the message.

"I'm sorry," the receptionist said, "but the gentleman insists he needs to speak with you. He says he's willing to wait down here for as long as it takes – until you're free."

Agnes closed her eyes and blew a sigh. "Tell him I'll be down shortly," she said, before putting down the phone.

She walked across to the window and flopped down onto one of the chairs. The river below was calmly making its way down towards the North Sea. It certainly looked a great deal more tranquil than she felt at this moment. The last person she wanted to see right now was Alan Johnson. Yet, she knew she would have to meet up with him at some point.

She rose to her feet and, grabbing her bag, she walked towards the door.

Agnes was a little surprised to find Brian was still on duty when she stepped into the lift. She had thought his shift would have been over by now. But who would take his place? With Larry in custody, maybe Brian had opted to stand in for him.

"Ground floor, please," she said.

"Ground floor it is," Brian said, pressing the appropriate button. "How're you this evening?"

"A little tired," she replied, not wanting to get involved in too much conversation. "A busy day, but now I'm ready for dinner."

"A busy day – I guess you've been to the mall?"

Agnes peered at Brian before she answered. What was it about Brian and shopping? He seemed to be obsessed with women's shopping habits. But then, who was she to argue? She loved looking around the shops. Maybe his mother was of the same frame of mind and had dragged him around the shops when he was younger.

"Yes, I've been all over Eldon Square," she lied.

By now, they had reached the ground floor and the doors slid open. Agnes spotted Alan sitting on the sofa near the entrance to the drawing room. He stood up when he saw her emerge from the lift.

"Enjoy your meal," the lift attendant said, as she strode away from him.

"Thank you, Brian," she replied, without a backward glance.

"What are you doing here?" Agnes said, as she drew close to Alan. "I thought we'd said everything there was to be said – at least for today."

"I couldn't leave things as they were," he replied.

His spirits lifted a little on hearing her last four words. Maybe there was a slight chance they would get together again sometime.

"Look, I know I was rude to you today and I'm really sorry about it. I don't know what came over me." He swallowed hard. "Can't we have dinner together and talk it all through?"

"Alan, it's been a very long and trying day. I'm feeling so tired, I don't think this is a good time. Besides, I'm not really dressed for going out for dinner. I've been wearing this outfit all day."

"Please, Agnes." He pointed towards the dining room. "We don't have to go out anywhere. We can have dinner here."

Just as he spoke, someone opened the door and emerged from the dining room door and the whiff of food wafted towards them. The smell made Agnes realise she hadn't eaten anything since that morning. But she had been so preoccupied all day, she hadn't even stopped to think about food until this moment.

Maybe she should wait until Alan said whatever he had come here to say and then enjoy a meal after he left. But, he could keep talking for the rest of the evening and the restaurant would probably be closed.

"Very well, we'll have dinner together. But I'll pay for my own meal."

Alan sighed as he followed Agnes across to the dining room. It wasn't the best way to restart the reunion with the woman he loved – but at least it was a step in the right direction.

* * *

Agnes was shattered when she returned to her room. It had been a long and rather trying evening. Alan had done his best to convince her he still thought the world of her. He had spent a great deal of time trying to assure her that he had no idea where his earlier outburst had come from and had sworn it would never happen again.

At that point, she had reminded him that he had promised her that once before.

During the evening, she had managed to switch the conversation to Larry Parker by asking whether the police had contacted Larry's parents. Alan had assured her that they had been with their son when he left the station.

"You know he's innocent, don't you?"

"No, Agnes, I don't," he had said, rather quietly. Yet, there had been an unmistakable firmness in his tone.

She had then steered Alan into explaining why the police had come to that conclusion. With some reluctance, he had gone on to explain that there appeared to be some friction between Larry and his colleagues. Though she had been itching to ask who, or how many of his so-called friends were involved and, more importantly, where he had discovered this information, she'd held back. Instead, she had made a mental note to speak to Mrs Telford, the staff supervisor, the following morning. It would be interesting to learn whether she was aware of this 'friction'.

When the meal ended and Alan called for the waiter to bring him the bill, she had interrupted; pointing out it was to be split between them. That hadn't gone down well and he had begun to argue about it. However, she reminded him of the deal they had struck before she agreed to have dinner with him. It certainly hadn't helped the fractured situation that John Alton just happened to have been eating at a table close by.

On leaving the dining room, Agnes hadn't failed to notice Alan looking longingly towards the lift. Had he hoped she would relent and invite him to stay the night? However, despite the evening going more smoothly than she had anticipated, she had bid him goodnight and a safe journey back to his home in Heaton.

Had she been a little too hard on him? Agnes knew she could be stubborn at times. Even Jim had told her several times how pigheaded she could be. Glancing down at her bed, she tried to push thoughts of Alan from her mind. The best plan was to switch off, get undressed, and snuggle under the duvet. First thing tomorrow morning, she would have a word with Mrs Telford. She had promised the staff supervisor that they would work together.

Next on the list would be to meet up with Larry's parents. She hoped Larry had heard her when she suggested his parents meet her for coffee at the hotel the following morning, or anywhere else they were happy to talk to her. With a bit of luck, they could point her in the right direction to a really good solicitor.

As Agnes switched off the light, she wondered why on earth she had volunteered to be so involved. She didn't need any of this. Her plan had been to live a quiet life with Alan, here on Tyneside. But, remembering how she and Jim had felt when their son, Jason, had been in the same position that Larry was now in, she immediately knew the answer.

Besides, tomorrow was a whole new day.

Chapter Twenty-Three

"I agree with you, Agnes. There are times when some members of staff don't get along with each other. But surely that happens in all work places?"

It was the following morning and Agnes was in the staff supervisor's office. Without going into too many details, she had explained to Florence what she'd learned from the police.

"Yes, it does. I'd be the first to admit that," she replied.

There was a time when Agnes's father had almost been forced to stand between two staff members to calm them down, due to a case of rivalry over a promotion opportunity. At the time, she had been helping out in the stock room, as a couple of people were off sick.

Back then, it had all worked out well. As he led the two young men to his office, her father had calmly told them that they were both worthy of promotion; whether it was this time around or the next. Whatever else he said was lost when the door had closed. Nevertheless, after that day, they became the best of friends and, in time, each had achieved a great deal in the business. But what might have happened if her father hadn't intervened and the two young men had continued with their grievance?

"Yet," Agnes continued, "what if what was once thought to be a mere disagreement, gradually became a little more intense, and then developed into a case of attempted murder?"

Florence sat back in her chair at the suggestion.

"I'm not saying that's what happened," Agnes quickly added.

"Nonetheless, you think it's a possibility."

Agnes nodded. She wasn't really sure whether it was a question or a statement.

Florence was quiet for what seemed an age.

"Well, as it happens," she said at last, "I do recall hearing something about an argument between Larry and another member of staff, but that was quite a while ago." She paused. "You must understand, Agnes, I'm not usually informed of these squabbles in an official capacity. It's just that I tend to keep my ears and eyes open as I wander around the hotel. That way, I pick up things I'm not really meant to know about. However, when it appeared to die down, I felt relieved that they had got over their disagreement – end of story, so to speak."

"Do you know who Larry had the argument with and what it was about?" Agnes hoped Flo's reply would shed a little light on the case.

"Yes, I do. It was with Peter Moffat, one of the porters." Florence sighed. "As I understand it, Peter was annoyed because he had to work on Christmas Eve. It seems he asked another porter to stand in for him, but he had refused. I think he already had something else planned that evening."

While the staff supervisor was speaking, Agnes was trying to recall whether she had ever seen this porter during her stay at the hotel. Then she remembered. The first time she came to the hotel, he had carried her luggage up to her room. He had seemed quite a pleasant young man; friendly and chatty. But then, being nice to the customers was part of a porter's job – especially if they wanted to receive a hefty tip. What they were like once they were out of earshot was another matter.

Now that she had a face to go on, she recalled seeing him two or three more times. On one occasion, he was arguing with another member of staff. She hadn't taken much notice at the time, but now, thinking back, he had looked rather angry about something.

Agnes scratched her head. She needed give this Peter Moffat more thought. But not now; there was something she wanted to ask Flo.

"I'm curious as to why it should have anything to do with Larry. Why would he get involved in a matter to do with the staff rota – especially when it didn't involve him or his shift?"

"But it did involve him – in a way," Florence said. "I don't know the full story. However, as I understand it, Peter wanted to join the group going to a restaurant and then a nightclub that evening, because a woman he liked would be there. Larry, who had organized the outing and had been collecting money from the participants each week, tried to calm Peter down. Instead, he became the target of Peter's anger."

Florence went on to explain that she had stayed out of the whole episode, hoping it would die down of its own accord.

"And it did." She looked away for a moment, as though giving it more thought. "At least, I thought it had," she continued, "as it all went quiet. Peter worked his shift and was off duty for New Year as per the rota. However, he left the hotel a couple of months ago. Apparently, he found himself another job – somewhere he wouldn't be expected to work over Christmas or New Year." She paused. "Yet, maybe if I had stepped in at the time, I might have been able to put an end to the argument before it boiled over."

Agnes was disappointed. She wasn't really sure what she had expected to learn, but she had hoped it would have set her on the path to finding out who might have a grudge against Larry. But this was merely a disagreement over the staff rota… or was it?

"Why didn't you tell me this yesterday?" Agnes asked.

If she had known about this skirmish the day before, at least she would have been prepared when Alan brought it up the previous evening. Though she still couldn't understand why he assumed Larry was guilty of murder, simply because he had tried to calm down a fellow worker.

"It never occurred to me," Florence replied. "Later yesterday afternoon, after we had spoken together, another detective turned up with more questions. He particularly wanted to know whether Larry had been involved in any quarrels, arguments, or any other sort of disagreements with his colleagues. Like I said to you, I told him that differences of opinion between members of staff happened all the time. Nevertheless, he was only interested in anything to do with Larry. Obviously the police have other reasons to suspect him."

"I see."

Agnes was thoughtful. Why hadn't the detective been interested to learn about quarrels between other members of staff? One of those quarrels might have actually involved Sue Matthews. But there was something else bothering her. She had the impression that the supervisor wasn't telling her everything. However, she decided not to persist at the moment. There was no point in spoiling their friendship. She needed Florence on her side – at least for the moment.

"As a matter of interest, do you happen to know who the detective was?" Agnes asked.

"Yes, his name was Detective John Morris. Do you know him?"

* * *

Agnes looked at her watch as she hurried along the corridor towards the drawing room. Larry's parents had agreed to meet her for coffee at the hotel. When they had phoned her earlier that morning, she had been more than a little surprised that they were happy to meet up at the hotel. She had thought they would prefer to meet somewhere more private.

She had almost reached the drawing room when John Alton suddenly stepped in front of her. In her haste, she hadn't seen him approaching.

"Ah! Just the lady I was hoping to see, before I left for another boring meeting."

He was dressed in a blue suit, though the colour was lighter than the one he had worn the previous day. He was also carrying a briefcase.

"I'm afraid I haven't time to chat at the moment," Agnes replied. "I'm meeting someone in a few minutes."

"I just thought that perhaps we could have dinner together this evening." He winked. "We could even have it served in my room –

it would, shall we say, be a little more private, if you get my drift. And don't forget I bought you champagne yesterday."

"I'm sorry, but I already have a date this evening." Agnes began to move to one side of him, but he quickly stepped in front of her.

"I think you're trying to play hard to get, naughty girl." He waved a finger at her. "I know you enjoyed our first little get-together."

She was about to tell him what she thought of his childishness, but someone beat her to it.

"You heard the lady. Now, get off to your meeting."

They both looked towards where the voice had come from and found Alan standing there. They had been so intent on their discussion that neither had seen nor heard him approach.

"It seems your father has you under his wing," John sneered.

"I am *not* her father," Alan retorted. "If you must know, I am a police detective."

Alton took one look at Alan and hurried away.

"There's something else you should know," Agnes called out, as John scurried towards the entrance. "You didn't pay for the champagne yesterday – I did. Check your damn bill!"

"Thanks for that," Agnes said, once they were alone. She screwed up her eyes. "But, why are you here?"

"I needed to talk to you, Agnes. Last night, at dinner, things didn't go as well as I'd hoped."

"Just what were you hoping for, Alan?"

He didn't reply.

"And what about the case? Shouldn't you be out there looking for the *real* killer?" She paused. "Besides, how did you know I'd still be here?"

"I didn't, this was only my starting point. If you hadn't been here, then I would have gone to the café near the bridge – your favourite port of call – and if you hadn't been there, then I would have given Ben a ring to ask whether he had dropped you off somewhere." Alan grinned. "Does that answer your question?"

"One of my questions, I suppose," Agnes relented. "But I *really* don't have time to talk now. As I told John, I'm meeting a couple of people in a few minutes." She looked at her watch. "Actually, they could be waiting for me at this very moment."

"Yes, I know. You're meeting Larry Parker's parents today."

"He told you?" Agnes gasped. "What pressure did you put on him to reveal that piece of information?"

Alan held up his hands. "None, I swear." He sighed. "Larry accidentally let it slip earlier this morning. But he didn't know where you were meeting them. Like I said, I wanted to talk to you and after his remark I decided to make the hotel my starting point."

Glancing over Alan's shoulder, Agnes saw a couple walking into the hotel. They made their way to the reception desk and spoke to the receptionist. After a brief exchange, the receptionist pointed the way to the drawing room.

Larry's parents had never met Agnes. However, they recognized the detective chief inspector and stopped walking the moment they laid eyes on him.

"What are you doing here?" Mrs Parker asked. "Did Mrs Lockwood ask you to join us?" She looked towards the drawing room. "Is she in there?"

"No, Mrs Lockwood didn't invite me. I'm here about something else," Alan replied.

"I'm Mrs Lockwood – Agnes Lockwood," Agnes broke in. "Chief Inspector Johnson is correct. He's here for another reason. We just happened to bump into each other."

She looked at Alan. "I'm sure we'll meet again – very soon."

Alan left the hotel with a smile on his face. Those last two words at the end of her statement had convinced him that it was possible they would get together again. Meanwhile, he would continue with the case against Larry Parker. To his mind, the lad was guilty. Yet he knew it would take a ton of evidence to prove that to Agnes.

Chapter Twenty-Four

Once Alan had left the hotel, Agnes shepherded Larry's parents into the large drawing room. Their uneasiness about the surroundings showed they had never been here before, despite their son working here. Agnes asked whether they would like coffee and scones, or prefer something a little stronger, given the circumstances. Once it was decided they would all go for the stronger option, Agnes called the waiter and placed the order.

"Mrs Lockwood..." Larry's mother was the first to break the awkward silence that followed.

"Please, call me Agnes," she interrupted.

"Then you must call me Janice," Mrs Parker replied, "and my husband's name is Paul." She paused before starting her question again. "Agnes, can I ask why you have such an interest in our son's welfare? Not that we don't appreciate you helping him," she added hastily, "but Larry is just a lift attendant here at the hotel, while you are a guest – a most respected guest, from what he's told us."

Agnes went on to explain how Larry had helped her out of a tight spot a couple of times in the past.

"But, more importantly," she continued, "I simply don't believe he attempted to murder Susan Matthews. He isn't that kind of person."

It had been on the tip of her tongue to reveal how her own son had been in the same situation only a few years earlier, but then she decided against it. She would rather Jason's case wasn't raked up all over again, were Larry's predicament ever to come to court.

While Agnes was in Australia visiting her sons, Jason had mentioned that his firm was thinking of expanding to the UK. Though he hadn't said he would opt for a position in the UK branch, she had high hopes he might, if given the opportunity. Therefore, she didn't want anything to get in the way of that, unless it was a last resort.

"We can't thank you enough for taking his side," Paul said. He glanced at his wife before looking back at Agnes. "Obviously, we've always been there for our son and, I hasten to add, we always will be. He's a good lad and we want to help him in any way we can. But," he swallowed hard, "in a situation like this, we're at a loss as to where to start. It was only when Larry told us you were helping him and would like us to meet up with you..."

He broke off.

His wife reached out and placed her hand over his.

"This has hit us hard, Agnes," she said. "I don't suppose you know what something like this can do to a family." Janice took a deep breath and blinked back the tears forming in her eyes. "But let me tell you this, we'll both do whatever it takes to prove our son is innocent."

Just then, the waiter arrived with their drinks.

"Right," Agnes said, once the waiter was out of earshot. "In that case, the first thing you can do is to give me the name of the best solicitor in Newcastle and I'll get in touch with him."

Janice looked at her husband for a second before turning back to Agnes.

"I'm sure Larry must have already explained to you that we could never afford to pay the costs of a really top-notch solicitor. They must cost a fortune."

"Yes, he did say something like that," Agnes replied. "But, we can discuss all that later. At the moment, our first priority must be to get Larry cleared of all charges and to do that, we need someone competent."

"You're right," Paul broke in, before his wife could say a word. "We must do whatever it takes. However, we don't really know too much about solicitors. We've never had the need for one… until now."

The two women watched as he rose from the chair and slowly walked across towards the window. For a couple of minutes, he stared at the quayside before swinging around to face them.

"Janice, what was the name of the solicitor who managed to prove the innocence of that young man accused of murder?" He looked at Agnes. "It must be a couple of years ago now. Everyone believed the lad was guilty, but the solicitor wouldn't let it go. He stuck at it."

He clicked his finger and thumb while he thought about it.

"Come on, Janice. You must remember the case? It was all over the news at the time."

"Yes, I do recall something, but I don't know…" Janice began, but then something sparked in her memory. "Wait, I believe you're talking about Gordon Fulton."

"Yes, that's him. Gordon Fulton," Paul agreed.

For a moment, Janice looked relieved that such an important man could be taking on Larry's case, but then her face dropped.

"What is it?" Paul said. "What's wrong?"

Janice looked at her husband and then at Agnes. "I've just remembered something else. I think I read somewhere that he had since retired."

* * *

Once the parents had left, Agnes hurried back to see the staff supervisor. She needed to contact Gordon Fulton as soon as possible and the quickest way to do that was to look him up on the internet. Though her phone had access to the internet, she preferred something with a larger screen and recalled having seen a computer sitting on Florence's desk. Hopefully, she would be able to look up the name of the firm Gordon Fulton worked for before he retired.

"If you can find the name of the firm, we might learn how to contact the man himself," Agnes said. She grabbed a chair and pulled it around the desk so she could see the screen. "Maybe we could persuade him to come out of retirement for one more case."

"I can't be certain, but I have an idea that Gordon Fulton owned the business," Florence said, tapping the name into the computer search engine. "By that, I mean when he retired, he probably closed the business."

Agnes sank back in the chair at the news.

"Hang on a minute. I think I've found something." Florence pointed towards the screen. "Look, here – it seems he has a daughter. She appears to have followed in her father's footsteps and reopened the old business. Perhaps we could start by contacting her."

By now, Agnes had sat back up and was peering at the screen.

"Call out the address and phone number," she said, reaching into her bag for her notebook. "I'll jot them down."

Chapter Twenty-Five

Alan left the hotel feeling a little easier in his mind after having spoken to Agnes. The air between them was certainly much clearer than it had been when he left the previous evening. Okay, they'd had a meal together and they had actually spoken to each other in a civilized manner. However, the whole episode hadn't been quite the same as it normally was. That was why he had put everything else on hold, until he called back to see her today. Not something he ever believed he would do. In the past, he had always put his job first and foremost.

But then, when Alan saw Agnes talking to, Alton – even thinking about the man now made him squirm – he had been about to turn around and walk away. For a brief moment, Alan had wondered whether she might have met up with Alton after he left the hotel last night, recalling that she had been keen to see him leave.

It was only because the conversation between Agnes and Alton suddenly turned a little heated and the voices grew slightly louder that he realised this wasn't just a little *tête-à-tête*. The man was pestering Agnes. At that moment, he knew he had to intervene. There was no way he would allow anyone treat Agnes in that manner.

Outside the hotel, Alan stepped into his car and switched on the engine. Now, if he and Agnes could come to some agreement on this wretched case, they might be able to pick up where they left off. But, as he and his sergeant both agreed they had the right man in custody, and Agnes believed otherwise, he knew there was always going to be some tension between them.

As he pulled away from the kerb and drove along the quayside towards the police station, he debated whether he should have mentioned the piece of evidence they had found when Larry was told to empty his pockets. Maybe, Agnes would then have realised she was on a losing wicket and stop trying to defend the lad. Though, knowing Agnes, it would most likely have made her even more determined to prove his innocence. She could be so stubborn about things – even when the evidence was staring her in the face. He sighed. Either way, at this moment, as far as his relationship with Agnes was concerned, he was in a lose-lose situation.

But, despite Alan being swayed towards believing Larry was guilty, there was still a doubt nagging away at the back of his mind. What if Agnes was right and Larry Parker *was* innocent? He reminded himself that she had been right before – on more than one occasion. Maybe, even if for only a short time, he should turn himself around and look at the case from a whole new perspective. For a start, could the evidence they found have been planted? The answer to that was yes, it was possible. But, if so, who could have planted it and why? The 'why' was obvious; to save themselves, whoever they were. Therefore, if the evidence *had* been planted, it meant the 'who' was still at large to kill again.

Back at the police station, Alan gathered his detectives together in the incident room. He hoped someone had found something new to go on, though he doubted it. Last night, before he left, he had instructed them to go through the evidence again. In other words, look for anything they might have missed the first time around.

"We don't want the case to fall apart once a solicitor gets involved," he had told them.

However, it seemed they had found nothing further, either one way or the other.

"Sir…" Andrews stepped forward. He glanced at the detectives grouped in front of the evidence board. "We believe we have the right man in custody." He paused. "And, unless I'm very much mistaken, I think you agree."

"I know, Sergeant. But we still need to be really sure." Alan glanced around his detectives, before turning his attention back to Andrews. "That's why I asked you all to go through the evidence again. I just think we should look at the case from a different angle. Is that so difficult?"

"But what about the piece of evidence we found in his pocket? Surely that proves he's guilty of the attempted murder of Susan Matthews, if not the other murders," Andrews said.

"That's *exactly* what I am talking about," Alan swiftly replied. "Yes, Sergeant, I agree with you, it does make Larry Parker appear to be guilty. But, at the same time, it could also mean that he had been framed. Is it possible that someone slipped the evidence into his pocket without him noticing?"

A long silence followed as the detectives tossed the concept around in their heads.

Detective Smithers was the first to speak.

"You're right," he called out. "It's possible, though it would have to have been someone Larry Parker knew well, to have got so close."

His statement was shortly seconded by his partner, Jones.

One by one, the detectives nodded to show their agreement to the possibility that the suspect might have been framed.

It appeared that Alan's team was on his side – except for one.

* * *

"What was that all about?" Andrews asked.

Alan was making his way back to his office when his sergeant caught up with him, having hung back to have a few words with the detectives.

"I thought we had it all sewn up. What's with this sudden change of heart? Unless Mrs Lockwood's been twisting your arm..."

Andrews broke off and chewed his lip. He had gone too far.

"What did you just say?" Alan swung around to face his sergeant.

"Sorry, sir, it's just that we all believed we had the right man in custody, including you, and now you're telling us to start all over again."

"I didn't tell you all to start again, Sergeant," Alan replied. He was trying very hard not to lose his patience. "I simply suggested that we should all look at what we had and make sure nothing had been missed."

Andrews was about to reply, but the chief inspector held up his hand when he saw Detective Morris hovering at the end of the corridor.

"Anything we can do for you, Morris?"

"I was on my way to ask whether you might have something you wanted me to do, while I'm hanging around the office," Morris replied, after a brief pause.

He nodded back towards the incident room. "The rest of them have gone off on their own, leaving me to take the calls – being that I'm the new boy on the block," he added, with a shrug. "You know what I mean."

"Yes, I do," Alan replied. "But you know, Morris that happens to us all when we first appear on the scene. We've all had to prove ourselves before being accepted into the fold."

He was aware that some of his detectives still hadn't got used to Morris and his rather lavish lifestyle. They all knew he came from a very well-to-do family and, while a few had accepted him, most of them still made the odd discourteous comment.

"I thought I might have been accepted into the fold, after my undercover work at the hotel," Morris replied.

"Sometimes it takes more than one job before you're acknowledged," Alan said slowly. "It depends on how the other detectives see it."

He would be the first to admit that Morris had done a good job while undercover at the hotel. In fact, some of the guys had taken him to the local pub for a few drinks to celebrate the success of his very first assignment. However, since then, Alan hadn't failed to notice that Morris was now always the one left holding the fort. Even at the dinner the other evening, when he suggested Morris go across and sit with the other detectives, they hadn't actually welcomed him with open arms.

"No, I'm afraid I haven't anything else for you at the moment." Alan scratched his head. "But I'll let you know if something turns up. In the meantime, you'd better get back to the incident room in case someone calls in."

Andrews had remained silent during the conversation between Morris and the DCI. He had been about to say something when Morris headed back down the corridor, but was cut short by Alan as he shepherded him into the office they shared, closing the door behind him.

"Now, what's going on?" Andrews asked.

"I don't know. But I feel something isn't right with Morris."

Alan walked across to the window and gazed down at the line of traffic travelling along the road below, before turning back to face Andrews.

"What do the other detectives have against Morris? Is there something we should know about?"

"I've no idea, sir," Andrews replied. "It's probably just like you told him out there." He pointed towards the door. "Sometimes it takes longer for newcomers to be accepted. Don't forget, I was hauled over the coals a few times before the guys acknowledged me as part of the team."

Alan laughed as he recalled the number of pranks played on Andrews before he was welcomed aboard.

"Yes, you're probably right." Alan nodded. "They had you jumping through hoops."

He walked across to his chair and sat down.

"Okay, now where were we before Morris arrived?"

"We were talking about rechecking the evidence against Larry Parker," Andrews replied.

He crossed his fingers that the DCI had forgotten his outburst regarding Mrs Lockwood.

"Yes, that's right. So, let's go through it."

Alan hadn't forgotten the remark his sergeant had made regarding Agnes but he decided to leave it alone – at least for the time being.

First, they discussed Susan's statement that she had thought the person behind her was Larry because he often crept up behind his friends and swung his arms around them. But she still didn't believe he was the man who attacked her. She had confirmed it when he called into the hospital to take her statement.

"His solicitor will have a field day with that," Alan said.

"Nevertheless, no matter what she says, she still didn't see the man's face, or hear his voice," Andrews persisted. "Larry could simply have been doing what he normally does. Only this time, his intention was to kill her. And don't forget, the pathologist believes the knife was thrust into the body by someone standing behind the victim."

They continued to talk it through. At one point, the two detectives even attempted to re-enact the scene, with one standing behind and thrusting their fist into the chest of the other. Though the two men were able to put up a fight, especially Alan, who was an ex-military man, it was still a possible scenario. All the victims had been women and may not have had the strength to fight off the killer.

From there, they moved on to when Larry signed out at the end of his shift.

"I just don't buy it," Andrews said. "How could he not notice what time he signed out? Surely he'd be interested in knowing how much overtime he'd be due – let alone check to see whether he would have time to catch up with the others."

Alan shrugged. He couldn't argue with his sergeant on that point. He had thought the very same thing at the time of the interview. They would need to go over that again with Larry Parker – only this time, without Agnes in the room. Though no doubt by then, he would have a solicitor sitting by his side – which, at the end of the day could prove to be even worse.

"Right, leaving that aside for the moment, what're we left with?"

"That would be the piece of evidence we found in Larry's pocket and what Morris unearthed when he spoke to the staff supervisor at the hotel," Andrews replied.

He recalled the DCI sending Morris to the hotel to talk to Mrs Telford about whether she knew of any conflict between Larry Parker and other staff members. Morris had looked very excited when he came back with the news that there had been a problem.

"I could kick myself every time I think about that day." Andrews thumped his fist on his desk. "How could I forget to ask for that information while I was with her?"

At the time, Alan had thought it strange that Andrews had been so lax. But he had been caught up with other problems, which was why he had let it go and sent Morris to speak to her.

"Shall we talk about the evidence we found on Larry, before getting to the information from Mrs Telford?" said Alan.

"Well, in that case, to my mind, that evidence alone should prove we have the right man in custody," said Andrews.

"I agree," Alan replied.

"Then, why the hell are we going through this nonsense if you agree with me that he's guilty?"

"I wasn't agreeing with you about him *being* guilty," Alan said, slowly.

He was trying hard to ignore his sergeant's second outburst towards him in one day.

"I was simply agreeing to your statement that the evidence found on Larry Parker *should* prove him guilty. But that isn't necessarily the case. What if the evidence had been planted to *make* him look guilty?"

Alan rose from his chair and began to pace up and down the room. "Think about it for a moment, Andrews."

Alan stopped pacing and looked at his sergeant. "Cast your mind back to when Larry emptied his pockets. Wouldn't you agree that either he's a damn good actor, or he truly *was* shocked when he saw the thing that he placed on the table?"

Andrews thought back to the scene. He had to admit, Larry Parker had looked rather stunned at what he found when he emptied his pockets. But then, maybe he *was* a good actor. Perhaps he was trying to fool them all with his expression of innocence.

"In that case, maybe I should check out whether he belongs to some amateur dramatic group," he retorted.

The sergeant looked away. He hadn't meant that to come out the way it did.

"I'm sorry, sir. I think this case is getting to me."

"I agree with you there, Andrews."

Alan was rather taken aback at his sergeant's second outburst in less than an hour. It was so unlike him. Yes, they'd had their differences over cases in the past. But they had talked it through and sorted it out. This time, something wasn't quite the same.

"Maybe you should stand back and let someone else take over until this case is closed," Alan suggested.

"No – sir," Andrews replied, quickly. "I need to work on this case."

Alan lowered himself into his chair. "Then tell me, what's going on? What's all this about?"

Andrews heaved a sigh. "Okay, where should I begin?"

"At the beginning." Alan shrugged. "Or even at the end. Sometimes blurting out the final aspect of a problem helps people to actually get started."

He sat back in his chair and waited until his sergeant was ready to speak.

Chapter Twenty-Six

Agnes wasn't sure what she should do first.

She needed to talk to a solicitor. Flo had looked up further information on the internet about Gordon Fulton and found he was well admired by his peers. There were probably lots of other solicitors in the city to choose from; however, it would be a random choice. Therefore, the daughter of the highly-esteemed retired solicitor seemed to be the best option. At least this one came recommended; well, sort of.

She had also promised to return to the police station this morning and update Larry on Sue's condition. Yet, looking at her watch, she found it was already lunchtime. She couldn't be in two places at once. So, where should she start?

Ben dropped her off outside a tall building on Grey Street. After throwing the options around in her head, Agnes had decided that engaging a solicitor should take priority.

She waited until Ben pulled away before she walked across to the door, which led into a rather impressive hallway. A long, elegant staircase leading to the upper floors was set in the centre, while a series of doors ran along either side. A notice board stood at the foot of the stairs, displaying the names of the various businesses in the building and on what floor each could be found. As it turned out, Emily Fulton, Solicitor, was located on the ground floor.

Agnes strolled down the hallway, looking at each door in turn, until she found the one she was looking for. She hesitated for one brief moment, before tapping on the door and walking into the office.

"Can I help you?"

The question came from a woman sitting behind a desk. Her fingers were poised over the keyboard of the computer in front of her. The woman looked to be in her late forties, or maybe early fifties. She was wearing a white blouse buttoned all the way up to the neck. A tweed jacket hung over the back of her chair, therefore Agnes surmised that she was wearing a matching tweed skirt. A nameplate sitting at the front of her desk gave her name as Mrs Amelia Gregg. Beneath her name, the word, *Secretary*, gave her position in the firm.

"Yes, you can. I'm here to see Ms. Fulton."

The secretary turned her head to check the diary lying next to the computer.

"And you are?"

"Mrs Agnes Lockwood."

There was a long pause while Mrs Gregg looked through the engagements for the day. Finally, she looked up at Agnes.

"Do you have an appointment? I don't seem to be able to find your name here."

"No, I'm afraid I don't." Without waiting to be asked, Agnes sat down in the chair in front of the desk. "Nevertheless, I really need to speak to Ms. Fulton today – now. It's rather urgent."

"I'm sure it is, Mrs Lockwood. But I'm afraid Ms. Fulton doesn't usually see anyone without an appointment."

"Doesn't usually? Does that mean she occasionally makes the odd exception?" Agnes paused. "Look, I'm sorry to be so persistent, I really do appreciate she's a very busy lady. But a young man is being accused of the attempted murder of one young woman and, very likely, the murder of two others. I believe he is innocent of all charges, but I'm going to need help proving it."

"What exactly does this young man mean to you? Are you related?"

The voice came from the other side of the room.

Agnes swung around in her chair to find a young woman standing by the open door leading into Emily Fulton's office. She hadn't heard the door open, so she had no idea how long the woman had been listening to the conversation.

"No, we're not related," Agnes replied. "I'm simply a guest at the hotel where he works. However, I believe he needs help."

"What about his parents? Why aren't they here?"

"I spoke to his parents this morning. They are aware that I'm seeking a solicitor on behalf of their son." Agnes paused. "Look, Ms. Fulton, does it really matter whether they're here or not? The important thing is that I speak to you about taking on this case."

"Why me? Of all the solicitors in Newcastle, why choose me?"

Agnes rose from the chair. "My first choice would have been your father. I was informed he was a really good solicitor, but I gather he's retired." She shrugged. "Then your name popped up. I thought that, being the daughter of such an excellent man, you might be anxious to carry on his good work."

Emily Fulton nodded. "One more question. Why didn't you make an appointment?"

"Simply because I could've been fobbed off for a few days by your secretary and I really wanted – no, I *needed* – to see you today."

The solicitor gestured towards her office. "Then you'd better come in, Mrs Lockwood." She glanced across to her secretary. "Hold all calls unless it's urgent."

"How did you know my name," Agnes asked, the moment the solicitor closed the door behind them.

"Look, does it really matter how I know your name?"

"*Touché!*" Agnes grinned.

"Please, take a seat."

Ms. Fulton pointed towards a chair that stood in front of the large desk, positioned in front of a huge window which looked out onto Grey Street. The tall pillars of the Theatre Royal could be seen almost directly opposite.

Agnes was rather surprised. She had thought the solicitor's office would have looked out onto the rear of the building. She must have gone in a full circle around the hallway while peering at the names on the doors, without realizing it. Agnes sat down and watched Ms. Fulton make her way around the desk towards her chair. On first sight, when she had seen her standing in the doorway of her office, apart from picking up that she was tall, had dark hair tied up at the back of her head and was wearing a trouser suit, Agnes had also thought that she looked rather smug. For one instant, she had wondered whether coming here had been a good idea after all and had considered walking away. Yet, for some reason, she had stayed. Why?

But now, watching Ms. Fulton sweep past her, Agnes knew why she had stayed. This woman wasn't trying to be smug at all. She simply had complete confidence in her abilities.

Once the two women were seated, the solicitor asked Agnes to tell the full story as to the reason of her visit.

"Don't leave anything out. I need to hear everything. By the way, you don't mind if I record your statement, do you? Like my father, I like to listen to it all again once the client has left."

"Not at all, please do," Agnes replied.

Once the recorder was switch on, Agnes sat back in the chair and began to recount the events of the last few days.

* * *

"What! I don't believe it!"

Andrews had only just blurted out four words, before Alan's outburst.

"What the hell happened?" Alan continued. "I thought everything was good between the two of you. Only a few nights ago, you were both at the dinner celebrating the Chief Superintendent's…" He broke off, as he cast his mind back to the evening in question.

On reflection, Andrews and his fiancée had been a little quieter than usual. At the time, Alan hadn't thought much about it, but now it was beginning to make sense. The couple hadn't taken to the dance floor very often and Andrews hadn't been keen to join his colleagues at the other end of the room. Normally, he would have swept Sandra over there like a shot, to join in the fun.

After all, Morris had been delighted when he'd been given the option, even though his colleagues hadn't looked quite so enthusiastic.

Alan quickly dismissed the thought. It was Andrews he should be thinking about at this moment, not Morris.

"Sorry, Michael, I had no idea there were problems between you and Sandra. Do you want to tell me what happened? Maybe there's something I can do to help the situation."

Alan sighed after his last remark. That was a laugh. What on earth could he do to help Andrews get back together with Sandra? He would probably end up making things worse. He couldn't even keep his own relationship with Agnes on an even keel. Who was he to give advice to anyone about their love life?

"It's the job," Andrews replied, after a long pause. "Well, partly," he added.

"Sandra believes you spend too much time at work?" Alan ventured.

"Yes, in a way." Andrews paused. "She understands that the job is important and is going to take up a great deal of time, but..." He broke off.

"But even when you aren't on duty, you're still at work." Alan finished the sentence for him.

Andrews nodded. "That's about it. I take it you've met with the same problem?"

Alan stroked his chin. "My ex-wife often complained about that. She told me several times that I never switched off."

"Was that the reason for your divorce?"

"No – not entirely," Alan said thoughtfully, staring down at his desk. "For some reason, we just didn't get along after we were married. It was great when we first got together and even while we were engaged – but it was never quite the same after the wedding."

He looked back at Andrews. "But this isn't about me. It's about you and your fiancée. For goodness' sake, if this is the woman you want to spend the rest of your life with, then you have got to put this right or you'll lose her forever. Take some time off. For once, forget about the job. Take her on holiday – go somewhere you've both only ever dreamed of going to. Believe me, Michael, you only get one chance in life at being happy. I…"

Alan broke off. Maybe he was trying to be too positive.

"However," he continued, "if, after all that, you still feel there are any doubts about your relationship with Sandra, then you must accept it and let her go. There'll be someone else out there waiting for you… Someone who won't give a damn about how many hours you spend thinking about the important work you do. Instead, that young woman will understand about the number of hours you need to spend at work. She might also be able to help you along the way with a few suggestions of her own – you know what I mean. A fresh pair of eyes, etc."

There was a long silence.

Andrews deliberated over whether Sandra might not be the right woman for him after all.

Meanwhile, Alan was focused on Agnes.

Though Agnes had been uppermost in his mind the whole time he had been pouring out advice to his sergeant, it had been his closing sentence which had really hit home. It had been her intuition which had helped the police close the last two cases. So, what if she *was* right about Larry Parker after all, and the police were barking up the wrong tree?

Just then the phone rang, making both men jump.

"Very well," Alan told the sergeant on the desk downstairs. "Tell her I'll be right down."

"What's going on, sir?"

"It seems Larry Parker now has a solicitor," he told Andrews, as he replaced the phone. "She'd like to see her client, but wants a quick word with me first."

"Mrs Lockwood doesn't hang around, does she? I wonder who she managed to rope in. Did you get her name, by any chance?" Andrews asked.

"Yes. It's Ms. Emily Fulton."

"Not… You don't mean Gordon Fulton's daughter?"

Alan nodded. "Yes, Andrews, I fear so."

"Ouch." Andrews grimaced. "Good luck."

"Good luck to you, too, Sergeant, because you're coming with me."

"I am?"

"Yes, you are!"

Chapter Twenty-Seven

Outside the solicitor's office, Agnes breathed a sigh of relief. She was confident she had found the right person to help Larry prove his innocence. Emily Fulton had listened carefully as she spilled out the reasons why she believed the young man who was being accused of murdering two women and the attempted murder of a third, was innocent.

The solicitor had been aware of the stabbings. She had followed the news bulletins over the last few days, most especially because the killings had taken place here in the city. However, she had been surprised to learn that the woman sitting in front of her was very the person who had not only discovered Wendy Hamilton in the Central Station, but had also recognized the man she had seen earlier with the victim. Her identity had been withheld from the press.

Ms. Fulton had promised to go to the police station right away. Agnes had offered to accompany her, as she needed to speak to Larry about Sue's condition. However, the solicitor had declined, saying it was best if she went on her own. But she had promised to pass on the news of Sue's condition to Larry, the moment she saw him.

Agnes tapped her foot on the pavement, pondering where to go from here. Earlier, she had been rushed off her feet, but now, here she was with nothing on the agenda. The Eldon Square was only a short distance from here; she could head up there and look around the shops. But, for the first time in years, shopping didn't appeal to her.

Just then, her phone rang. It turned out to be the estate agent. He was interested to know whether she had come to a decision about the apartment she had viewed recently.

"I'm afraid I haven't come to a decision yet. I haven't had the chance to speak to my partner about it."

The agent rambled on for a few minutes, telling her about the number of other people interested in the property. "If you don't make an offer soon, I'm afraid you'll miss out."

"Then, if that were to happen, I'll assume the apartment wasn't meant for me."

Agnes hung up and flung her phone back into her bag. That apartment was exactly what she had been looking for. It had everything she wanted. But, due to this murder investigation, she hadn't really been in a position to tell Alan about it. Whenever she thought the time was right to mention it, something had reared its head and ruined the moment. Then, there had been that awful row.

After their argument, she had been so angry that she had thought about going ahead anyway – buying it and moving in on her own. What the heck? This was her life. Besides, it wasn't as though she couldn't afford it. If he got over his tantrum and decided he wanted to join her, then he could do so.

But the one thing holding her back at the moment was the thought of living there alone under those circumstances. The notion of peering down to the quayside and seeing the places she and Alan had visited together, made her think of herself as another Miss Havisham, the character from the novel, *Great Expectations*; a woman who lived her life in the past. Now that she and Alan were beginning to talk to each other again, she felt she ought to at least run it past him. If he didn't like the idea of living there, then she would make a decision for herself.

Agnes stood for another couple of minutes, looking up and down Grey Street, trying to decide where to go from here. Maybe she should go back to the hospital and see how Sue was progressing. But what if Keith was there? She didn't want to interrupt the couple again. The pathologist had been very kind and understanding when she had arrived the day before. Nevertheless, it was obvious that they had a thing going for each other. It was good that each had found someone special, but at the same time, it was a shame they'd had to meet under such awful circumstances.

It was then that Agnes suddenly made up her mind to walk down Grey Street to the quayside. The small map in her hotel room showed a road leading from the foot of the Tyne Bridge, right up to Grey's Monument; a short distance from where she was now standing. She had no idea how long it would take. But did it really matter? There was nowhere else she had to be.

On her way down Grey Street, she was delighted to see how the buildings had been preserved. Perhaps inside, they had changed over the years to suit the new owners. But from the outside, they looked exactly the same as they did when they were built all those years ago.

By now, Agnes had reached Dean Street. It seemed rather quiet. It was certainly quieter than she had expected a road leading from the hub of the city to the busy quayside to be. But, as she approached the Side, the road to the quayside, she heard raised voices coming from somewhere close by.

"Just stay away from him! If I see you near him again, I'll..."

The voice broke off.

Agnes hesitated, wondering whether she should continue on her way and look along the small road leading off from Dean Street, or take several steps back and pretend she hadn't heard anything. However, she wasn't given the choice, as a woman stormed around the corner and almost collided with her. She was shocked to find it was the same woman who had looked daggers at her earlier in the week, when that pompous newspaper photographer, Harold Armstrong, had blown a kiss at her on the quayside.

Seeing her up close for the first time, Agnes realized she was quite attractive, or she would be if she wasn't expressing so much anger. She was wearing a different outfit to the one she was wearing the other day, but it was still at least three sizes too small for her. The blue pencil skirt was almost bursting at the seams and was about six inches above her podgy knees.

Agnes hoped the woman wouldn't recognize her. But no such luck. "And that goes for you, too! Stay away from my man," she almost spat out the words. "Why're you all pestering him? He doesn't want your attention. Leave him alone – or, I'm warning you, you'll be sorry."

The woman stepped around Agnes and headed off up Dean Street. "What the hell was that all about?"

By now, the lady who had been the victim of the woman's tantrum had reached the corner of the alleyway. She was visibly shaken by the ordeal.

"Who is that lunatic? For a moment, I thought she was going to punch me in the face," she added, gazing up the road at the woman marching away. "Thank goodness she heard someone coming and backed off."

She looked back at Agnes. "Sorry, my name is Jane."

Agnes smiled at the young woman in front of her. She was also wearing a mini-skirt, but it suited her slim figure.

"I'm Agnes, she replied, "but, answering your question, the woman is – she's the lady friend, or maybe the wife, of Harold Armstrong, the newspaper photographer."

"Oh – that creep!" Jane pulled a face.

"By that, I gather you've met him at some point."

"Oh, yes. He tried it on with me recently, but I wasn't having any of it," Jane said. "He seemed to think I would be impressed because the photo he had taken was all over the news. To his mind, he was famous."

"Yes, he foisted himself on me, too," Agnes said, recalling the day he had joined her at the table outside the café. "However, after I managed to get rid of him, his lady friend," she gestured up the road, "caught him blowing kisses at me. She was livid. She seemed to be under the impression that I was chasing him, and not the other way around. Someone should put her straight before she does someone some harm."

Agnes was thoughtful as she continued walking down the road towards the quayside. Before they parted, there had been a brief discussion as to whether the woman was married to Armstrong or just a hopeful bride-to-be. Jane had said that she hadn't seen any rings on the woman's fingers when she had threatened her. Therefore, as far as she was concerned, they weren't married.

Nevertheless, Agnes thought it was possible Jane could have missed seeing a narrow gold band on one finger when she was trying to dodge a blow from a clenched fist hurtling towards her. Not that it was relevant whether the woman was married or not. In either case, she should not be behaving in such a manner. Like Jane said, she could end up harming someone.

Agnes stopped walking when another thought popped into her head. Was it possible that this woman was the killer the police were looking for? What if Armstrong had also tried to chat-up the murder victims? The woman might have believed they were flirting with her man and killed them in a rage of jealousy. Thinking back to when she had come face to face with the woman only a few minutes ago, the hatred blasting from her eyes made Agnes believe it was more than a mere possibility.

For a moment, Agnes was tempted to turn around and look back up the road to see whether the wretched woman was hovering around somewhere. But she decided against it. The best thing to do was to continue walking towards the quayside without giving the impression that she was anxious about whoever might be lurking behind her. Once she was there, she would be safe. At this time of the day, there would be too many people around to witness an attack on her.

Agnes heaved a sigh of relief when she finally reached Sandhill. The quayside was only a short distance away. She was safe; at least for the time being.

* * *

Agnes took a long sip from her wine glass. By now, she was sitting inside her favourite café close to the Millennium Bridge.

Normally, on such a lovely, warm day, Agnes would have chosen to sit at one of the tables outside the café and gaze at the River Tyne.

However today, given the circumstances, she wanted to spot whoever passed by the café, without them seeing her first.

Her first thought had been to go straight back to the hotel, head up to her room and lock the door. But, after thinking it through as she slowly made her way along the quayside, she decided that might not be such a good idea. If the wretched woman *was* following her, it would give further evidence of where she was staying.

Despite trying to stay calm and look like someone without a care in the world, Agnes kept her eyes glued on the windows of the café. The seat she had chosen was in the best position for scrutinizing people coming from all directions. However, there was no sign of the woman she had encountered earlier, which meant she hadn't followed her.

But then Agnes had another thought. It could mean that the woman had trailed Jane up Dean Street towards the city centre. Was it possible that someone would find Jane lying dead in some alleyway? Agnes picked up her phone to call Alan. This had gone too far; she needed to talk to him about what she knew.

However, something Jane had said flashed through her mind and she lowered her phone. It was about the woman clenching her fists as though to strike her. That must mean the woman had been standing in front of Jane, whereas the other victims had been attacked from behind – with a knife. Therefore, maybe she wasn't the killer after all, though she was still a rather nasty woman, who should be reported to the police.

Agnes sighed. It was time to go back to the drawing board.

* * *

The DCI and his sergeant made their way downstairs to meet up with Larry Parker's solicitor. Though Ms. Fulton was relatively new to the position, both detectives were aware of her reputation for getting the job done.

"I suppose she has a high standard to live up to," Andrews said. "Her father was one of the best solicitors in Newcastle."

"I would say he was *the* best," Alan replied, recalling some of the cases Gordon Fulton had worked on in the past. "And I'm sure his daughter is not planning to let him down." He took a deep breath. "We must either make sure we have a strong case for charging Parker with murder, or release him."

By now, they had reached the ground floor. Ms. Fulton was waiting by the desk near the entrance.

"I'm DCI Johnston and this is Sergeant Andrews," Alan said, as they approached her. He held out his hand. "It's good to meet you."

She smiled as she shook hands with the DCI. "Yes, I know who you are. It's nice to meet you – both," she added, glancing at Andrews. "Nevertheless, you will understand that this is not a social call. I'm here to speak to my client, Larry Parker. However, before I talk to him, I'd be interested to learn *your* version of the events leading to his arrest."

Your version; Alan winced.

Her straight-to-the-point attitude reminded him of her father, Gordon Fulton. He was a man who never minced his words and it appeared his daughter had learned a few things from him. In this instance, to put the police on the wrong foot by making it appear they had concocted some story to get the case over and done with.

"Perhaps we should talk in here." Alan gestured towards a small office to his right.

The DCI didn't say anything further until they were seated.

"Ms. Fulton, I appreciate that you're here to look out for your client. However, let me assure you, Parker has been detained because of what we were told by the one victim who…"

The solicitor was about to break in, but Alan held up his hand. "I believe you wanted to hear our version of events. Therefore, please do me the courtesy of allowing me to finish. As I was saying," he continued, "the one victim who managed to survive the terrible experience has told us her attacker approached from behind and thrust his arms around her, before stabbing her."

Alan droned on at great length, explaining the reasons why Larry had been kept in custody. Ms. Fulton might well have learned a lot from her father over the years, but he had picked up a few lessons elsewhere. This particular one was something he saw on the TV show, *The West Wing* – take a long time to answer a question and do not allow any interruptions. With a bit of luck, by the time the end of the statement was reached, the person who had asked the question would have forgotten what it was they wanted to know. Or would not give a damn one way or the other.

The solicitor rolled her eyes several times during the course of his long conversation. He had repeated a few things numerous times, though he had craftily worded them differently.

"And there you have it, Ms. Fulton. Now, what would you like to say?"

"I think I had better talk to my client," she said, rising to her feet.

"Yes, that's probably a good idea," Alan replied. He rose from the chair. "My sergeant will escort you to the interrogation room. I'll have an officer bring Parker to you."

"Isn't there somewhere a little more private? I would rather speak to Larry without the fear of anyone watching through some two-way mirror."

"I could have him brought to this room," Alan said. "Would that suit you better? Or do you think there might be a camera poised somewhere above, staring down at you?"

"This room will be fine, thank you," she uttered, lowering herself back into her chair.

"Well, that certainly shut her up," Andrews said, as they walked back to their office. "I thought you were never going to stop talking. You made it sound as though we have much more evidence against Parker than we do."

"That was the point," Alan replied. "Agnes will have already told her the full story when she approached Ms. Fulton to take on the case. Therefore, I needed her to believe we had learned a great deal more over the last few hours." He paused. "But apart from that, I don't take kindly to being talked down to by someone trying to boost their own self-esteem – especially when they're new to the game. I'd be the first to admit, her father was a great solicitor and I think she will be, too – one day. But, in the meantime, Ms. Fulton needs to work on her approach to the opposition a little more carefully."

Chapter Twenty-Eight

Now, assured that the angry woman friend of Harold Armstrong hadn't followed her, Agnes slowly made her way back to the hotel. Her first port of call was to speak to the staff supervisor, to bring her up to speed.

Flo appeared to be delighted when she learned that Gordon Fulton's daughter had agreed to take on the case.

"Yes, I feel she will be more than capable of standing up to the police," she said, thoughtfully.

Agnes nodded in agreement. She then mentioned the angry woman she had seen on Dean Street on her way back to the hotel.

"At first, I had the idea that she might be the killer. But after thinking it through, I changed my mind. What we know about the murderer didn't fit in with this woman's approach." She thought for a moment. "Why would anyone want these young women dead? Could it be some kind of vengeance? Maybe they upset someone without realizing it."

"Could be," Flo agreed, quietly.

"Well, I must let you get on," Agnes said, as she stood up and moved over towards the door. "I'm going upstairs, to have a long think."

Up in her room, Agnes sat down near the window and looked down at the people bustling around on the quayside.

Brian, the lift attendant, had been a little chattier than his usual self. Perhaps he was trying to make up for Larry's absence – though, if that was the case, he had a long way to go. Larry's banter came easily, whereas Brian's chatter always seemed a little forced. Still, the lad was doing his best for the guests and the hotel. She hadn't failed to notice that he had volunteered for extra shifts these last couple of days.

Her eyes drifted towards the table. The two photos taken by Harold Armstrong at the Central Station stared up at her. She had meant to clear them off the table and put them in a drawer. However, for some reason, they were still lying there. Now, focusing on the enlarged picture of the man she had seen in Whitley Bay, she was seeing it in a whole new light. Could it be that the man wasn't watching her after all, but was looking at someone standing directly behind her? It would make a whole lot more sense. Why hadn't she thought of that before?

Agnes stood up and walked around the room, trying to recall the scene at the Central Station. But, truthfully, she couldn't remember turning around to see what was going on behind her. She had been so concerned about the poor young woman who had been stabbed that she hadn't even noticed the newspaper photographer. Maybe Alan could put out a new statement to the newspapers and the TV stations, asking whether anyone had seen this person hovering around. She shook her head as she thought it through. That was stupid. Of course people were hovering around. It was a train station. There were always people drifting around train stations.

Agnes turned her attention to the other questions running through her mind. If she was right, why was the man looking at this person so intently? Did he recognize him, or her, from somewhere else? Perhaps they were friends. However she quickly dismissed that notion. The expression on the man's face wasn't one of pleasure at seeing a friend. Instead, there was a definite a look of hatred in his eyes. Did he have reason to believe that whoever he was looking at had stabbed Wendy? Was that why he had been found floating down the River Tyne not long after?

Agnes poured herself a glass of wine before returning to her seat by the window. If her assumptions were correct, then that would let Larry off the hook. She was about to pick up her phone to call Alan and let him know her latest thoughts, but then changed her mind. If

Larry had happened to be off duty that day, it would only give the police further ammunition against him.

Instead, she thought back to the day she visited Whitley Bay, trying to recall who had been operating the lift that morning. It had been Larry; when she told him where she was going, he had laughed, asking her to bring him a stick of rock from the coast. She had totally forgotten about his request until this moment. However, that wasn't really what concerned her. It was the fact that Larry had already gone off duty when she arrived back at the hotel that afternoon. It had been Brian who had taken her to the fourth floor. While the lift travelled upwards, he had commented on how Larry had wanted a couple of hours off and he had received a call asking if he could come in early.

"I was quite happy to agree," he had said. "A bit of overtime now and again is always good."

Therefore, it appeared Larry wasn't at the hotel when Wendy was stabbed. Agnes was quite shaken. Could it be she had been wrong about him? Might he have killed those two women and attempted to kill Sue Matthews, after all? If that was the case, the man in the photograph at the Central Station could have been looking at Larry Parker.

Agnes swallowed hard as she realised it was possible that she was protecting a killer.

Chapter Twenty-Nine

Agnes sat for a long while, weighing up the pros and cons as to whether Larry was involved in the killings.

Yes, Larry could have been the person standing somewhere behind her. The very person the man in the photo was looking daggers at. But surely, if it had been Larry, he would have recognised her and scurried away for fear of her suddenly glancing around to see him standing there. However, on second thoughts, she was well aware that the young man was very good at coming up with suggestions, ideas or anything else needed to fit any situation. His quick thinking had helped her out of a couple of sticky situations in the past, which was why she had been so eager to help get him out of this mess.

Yet, could it be she had she been wrong about him? Perhaps he *was* guilty of murder, after all. For a start, it appeared he was away from the hotel when two of the stabbings took place. Who knows, he could also have been off duty at the time Janet Cunningham was murdered! If only there was someone she could talk it through with… Of course, there was Alan. But, the way things were between them at present, he was likely to say, "I told you so. Leave it to the police from now on."

She could speak to Flo. Yet, there was something about her attitude that Agnes was a little concerned about. But at the moment, she couldn't put her finger on it. Nevertheless, she needed to confirm Larry's whereabouts at the time Janet Cunningham had been attacked and the only person who would know whether he was in the hotel, was Flo. She picked up the phone and asked to speak to Mrs Telford.

Flo informed her that Larry was off duty for a short while, the day Wendy Hamilton was stabbed.

"He had couple of hours owing, and he asked whether he could take time off that afternoon. Brian Hockley was happy to stand in for him," Flo explained.

"What about the day Janet Cunningham was murdered?" Agnes asked.

"Let me just check." There was a short silence. "Yes, he was on duty that day. In fact, he agreed to stay on to cover for Brian Hockley. But as you know, Brian arrived early."

"Yes. Thank you, Flo."

When the call ended, Agnes poured herself another glass of wine and moved across to the sofa.

Looking at this case from the beginning and assuming Larry wasn't the killer, who else could be in the frame? Who could possibly have some kind of vendetta against these three young women? One woman might have upset the killer at some point and caused him to want to frighten her; but three!

The first person to come to mind was the woman she had seen earlier that day; Harold Armstrong's lady friend. There was a jealous woman, if ever there was one. Each of the murdered women could have been approached by her man friend, Harold Armstrong. Yet her method of attack didn't quite fit.

Agnes shook her head. This was hopeless. How could she possibly know who these women had been associating with? The age differences between her and all three women meant they would never have met up at the same hotspots. Agnes frowned. 'Hotspots'… where did that come from? She sighed. Never mind. Obviously she had picked it up somewhere down the line. It probably meant pretty much the same as going to the same restaurants or theatres. But getting back to the case, the person who stabbed them must have been about their age;

someone who visited the same hotspots. That immediately brought her back to Larry Parker.

But, for heaven's sake, several of the people working in the hotel were of the same age and went to the same clubs. For instance, there was Brian Hockley, the other lift attendant and all those working in the restaurant, or the bar. Not forgetting the personnel working behind the scenes, such as the domestic staff. At the end of the day, any of them could have been involved in the stabbings. Any of them could have had a grudge against the three women. Nevertheless, only Larry seemed to fit the bill.

* * *

Alan sat behind his desk trying to pull all the pieces together. This case was going nowhere. A short while ago, Superintendent Blake had called him into his office – no, maybe *hauled* him into his office would have been a more accurate turn of phrase. Either way, it had definitely been more of a command than a polite invitation.

Blake had not been at all happy at how the case seemed to be on hold.

"For goodness' sake, man!" he had roared. "You have the murderer in custody. Reading the report, it strikes me Larry Parker is guilty. Why are you still hanging around? Case is closed. I have a press conference tomorrow morning."

Though he'd had the urge to yell back at the superintendent, Alan had held his tongue. He only had a few years to go before he would retire with a good pension. That, together with his army pension, would allow him to see out his days in comfort. Therefore, there was no way he was going to let this man get the better of him as he could lose everything. However, neither was he prepared to allow Blake to have the upper hand.

"The thing is, sir, we're working on some new evidence and I felt sure you'd want us to check it out fully before you actually spoke to the press."

At that point, he had paused for a second before striking where he knew it would hurt Blake the most.

"After all, you wouldn't want to give out the wrong information at your press conference – would you, sir? But of course, if you are happy that we have the right man, then go ahead."

At that point, Blake had coughed a few times to clear his throat before agreeing the DCI definitely needed more time.

But now, back in the office, instead of experiencing a sense of relief, Alan was stumped about where to go from this point. Since Agnes had arrived back on Tyneside, he had found it helpful to talk things through with her. She seemed to be able to look at a case from a whole new standpoint and very often came up with some concept he and his team had missed. If only he could talk it through with her now. Between them, they might have come up with something they had both overlooked earlier. At the end of the day, that one thing could possibly prove Larry Parker's guilt, or even his innocence.

Alan sighed. But how could he seek her advice now? Their relationship appeared to be on a knife-edge; though things had looked a little more positive when they met earlier today. If only he hadn't been so jealous of that wretched man, John Alton. Clearly, as he had seen for himself that morning, there hadn't been anything going on between them. The whole affair had been a figment of his imagination. Yet he had allowed it to take over and almost ruin their relationship.

A couple of minutes later, Alan came to a decision.

The sergeant looked up from his laptop in surprise when the DCI leaped from his chair.

"I'm going out!"

"Where're you going?"

"Nowhere."

"You're going out – nowhere?"

"Isn't that just what I said?"

Andrews nodded. But then he had another thought.

"Sir, what should I tell Superintendent Blake if he should ask to see you again?"

Alan was about to stride off down the corridor, but instead, he swung around and pulled a face.

"Okay, got it, sir."

Chapter Thirty

Alan pulled up outside the hotel and clambered out of his car. On his way up the stairs, he considered whether he should have called first. Perhaps she wouldn't even open the door.

However, he needn't have worried. She looked quite pleased to see him.

"Come in, Alan," she invited and pointed towards the bottle of wine. "Want some, or are you still on duty?"

Alan nodded as he lowered himself onto the sofa. "Yes, I'm still on duty. However, I'd love to join you – but make mine a small one."

Agnes poured him some wine and topped up her own glass, before joining him on the sofa.

There was a long silence, then they both began to speak at once.

"You first," Agnes said. "After all, you could be called away any minute."

Alan took a deep breath.

"Agnes, I'm really stuck on this case at the moment." He sighed.

Never in his life did he think he would purposely set out to seek advice on a police murder investigation from a… an… amateur sleuth. Perhaps this wasn't such a good idea after all. Yet he was here now, so he might as well get on with it.

"I just thought that maybe, if I could talk it through with you, we might be able to come up with something we missed the first time around."

"Funny you should say that," Agnes replied. "It was only a short while ago that I realised there were a few things I wanted to talk over with you."

"Okay, where do we start?" Alan asked.

"Where did we leave off?"

Alan shrugged. He really didn't want to go down the road of when Agnes was with Larry at the police station.

Realizing they were going to waste time going through a load of nonsense, Agnes went across to the table and brought back the photo of the man who had later been found floating in the Tyne.

"Take another look at this," she said, thrusting it at Alan.

"Yes, yes, the man appears to be looking at you. Why am I looking at this again? We've gone through all this before."

He handed the picture back to Agnes.

"That's why I'm asking you to take another look at it," she replied, shoving his hand away. "Look again."

"What am I looking at?"

"Look at the man's eyes. At first, I thought he was looking at me. But now I believe he is staring at someone *behind* me."

Alan focused his attention on the man's eyes, as Agnes continued.

"And I think that's the reason why he was murdered." She stabbed her finger on the photo. "Don't you see, Alan? If what I am saying is correct and he *had* recognised the person behind me, then that person couldn't take the chance that the man wouldn't speak to the police."

"Slow down, Agnes." Alan scratched his head. "I think I can see where you're coming from." He looked at the photograph again. "But, if that *is* the case, how can you be sure that the person behind you didn't recognize you, too? I mean, he could've spotted you watching the couple in Whitley Bay, and then seen you again on the train." He paused. "Or anywhere else, for that matter," he added.

"Yes, I agree, he might well have done." For a moment, Agnes reflected on her earlier thoughts of how the killer might really be Larry after all. "Nevertheless, it's obvious the person was confident that I hadn't seen them and therefore couldn't pass on any information to the police."

"How can you be so sure? We're dealing with a ruthless killer here."

"Because, Alan, I'm still alive. If he, or she, had been in any doubt, I would be dead by now."

Alan was stunned. How could Agnes remain so calm, given what she had just said? He picked up his glass and swallowed the remaining wine, before refilling it.

"You told me that you were still on duty," Agnes said.

"I was when I walked in here, but not any more. I have just signed myself out." He shook his head. "Agnes, have you any idea how worried I am about you? I don't know what I would do if I were to lose you now. Can't you stay away from this case? Actually, come to think of it, that goes for any police investigation."

"I certainly can't step back from this case, Alan. I'm in too deep now." Agnes smiled. "As for any other inquiry – I can't promise anything."

She took a sip of wine. "Now then, what did you want to talk to me about? Have your team come up with anything new I should know about?"

"No, unfortunately, we don't have any new evidence one way or the other. I simply wanted to talk over a few things with you. I thought that if we could put our heads together, we might come up with something." Alan paused. "Apart from your new thoughts about the photo, is there anything else you want to talk about?"

Agnes looked down at the floor for a few seconds. "I don't know whether I should be telling you this, but it seems that Larry wasn't on duty here at the hotel at the time of two of the attacks."

"So you've come to your senses," Alan said. "We *do* have the right man in custody. Why didn't you tell me this earlier?"

"Because I knew you would react exactly like this," Agnes said angrily. "Okay, Larry wasn't on duty at those particular times, but nor were several other people working here at the hotel. I thought you came to see me to talk things through, yet you're sitting here trying to score points against me."

She sighed. "To tell you the truth, I wish I hadn't invited you in. I was stupid to think I could trust you." She nodded towards the door. "Maybe it would be best if you left right now."

"Is that what you really want?"

"Yes, Alan. But before you go, at least give me something. Tell me why were you so sure you had the right man in custody? I mean, before I gave you the information about Larry being off duty at the time of the attacks?"

Alan hesitated. There was no need to say another word. He had everything he needed to charge Larry with the murders of Wendy Hamilton and Janet Cunningham, as well as the attack on Sue Matthews. Yet, he had come here to exchange information. How could he go back on his word? Besides, what could Agnes do about it now? The evidence had come from a reliable source.

"It was all down to what the staff supervisor here at the hotel told Detective Morris."

Chapter Thirty-One

"No!" Agnes leapt to her feet. "Flo didn't say that at all!"

"Who the hell is Flo?"

"Flo – short for Florence, she's the staff supervisor. She told me exactly what she said to your detective and it wasn't anything like what he passed on to you."

Alan's jaw dropped. A long silence followed, as Alan tried to come to terms with the fact that Detective Morris had given him false information. Why on earth would he do that? This was a murder inquiry. A young man's life was on the line.

Meanwhile, Agnes lowered herself back onto the sofa and waited until Alan was ready to hear the true account of what had happened.

"Okay, what did she tell you?" Alan said, recovering slightly.

Agnes explained exactly what Florence had told her.

"So you see, the argument wasn't between Larry and Sue. Actually, it had nothing to do with Sue. If you don't believe me, then feel free to go downstairs and speak to Flo yourself. This is important, Alan. You're basing your whole case on a lie."

"But why would Morris make up such a story? For heaven's sake, why would he tell me there'd been a big argument between Larry and Sue when it was between Larry and another man – a man who doesn't even work here any more?"

"I don't know," Agnes replied.

But then she had another thought. "What if he's somehow involved in these murders? He could even be our killer." She bit her lip as she waited for his reaction to her outrageous theory.

"Morris – a killer? I don't believe it!" Alan retorted. "He's a police detective and..." He broke off when he thought back to an incident earlier that day.

Morris had been hovering around at the end of the corridor. It was only by chance he had spotted him. At first, Alan had thought he was trying to listen in on the conversation between him and his sergeant, but then had quickly dismissed the notion. For goodness' sake, Morris already knew everything about the case – unless he believed there was some evidence being kept from him. But why would he have reason to think that?

By now, Alan was pacing up and down the room with the thoughts of Morris's recent behaviour tumbling through his head. He recalled how the rest of the team seemed to have something against their fellow detective. He had thought it was because Morris had gone back to wearing his rather expensive suits, since his return from a visit to his parents, but maybe there was something more to it. He had preferred to stay out of it, but perhaps he should have made a few discreet enquiries.

"So, you think it *is* possible Morris could be involved?" Agnes interrupted his thoughts.

"I don't know," Alan admitted, returning to the sofa. "I can't believe he's capable of murder. Yet," he clicked his tongue, "he was acting strangely earlier today."

"So, what happened today?"

Alan told her about the encounter in the corridor at the station. "Come to think of it, I've seen him doing that a couple of other times, when Andrews and I have been discussing something."

"Then you must speak to him right away. Find out what's going on – why he lied to you about what Flo told him."

"I doubt Morris is going to scarper off anywhere. Quite honestly, I can't believe he's our murderer."

Agnes smiled.

"So, what are you smiling about?"

Agnes winked. "Because you've finally agreed that the person you and the police are looking for, is *our* killer."

Alan was silent for a long moment.

Making a decision, he stood up and grabbed his jacket.

"I'm going back to the station before Morris goes off duty. I think he and I need to have a little chat."

Agnes was about to say something, but Alan beat her to it. "And, before you ask, no, you can't come with me." He paused. "But I promise I'll come back and tell you how it went."

"Before you shoot off, Alan, is there anything else you haven't told me?"

"Well, yes, there is, actually…"

* * *

The moment he was clear of the hotel, Alan pulled out his phone and called Andrews.

"I need to speak to Morris. Make sure he doesn't go off duty before I get there. I'm heading back now."

"Is there a problem, sir?"

"You bet there is. I'll tell you about it when I get there."

Thankfully, the roads weren't too busy and it wasn't long before he reached the station.

Once inside his office, he picked up his phone and ordered Morris to drop whatever he was doing as he needed to speak to him right away.

"What on earth has happened?" Andrews asked.

"You'll hear about it in a few minutes," Alan replied, slamming the phone back down.

A couple of minutes later, Morris arrived.

"Come in and close the door," Alan said.

Morris looked at the chair in front of the DCI's desk, but, as he wasn't invited to sit down, he remained standing.

"Would you tell me exactly what you learned from the staff supervisor at the hotel?" Alan said.

"I told you…" Morris began.

"I know what you *told* me and what you wrote in the report," Alan interrupted. "But this time, I would like you to tell me the truth."

Morris shuffled his feet before he spoke.

"Larry Parker did have a bit of an argument, but it wasn't with Sue. It was with one of the porters."

He turned his head and glanced at Andrews before looking back at Alan. "Look," he continued. "We all know the lad is guilty, I just thought that I could help to speed things up a little."

"You thought that by passing on false information, you'd be speeding up the process," Alan replied, through clenched teeth. "What do you think would have happened if the case gone before the court? Any solicitor worth his socks would have checked out the statement with the source and passed on the information to the barrister. The police would have been brought up for fabricating evidence!" Alan's fury showed in the rising volume of his voice.

"I'm sorry, I didn't think it through. I just thought that an extra piece of evidence would help you with the case," Morris whined, "especially as he had the necklace in his pocket."

"You didn't put that there, by any chance, did you?" Alan snapped. "You know, just to help the case."

"No! I swear. You don't really believe that, do you?" Morris closed his eyes for moment. "I've blown it, haven't I?"

"You certainly haven't done anything to help yourself!" Alan retorted. "Have you done anything else that could hinder this case?"

Morris hesitated for one brief moment before replying.

"No, sir," he mumbled.

Alan took a deep breath, unsure whether to believe him. "Very well, go back to the incident room and rewrite that report. Then, get on with your job – while you still have one!"

"Do you believe him – about not having any further secrets about the case?" Andrews asked, once Morris had left.

"I think there's something he's not telling me. I thought he looked a little cagey when I asked him."

"What are you going to do about the false report?"

Alan stood up and walked across to the window. "I don't know," he said. "I just don't understand why he would even think of doing something so stupid." He swung back around to face the sergeant. "Maybe that's why he's been acting a little strange lately – you know, hovering around in the corridors. Perhaps he was trying to listen in to our conversations, to learn whether we knew what he'd been up to."

"It's possible." Andrews agreed. "Thank goodness you found out about it before Ms. Fulton did. She could have made a really big thing out of something like that."

"I think she would *definitely* have made a big thing out of it," Alan replied.

Chapter Thirty-Two

Agnes sat by the window and thought through what Alan had told her before he left. When Larry had been asked to empty his pockets, he had pulled out Sue's missing necklace.

Alan had admitted Larry had been happy to oblige and had looked extremely surprised when he saw it. Nevertheless, she had to agree it was quite damning evidence. If anything, it made her earlier suspicions that Larry could be guilty sound more convincing.

Yet Agnes still had a nagging doubt. What if someone really was trying to frame him? After all, with the police seeking evidence against him, someone out there might be trying to give them a helping hand.

Agnes rose from her chair and moved nearer to the window as she gave the problem more thought. Was it possible that the killer had paid Morris to give false information to the police? If that was the case, might the killer have also paid the detective to plant the necklace in Larry's pocket? Yet, until she heard further from Alan, she couldn't really go down that road.

She wished she knew how long she would have to wait for Alan to come back with an update about Morris's involvement – that is, if he were to come back at all. Though he'd said he would inform her of the outcome, Agnes still wasn't fully convinced that they were working together on this case – certainly not in the way they used to. For instance, their meeting today had ended up more a case of 'tell me what you have and I'll give you something', rather than actually putting their heads together. Therefore, if she wanted to get to the truth about the murders, she needed to carry on without him.

But where on earth should she start? She had already been involved when she found Wendy Hamilton in the Central Station, and that hadn't led her anywhere. Therefore, perhaps her next step should be to look into the attack on Susan Matthews.

At least Agnes had met the young woman during her stay at the hotel, as well as some of her colleagues. Perhaps a little informal chat with a few of them could throw some light on where Sue went and who she met up with when she was off duty. It was more than likely that the police had already spoken to Sue at the hospital. If Alan was in a good mood when she next saw him, he might reveal what was said. Meanwhile, sitting around in her room wasn't going to help.

"Ground floor, please," she told the attendant, as she stepped into the lift.

"Off out shopping again?" Brian grinned.

"No, not today!" She laughed. "It's too nice to wander around shops. I thought I would take a stroll along the quayside, then come back and enjoy a cool drink in the drawing room."

"Sounds like a good plan," he replied.

"Do you enjoy your job, Brian? I mean, don't you ever get bored going up and down in the lift all day?"

"Some days are better than others," he admitted. "By that, I mean some guests are friendlier than others." He shrugged. "But, at the end of the day, a job is a job. And, you never know, if I do well, it could lead to a promotion to something better."

Agnes nodded. It was much the same response she'd had from Ben when she asked him whether he liked being a taxi driver – apart from the promotion bit.

By now, they had reached the ground floor. The doors swept open and Agnes stepped out of the lift.

"Why do you ask?"

"No reason," she replied, turning back to face Brian. "Just making conversation, I suppose."

She hesitated. That was true. Nevertheless, when he had mentioned the word 'promotion', her mind had been set in motion.

"However, Brian, merely out of curiosity, where would such a promotion lead? Maybe I could be of some help."

"That would be brilliant, Mrs Lockwood." He tapped his chin. "Well, it would certainly take me above a senior porter's position."

"Above a senior porter's position," Agnes repeated. "Oh, Brian, that sounds very impressive."

Despite her enthusiasm, Agnes had no idea as to how far up the chain of command at a hotel a senior porter was. Yet, maybe it wouldn't do any harm to sound impressed, at least for the moment.

"So, to what heights, exactly, would a promotion take you, Brian?"

"Difficult to say, Mrs Lockwood. It would depend on what job is on offer at the time."

"Oh yes, I understand. When someone leaves, other staff members have the option to apply for the post, if they're interested."

"That's it. Obviously, no one would apply for a post beneath the one they have already, or a job they wouldn't enjoy."

"Obviously," Agnes agreed. "So, have you got your sights on anything further up the scale at the moment?"

"I'll apply for Larry's job, when the vacancy is announced."

"But you're already a lift attendant." Agnes sounded surprised.

"Ah, but Larry is the *senior* lift attendant. I'm the junior."

"I'm sorry, I had no idea there was a senior and a junior operating the lift. I always thought you were both on the same level."

"No worries. There isn't a great deal of difference, we both take people up and down the hotel. But the senior gets the choice of shifts and, of course, more money. But not only that, he or she would be able to apply for something even higher."

A buzzing sound coming from inside the lift told Brian that some people were waiting to come downstairs.

"Got to go now," he said. "Nice talking to you."

Agnes's mind was working overtime as she walked across the reception area towards the door. She hadn't realised that the staff were given the option to apply for a vacant position at the hotel before it was advertised. It made sense, though. Both the manager and the head of the department needing the replacement would already be aware of the applicant's capabilities. However, there was something about this idea that worried her a little.

Petty as it sounded, was it possible that someone had framed Larry because they wanted to apply for his job as senior lift attendant?

Chapter Thirty-Three

Agnes spent what was left of the afternoon strolling along the quayside, while considering who might apply for Larry's position, should he be forced to leave if found guilty of murder. The most obvious person was Brian. He was next in line; unless the management didn't think he was quite ready for promotion.

However, would Brian have volunteered so much information if he was guilty of framing Larry? Surely he would have remained silent. Besides, according to his timesheets, all verified by the staff supervisor, he was at the hotel when the attacks took place. Therefore, who else might apply for Larry's job?

It would need to be someone further down the chain. According to Brian, staff were given the option to apply for a better position; a higher position. But, what if there was someone at the hotel who was already in a senior post and wanted to move sideways? It could be that someone who was very unhappy with their present position might want to move to a completely different post. Yet, would that someone really attempt to kill an innocent young woman and then frame Larry as the murderer, just because they wanted his job? Why not just murder Larry in the first place? That way, the lift attendant's job would need to be refilled almost immediately. They wouldn't have had to wait for the outcome of his trial before the job was advertised.

The more Agnes thought about it, the more convinced she was that none of it had anything to do with the promotion prospects at the hotel. Someone, somewhere, wanted to see Larry suffer by being charged with murder and sent to prison for a murder he didn't commit.

Agnes stopped walking and clasped her hand to her forehead. Oh, my goodness! Had she got it all wrong? Was it possible that the murders weren't about some vendetta against the murdered women?

Could this whole thing be a vendetta against Larry?

* * *

"Where do we go from here, sir?" Andrews asked.

He had given the DCI a few minutes to calm down after Morris had admitted lying in his report.

Alan shook his head. "You know something, sergeant, I have no idea. Apart from the necklace in Larry Parker's pocket, we haven't anything else to go on." He paused. "And, at the end of the day, that might well have been planted."

He stood up and walked across to the window.

"We haven't learned anything from the IVF department at the hospital – well, nothing helpful, anyway – or from Wendy Hamilton's parents, regarding her pregnancy. Both inquiries were a dead loss."

The moment Keith Nichols had informed him of Wendy Hamilton's IVF treatment, he had sent Detectives Jones and Smithers to the hospital to find out if they could flush out anything that could be of help. However, the department had not divulged any information. Apparently, it was all highly confidential. Therefore, they hadn't learned anything they didn't already know.

As for Wendy's parents, they had been so shocked to learn of their daughter's pregnancy, coming so soon after the news of her death, that they hadn't been able to utter a word. The officer who informed them was so worried about them that he had been forced to speak to the next-door neighbour, asking whether the couple had a relative close by who could come and spend some time with them. Fortunately, the neighbour came up with the address and phone number of a niece.

Alan scratched his head. This case wasn't going anywhere. He looked down at his watch and saw that it was almost six o'clock.

"Let's call it a day, Andrews. Get back to that lovely woman of yours and tell her that you need her. Job or no job, your life with her is important. Don't let it slide."

"Where are you going?" Andrews asked. He wasn't stupid. He hadn't failed to pick up the signs of the rift between his boss and Agnes Lockwood.

"I'm going to the hotel, if you must know," Alan replied. "We all need to be humble at some time or another."

* * *

"Are you alright?"

Agnes had been so deep in thought that she hadn't noticed Alan's car pull up at the side of the road.

"You look so shocked. Has someone been pestering you?" Alan glanced around the area as he spoke.

"No, I'm okay," she replied. Agnes took a deep breath. "Alan, we really need to talk."

"Yes, I know."

"But please, not here."

At first, Alan thought she didn't want to talk here because they were in such a public place. But then, seeing a piece of police tape still hanging from the barrier, he realised that this was the spot where the body of the still unidentified young man had been pulled from the River Tyne… The very place where he had tried to be so damn clever by saying the body must have been dropped into the river some miles upstream, before really thinking it through.

Had he given it some thought, he would have figured out what really happened. But instead, when Agnes had come up with some other reason as to why the body had taken so long to reach this point, he had scorned her idea, until the pathologist had intervened…

Alan shut down his thoughts. Did he really want to go down that road all over again? Maybe this time he should listen to what Agnes had to say.

"Okay, where?"

"Over there." She pointed at the hotel. "In my room, where we won't be overheard."

Alan nodded. "Okay. You go on ahead. I need to move my car before I get a ticket."

Once they were settled upstairs, Agnes spilled out her latest thoughts on the case.

"At first, I thought that someone might have something against the women."

She went on to tell him about the rather self-important photographer and his extremely jealous lady friend. "However, I'm now wondering whether someone has a grudge against Larry."

"You could be right, Agnes."

"I could?" She had half expected him laugh off her latest notions.

"So far, our investigations haven't led anywhere," he said. "We still don't even know the identity of the man we fished out of the river. Not one single person has come forward to identify him."

Alan went on to tell her that the IVF department hadn't been any help, as they had refused to name the donor.

"It's all to do with confidentiality," he spluttered.

He then told her how Morris had confessed to lying in his report regarding the argument involving Larry.

"Oops," Agnes said. "The bit about Morris, I mean," she added. "I can understand where the IVF people are coming from."

"You can?"

She nodded. "Some of these people wish to remain anonymous, even to the recipient."

Alan sighed. "I suppose you're right. But it still doesn't help our case."

"So, getting back to your detective, what have you decided to do about him?"

"I haven't made up my mind." Alan blew out his cheeks. "I should at the very least mention it on his file – if not report the incident to the superintendent. But, at the same time, I don't really want to ruin his career. I think he's learnt his lesson."

"I hope so. He could have helped to put an innocent man in prison." She thought for a moment. "By the way, changing the subject slightly, how did you get on with Ms. Fulton?"

"That is a whole new story," Alan replied. "Can we talk about it over dinner? I'm starving."

Chapter Thirty-Four

The restaurant was rather busy that evening. However, as Agnes was looked upon more as a resident than a guest, there was always a table booked under her name.

"That was wonderful," Agnes said, as the waiter cleared the table. "Please pass on our compliments to the chef."

"I will indeed, madam," he replied. "Would you like coffee?"

"Yes, please," she replied.

She wasn't really bothered about having coffee, but she didn't want to leave the restaurant; not yet, anyway. The buzz of the people around her was invigorating. Which, at the same time, made her wonder whether she would really be happy tucked away in that apartment she had viewed a few days ago. Was she ready for that kind of seclusion? Maybe Ben was right, after all; she did have everything she needed here at the hotel.

"What're you thinking?" Alan said, interrupting her thoughts.

Agnes took a deep breath. "Earlier this week, I went to look at a penthouse apartment. It was really wonderful and had everything we could wish for."

"*We*...? By that, I suppose you mean you and me?"

"Yes, you and me, who else would I be talking about?"

"Then why didn't you tell me about it?"

"I'm telling you about it now." She sighed. "If you mean why didn't I tell you earlier, then let me remind you that I tried to, twice. But you were…" Agnes broke off. This was going nowhere. "Look, Alan, I'm telling you now."

"Sorry, Agnes."

Alan recalled the day she had been anxious to tell him something, but he had kept putting her off.

"Well, you can see it from outside the hotel as it overlooks the quayside. I'll point it out to you before we head off upstairs."

She went on to describe the interior, before pulling out her phone and showing him the photographs she had taken.

Alan had to admit, the apartment looked great and he fully understood Agnes's enthusiasm. Yet he felt there was a 'but' about to unfold.

"But…" she glanced around the room before continuing, "being here in the restaurant tonight with all these people milling around, has left me wondering whether I'm ready to be cut off from the outside world."

"You wouldn't really be cutting yourself off, Agnes. I'm sure you would be out and about just as often as you are now. I can't imagine you sitting around in the apartment all day."

"I know. It's just that if I get bored in my hotel room, I can go downstairs to the sitting room, where there are usually a few other people I can talk to."

But, thinking about it now, she realized that she didn't really chat with the other guests. Many of them were in groups. It was seldom that anyone stayed here on their own, unless they were company representatives – like John Alton, and she would rather forget about him.

"Maybe I'll go back and take another look around. I must admit, I was really taken with the place when I saw it the first time." She smiled. "Perhaps you might like to go with me… give me your opinion."

"I would love to, Agnes."

"Right, then I'll make an appointment with the agent."

Just then, the coffee arrived.

* * *

The following morning, Alan was the first to arrive at the station. He had enjoyed the previous evening with Agnes. Being back with her was everything he could wish for. However, he hadn't slept well because there was one thing niggling at him – the penthouse apartment. It really did look outstanding. It was the sort of place he had only ever seen in magazines, but never thought he would actually get to live in. Those kinds of luxury properties were way out of his price range. Even if he were to sell his house in Heaton, he still wouldn't have anywhere near the cost of something like that.

He hadn't thought about the money side of it while Agnes was giving him the details. That part only came to light the moment he rested his head on the pillow. But he couldn't go back on his word now. If that was what she wanted, then he would just have to work his socks off to pay for it – even if he was stuck with Superintendent Blake for the rest of his life!

"I took your advice, sir," Andrews said, as he strode into the office.

He was thirty minutes late.

"I went to see Sandra and we've talked things through. I believe we have managed to overcome our problems."

"I'm very glad to hear it."

"So, what's on for today, sir?" Andrews asked.

There was a long silence.

"I've decided to release Larry,"

"What! I don't believe it!" Andrews said. "He's our only suspect and you tell me you're going to release him?"

"Yes. However, I want him under surveillance at all times." Alan took a deep breath. "But that's not because I think he's guilty and will strike again. It's to make sure that if someone else is attacked, then we'll know exactly whether Parker is responsible or not."

"But…"

Alan held up his hand. "I know exactly what you're going to say. "You're wondering why we would put some other woman's life at stake, to prove a man's innocence."

Andrews nodded.

"So you think that if we keep Parker in custody, everyone on the streets of Newcastle will be safe? But, what if Larry really is innocent and he's being framed? The real murderer will have got what they wanted."

Alan paused for a moment. "Look, sergeant, I know it's not the best idea, but what else can we do? Besides, I'm going to have every man we can spare out there on the streets keeping a close eye on the community."

"Don't we do that anyway, sir?" Andrews still wasn't convinced.

"Yes, we do," Alan replied. "But, had they all kept their eyes peeled, maybe we wouldn't have two women lying in the mortuary."

He blew out a large sigh. "That's not fair. I know the men are overstretched. Perhaps if the government spent a little more money on putting additional men on the beat, then we wouldn't be in this bloody situation in the first place."

Andrews nodded in agreement. He couldn't argue with that.

Just then, Alan's mobile rang.

Chapter Thirty-Five

Agnes had been a little surprised that Alan had risen and left the hotel before even having breakfast. When she had mentioned it, he had tried to reassure her by saying that he simply wanted to get an early start. But, though she hadn't said anything, she hadn't been convinced.

She hadn't failed to notice that Alan hadn't slept well. How could she? He had tossed and turned all night, occasionally banging his fist against his pillow. Could it be that the case was getting him down? However, she aware that Alan had been a detective for quite some time, so why would this case make him more uneasy than any other he had worked on in the past? He was a chief inspector, for goodness' sake. No! There had to be something else on his mind – but what?

Once breakfast was over, she rang the estate agent to make an appointment to view the apartment again.

"Perhaps we could make it very late this afternoon," she suggested. "Providing no one has snapped it up in the meantime?"

The agent assured her that the apartment was still on the market. "Though," he added, "there has certainly been a great deal of interest."

"Yes, I'm sure there has," she replied. "It's a lovely place."

Once a time was agreed, she told the agent that she would meet him there. That settled, she called Alan to give him the information.

"I understand things are busy for you at the moment. If you don't have time to pick me up, just let me know and I'll get a taxi. I'll meet you there," she told him.

That settled, Agnes sat down and began, once again, to go through everything she knew about the case against Larry.

The original suspect, the man she had picked out in the photograph, was out of the equation, as was Harold Armstrong's overpowering girlfriend. Or at least she was for the moment. From what Agnes had surmised the other day, that particular woman liked to strike from the front, rather than sneak up from behind. Therefore, who was left, apart from Larry Parker? Everything pointed towards Larry. But then, if he really was being framed, that would be exactly how it was intended to look.

Someone was working really hard to prove he was guilty.

Then there was the mystery of Wendy Hamilton's pregnancy. Why had she been so determined to have a baby when she was only seventeen? Agnes decided to put that at the back of her mind for the time being. Even Wendy's parents had been totally unaware their daughter was carrying a child and, with the man who had been accompanying her at Whitley Bay now dead, she doubted the police would ever find the answer to that particular puzzle.

The next victim was Janet Cunningham. Again, no one had been able to understand why she had been murdered. According to her family and friends, she didn't have any enemies. However, maybe there was something going on in her private life that they weren't aware of.

Last, but not least, there was Sue Matthews. Thankfully, she was doing very well. Alan had forwarded that piece of news on to her the previous evening. He had spoken to Keith Nichols regarding his postmortem on Janet Cunningham. Apparently, the results had been very much the same as in Wendy Hamilton's case, in that the knife had been thrust into the young woman from someone standing behind the victim. The only difference being, Janet wasn't pregnant.

Before hanging up, Alan had enquired about Susan Matthews. Keith had responded by saying Sue was doing so well, it was likely she would be discharged from the hospital very soon. Agnes had heaved a sigh of relief at that piece of news.

Turning her attention back to Larry, Agnes recalled him saying he had never met the first young woman who had been stabbed, though he admitted he had seen Janet, the young woman from the coffee shop. He had even sworn he was innocent of all three attacks. How could she have doubted him? Yet, who else was there?

Agnes counted the names on her fingers as she went through other possible candidates. First, there was Brian Hockley, the lift attendant. He could well be in line for promotion to senior attendant, should Larry be ousted from his post. Or might it have been the wretched lady friend of Harold Armstrong, after all? Agnes recalled the woman's words on the quayside. "After all I've done for you!" she had screamed at the photographer. What did that mean? Had she attacked all three women so he would get a big news story?

Thinking it through, she recollected that the reporter always seemed to be around when the stabbings took place. Was that merely a coincidence? Or did he already know in advance when someone was going to be attacked? Had his lady friend informed him that trouble was brewing before it actually happened? If so, how could she know?

On the other hand, was it possible that Armstrong had attacked the three women himself? Instead of getting answers to the puzzle, she had only generated more questions.

Agnes stood up and walked across to the window. Gazing down at the quayside, she suddenly spotted Armstrong's lady friend. She appeared to be talking to someone, but Agnes couldn't see who it was. However, as the woman marched off, someone stepped into view... it was Detective Morris. Perhaps she had upset someone else with her bad temper and threatening behaviour and they had called the police.

Agnes thought it strange that the police would send a detective to speak to the woman, rather than a uniformed officer. But, she dismissed it from her mind. She needed to focus on her three suspects. So far, she had three; however, two of them probably had no idea about Larry's habit of creeping up behind his friends, whereas it was more than likely that Brian was aware of Larry's custom. Yet surely, as she had concluded earlier, he wouldn't have been so forthcoming if he was guilty. Therefore, who else was in the equation?

She was just about to throw up her hands in despair, when another name suddenly popped into her mind. A name that had cropped up earlier in the week, but had since escaped her mind.

* * *

"You're releasing my client?"

Emily Fulton flopped back in her chair at the news. That was the last thing she had anticipated. When her secretary gave her the news that Chief Inspector Johnson wanted to see her, she thought the police had more evidence against her client. Instead, it turned out they were releasing him. She screwed up her eyes.

"Okay, Chief Inspector, out with it. What's going on here? What am I missing?"

"There isn't anything going on and you haven't missed anything." Alan glanced at his sergeant before continuing. "We just feel we don't have enough to hold your client at the moment."

"I see."

It was obvious from her expression that she would like to ask a few more questions, but she held back.

"In that case I would like to see my client."

"No problem. Sergeant Andrews will take you downstairs. You can give him the good news."

"You mean you haven't told him he's about to be released?"

"I thought you might like to do that, Ms. Fulton."

"Did she say anything on the way downstairs?" Alan asked, the moment Andrews stepped back in the office after escorting Parker's solicitor to where he was being held.

"No. Well, nothing to help our case," the sergeant replied. "I think she was still getting over the fact that her client was being released. She mentioned the warm weather and that was about it." He took a deep breath. "So, where do we go from here?"

"I think you asked me that earlier, Andrews and, to tell you the truth, I still have absolutely no idea."

Alan stood up and wandered across to the window.

"So, what are you thinking about at the moment, sir?"

"I'm wondering how the hell I am going to pay for the apartment Agnes is taking me to look at later this afternoon."

"An apartment? That doesn't sound too expensive," Andrews replied. "There are apartments all over the place these days. As I understand it, an apartment is simply the American word for a flat. You know the sort of thing I mean – a small, self-contained place."

"If only," Alan mumbled to himself.

"Sorry, did you say something?"

Alan didn't reply. His attention was fixed on the apartment building in the distance. Agnes was expecting him to pick her up to view the property, unless he was tied up with the case. At a pinch, he could tell her that some fresh news had emerged and he wouldn't be able to meet her after all. But could he really do that? He was a man of his word. However, there was still plenty of time; something could still happen before four o'clock.

Chapter Thirty-Six

Agnes was still thinking about the man who had popped into her mind earlier, when she suddenly saw him. He was walking across the Millennium Bridge towards the hotel. Though she kept her eyes focused on him, she was aware it didn't necessarily mean that he was coming here. He could be going anywhere. However, if he was planning to call into the hotel, then she would like to, sort of, bump into him somewhere downstairs.

Agnes quickly thought it through. She could hang around in her room and watch where he headed once he stepped off the bridge. But, by doing that, she could miss out on her mission to meet up with him as, by the time she got downstairs, he could have entered the hotel and disappeared into the staff room, or wherever else he was going. Maybe her best option was to go down to the reception area now. With a bit of luck, she would already be there when he walked in.

Once she was out of her room, Agnes decided to take the stairs. If she opted to take the lift, there was a chance that Brian would be on duty. If that was the case, then he might keep her talking after they reached the ground floor. That was all very well some days, but not today; at least, not at this moment. She needed to be on her own when, or should that be *if*, the man she wanted to meet walked into the hotel.

She had almost reached the ground floor when Agnes saw her suspect swagger through the automatic doors. He waved cheerily at the two receptionists, before striding towards the corridor which would take him to the staff room.

"Oops! Can you help me?" Agnes called out as he approached her.

The young man hurried across to her and helped her down the last stair.

"Thank you," Agnes said. "I don't know what happened, but for a moment I thought I was going to fall."

"Where are you going? I'll help you."

"I was on my way to the drawing room. But I'll be fine now. I don't want to put you to any trouble," Agnes replied. "I think I lost my footing."

"No trouble at all, Mrs Lockwood."

"You know me?" Agnes was surprised. Not that he recognised her, but that he knew her name.

"Yes, I used to work here," he said, as he took her arm and led her across to the drawing room.

Though Agnes knew exactly who he was, she gave him a long, puzzled stare.

"Yes, I remember you now, you were a porter. Now, what was your name? No, don't tell me. Let me think about it for a moment or two." She tapped her chin. "Peter? Yes, that's it, Peter. I remember meeting you on the first day I arrived at the hotel."

"Yes, that was me. I carried your luggage upstairs. I'm surprised you know my name, though."

"That's because I always take notice of the name pinned on the uniform of the staff. Probably much the same way you remember the name of the guests – by the name fastened to their luggage."

He nodded. "Very true, Mrs Lockwood, but you're still here, whereas I'm not. I guess you like the Millennium Hotel."

"Yes, I do."

By now, they had reached the drawing room. However, Agnes wanted to keep him talking for a little while longer while she had the chance.

"Have you got a few minutes to spare, Peter? I was feeling a little lonely upstairs, which was why I came down here. I was hoping to meet up with a few of the guests, but it seems everyone is out enjoying the warm weather. Besides, I would be interested to learn about your new job."

He looked at his watch.

"We could have a glass of something, while we talk," she said persuasively.

He looked up from his watch. "Well, come to think of it, I have got some time to spare and a glass of whisky would go down a treat."

"Good," Agnes replied. "Let's sit down. I'm sure the waiter will appear very soon."

Agnes had become aware over the months she had stayed here, that when guests started drifting into the drawing room, a waiter always descended shortly afterwards. She had since worked out that the news was passed on from the reception staff across the hall. Probably part of the management's ploy to get the guests to spend more money. So she smiled at the waiter who had appeared within seconds of their making themselves comfortable on a squishy leather sofa.

"Whisky, wasn't it?" Agnes looked at Peter.

Peter nodded.

"A large glass of the best single malt whisky you have, and I'll have a gin and tonic."

The waiter nodded as he jotted it down on his pad.

"Thank you, James," she added, peering at the name pinned to his uniform.

"So, Peter, what made you leave the hotel in the first place?"

Agnes decided to jump in while the iron was hot, as the saying went. Yet, at the same time, she hoped the waiter would return very soon with their drinks. A strong drink might help Peter to say more than he had intended, especially if he was trying to hide something. Besides, it wasn't as though the waiter had a whole list of orders. There were only the two of them in the room, unless the bar was full.

"Weren't you happy here?"

"On the contrary, I quite enjoyed my job. It's just that there were a few things I didn't agree with."

"Such as?"

Peter fell silent.

Perhaps she should have waited until the drinks had arrived before she began to probe. Fortunately, the waiter appeared, so for the moment she was off the hook.

"Cheers!" she said, holding up her glass in front of Peter.

"Indeed, cheers," he responded, picking up his glass.

Peter took a sip of his drink and savored the taste. His budget didn't run to this sort of quality. He intended to enjoy every single drop.

"Oh, it wasn't anything serious," he said, placing his glass on the small table in front of them. "I simply got a bit fed up with having to work evenings, weekends and Bank Holidays, when the rest of my mates were all out enjoying themselves."

"I understand," Agnes replied. "It can be difficult. But you would have known about the shift pattern before you took the job."

"Yes, I did. But I wanted the job, so I suppose it was my own fault."

He picked up his glass and took a long drink.

"Yet, at the end of the day, the shift pattern seems to work out better for some staff members than others."

"Oh, how's that?"

Agnes hoped he was beginning to open up.

"It seems to depend what job you're in. Apparently, being a porter means you're a Jack of all trades. During my time here, I was asked to stand in for all sorts of posts. I did it without question, providing I didn't have anything planned. Yet, whenever I asked someone to stand in for me, it was out of the question."

"How often did this happen?"

"All the time," Peter replied.

Agnes was a little taken aback. She picked up her glass and took a long swallow. That was the last thing she had expected to hear. She had thought his main problem had been the episode at Christmas.

"You mean no one *ever* stood in for you? Not once?"

He frowned. "Well, perhaps a few times."
"Why do you think that was?"
He shrugged.

Agnes looked across to the window and took a deep breath. This was going nowhere. Why wouldn't anyone stand in for Peter, when he had always helped them out? Then another question popped into her mind.

"Then, for goodness' sake, Peter, why on earth are you visiting your ex-colleagues, if none of them ever helped you out during the time you worked here? It doesn't seem to make any sense. I'd have thought you wouldn't want see any of them ever again."

Peter took a sip from his glass.

"That's because it wasn't their fault – not entirely, anyway."

* * *

Agnes sat in the drawing room for some time after Peter left, trying to sort things out in her mind. When she enquired what he meant by, 'it wasn't their fault', he had been reluctant to reply. However, with a little coaxing and a few more sips from his glass, he had gone on to say that whenever someone was willing to help him out, they suddenly changed their minds at the last minute. Usually, making up some excuse that they had forgotten they were going out somewhere, so wouldn't be able to stand in for him after all. When she had asked why he thought they weren't telling the truth, he told her it was because they couldn't look him in the eye when passing on the news.

"Christmas was the last straw," he had added. "When the two people I asked to help me out both refused, I felt it was time to look for another job. Then the lift attendant stepped in to have his say. What the hell did it have to do with him?"

With a little more gentle prodding, Peter admitted he hadn't really expected either of the two people he had asked to give up their time off on Christmas Eve. Nevertheless, it was obvious that he had been disappointed, as he went on to tell her that he had linked up with a nice young woman and wanted to take her out somewhere special.

Flo had got that wrong. She had been under the impression that he wanted to go on the staff outing.

He had also told her that he had been sorry to leave the hotel, as it was a good place to work. He had even mentioned how the chance to apply for promotion was an extra bonus. Not all firms worked that way.

Agnes hadn't failed to notice that it was the second time the subject of promotion had popped up in conversation over the last couple of days. Could that have something to do with these stabbings? It sounded ridiculous, even to her. But in this day and age, murders were being committed for a lot less than a chance to step up the ladder.

But, putting that aside for the moment, why were the other members of staff refusing to stand in for Peter? Though he hadn't said as much, Agnes had picked up the impression that someone in the hotel had been trying to push him out of his job. Could it be that whoever it was had wanted his position? She stood up and walked across to the window. If only she had enquired how far up the scale he had been when he left the hotel. But she hadn't thought about it at the time. However, thinking it through now, if he had been head porter when he left, who would benefit from his departure? Or, looking at it from another angle, exactly who might have benefitted if Larry had left the hotel, leaving his post up for grabs?

Oh, get a grip, Agnes, she told herself. She was really going around in circles now. Hadn't she gone down this road before? There was nothing else for it. She needed to talk to someone who knew about how the staff promotion thing worked. Her first thought was Flo. Being staff supervisor, she would know who was leaving and how everyone was placed on the promotion scale. However, Agnes was reluctant to speak to her today. She had become little suspicious about some of Flo's remarks. Maybe all this was getting to her and she was being overdramatic. Nevertheless, Agnes made the decision to bypass the staff supervisor in this instance and have a quiet word with the manager. If he didn't already know what was going on in his hotel, then she would put him straight!

Chapter Thirty-Seven

Brian Hockley was standing by the lift as Agnes walked out of the drawing room.

"Hello, Mrs Lockwood," he gestured towards the lift. "Going up?"

Though he sounded bright enough, Agnes felt there was something not quite right about his tone. Had he seen her and Peter talking together in the drawing room and was wondering what was going on? Peter had made it clear to her that he and Brian weren't the best of friends.

"No, not yet, thank you," she replied. "I want to have a few words with the reception staff, and then I think I might go out for a breath of fresh air."

"No problem," he replied. "I don't blame you. It's a lovely day."

Agnes kept her voice low when she reached the desk. She didn't want everyone to know about her talking with the manager. Especially Brian, as it wouldn't take long for the whole hotel to hear about it. Thankfully, the staff on the reception desk had more discretion.

By a stroke of good timing, someone upstairs called for the lift just as the receptionist picked up the phone to inform the manager that one of the guests wished to speak to him, enabling Agnes to slip into the office without Brian taking note.

Mr Jenkins asked her to sit down and, once the pleasantries were over, she came straight to the point.

"You'll be aware that Larry is in a spot of bother," she said.

He nodded. "From what I've heard, it's a lot more than a *spot* of bother." He tapped his fingers on the desk. "It's causing a quite a problem at head office."

"I'm sure it is," she replied. "However, I don't believe he committed the murders and I would like you to help me to prove it."

"I would be delighted to help, but what can I do?"

"First of all, what can you tell me about Peter Moffat? He was a porter here at the hotel until a couple of months ago."

The manager screwed up his eyes. "I don't know too much about the goings-on of individual members of staff. Mrs Telford deals with all that." He reached across the desk for his phone. "I could ask her to join us."

"I'd rather you didn't," Agnes said quickly, maybe a little too quickly. She smiled. "What I mean is, she's busy at the moment. I'll catch up with her later."

There was a puzzled expression on Jenkins's face as he sat back in his chair. "What's going on? What am I missing?"

"I don't know," Agnes replied. "Tell me what you know about Peter Moffat and then, perhaps, I'll be able to tell you whether you're missing something."

Agnes stared across the desk at the hotel manager.

"Okay," Mr Jenkins said, after a long pause. "To the best of my knowledge, he was a good worker. He was sociable with the guests, which is most important for the hotel."

"Yes, I can understand that," Agnes nodded. "Can you tell me what position he held when he decided to leave the hotel?"

Mr Jenkins rose from his chair and walked across to a filing cabinet. Pulling out a file, he opened it and thumbed through a few sheets of paper.

"He was head porter," he read out. "It seems he was good at his job and rose through the ranks quite quickly."

"Yet, you still didn't think to question why a young man with such potential suddenly decided to leave." Agnes shook her head in dismay.

"Mrs Telford will have looked into it," he mumbled. "She…"

"For heaven's sake, *you* are the manager of this hotel, not Mrs Telford," Agnes interrupted. She heaved a sigh. "Can you, at least, tell me where Peter's career might have led him, should he have stayed here at the hotel? In other words, as head porter, what would been his next step up the ladder?"

Mr Jenkins walked back to his chair and sat down, his head still bent over the folder.

"I believe, as head porter, he would have been able to apply for the job of senior lift attendant, should the post become vacant. Judging by his record, he could well have been given the job. He seems to have done well here at the hotel."

"As a matter of interest, Mr Jenkins, who else would have been in a position to apply for the post?"

He thumbed through the papers.

"Well, for a start, there's Brian Hockley." He looked up at Agnes. "He's the assistant lift attendant at the moment."

"Yes, I know," she replied. "Is there anyone else?"

"I suppose some of the bar or restaurant staff might fancy a change of direction," he said, glancing back down at the folder. "Some of the domestic staff would also be eligible to apply. But some of them haven't worked here very long. Therefore, it's hard to tell whether they would be right for the post."

"Has Brian Hockley worked here very long?" she enquired.

She was trying to remember who had been working with Larry when she had first arrived at the hotel. It certainly hadn't been Brian.

"No, actually he hasn't," the manager replied. "He only arrived a few months ago. Our other employee left as he was moving south – London, I believe."

"Does that mean Brian walked straight into the lift attendant's position? I mean, didn't anyone already at the hotel apply for the job?"

"It appears not." He heaved a sigh and threw the folder down onto his desk. "Look, Mrs Lockwood, where exactly is this going?"

"Didn't you find that a little surprising?" Agnes asked, ignoring his question. "I would have thought at least one person would have applied for the post."

"Yes, I suppose it is, now that you mention it." He tapped his chin. "I just didn't think about it at the time. I leave all that sort of thing to the staff supervisor." He sat back in his chair. "Anyway, you still haven't told me what this is all about."

Agnes took a deep breath.

"As I said earlier, I don't believe Larry Parker had anything to do with the recent murders. Nevertheless, I do think they were committed by someone else working at the hotel."

"Why would anyone working here commit murder?" Mr Jenkins exclaimed. "What would be the motive behind such acts?"

"I think it's all to do with your promotion system. Don't get me wrong," she added quickly. "I think it's good that your members of staff are given the chance to apply for a promotion before it's advertised publicly." She swallowed hard. "However, I'm wondering whether someone might have gone a step too far to achieve their ambition."

"Are you saying that three people were attacked by someone working at this hotel, merely because they wanted a promotion? I can't believe it! You must be mistaken."

"I agree, it sounds insane when you say it out loud. There must be something I'm missing." Agnes shook her head. "But I still think that this promotion thing fits in somewhere – even if only as a bonus."

* * *

Brian was showing a couple of hotel guests into the lift when Agnes emerged from the manager's office. *Just my luck*, she thought. A few seconds later and they would all have been on their way upstairs. It crossed her mind to slip back into the office on the pretext she had forgotten something, but it was too late, as he had already seem her.

"Are you going up, Mrs Lockwood?"

"No thank you, Brian. I'm just about to go out."

Agnes got the impression he would like to have said something further, but, with people waiting in the lift, he simply nodded before stepping inside and closing the doors.

Outside the hotel, Agnes glanced over in the direction of the penthouse apartment she and Alan would be viewing later that afternoon. She had pointed it out to him the previous evening, but though he had looked impressed, he hadn't really said anything – well, nothing about the apartment. He had simply changed the subject. She hadn't thought much about it at the time, believing he had other things on his mind, such as the case he was working on. But now, on reflection, maybe he wasn't keen on the move after all, despite him reassuring her that she was doing the right thing when she had mentioned her doubts.

"Men," she muttered. "Why can't they ever give you a straight answer?"

Agnes looked down at her watch. Where had the day gone? She was due to meet the agent in about two hours. Looking up from her watch, she noticed the café across the road. It was where Janet Cunningham had worked right up until the day she was murdered.

Though it was on the doorstep, Agnes had only been there two or three time. She much preferred the one positioned right next to the river. Maybe today was the day to pay this one another visit.

She crossed the road and walked towards the café. At first sight, it appeared that all the tables were taken. However, as she drew nearer, a couple of people stood up, pushed back their chairs and gathered their belongings together. It seemed luck was on her side.

The moment she sat down, a young waitress appeared and began to clear the table.

"I won't keep you a moment," she said, gathering the dirty crockery together and placing it on her tray.

"No rush," Agnes replied, looking at the name pinned to the apron of waitress. "I only want a coffee, anyway."

"Is there any particular coffee you would like?"

"No, whichever is easiest."

"Fine, I'll be back in half a tick."

The waitress was true to her word. In no time at all, she was back with a tray holding a steaming mug of coffee, a jug of cream and a bowl of sugar.

"Is there anything else I can do for you?"

"Yes, I think there is, Pauline. Perhaps you could sit down and tell me whatever it is you know about your friend Janet that you decided to withhold from the police."

Pauline glanced around at the tables nearby. Assured that no one had overheard, she turned back to Agnes.

"I don't know what you're talking about," she said frostily. "Janet was my friend. I told the police everything I knew."

Agnes picked up the cream and poured a little into her coffee.

"Not everything," she replied, slowly replacing the jug on the table. "I think you held something back. Was it to do with her latest boyfriend?"

"I told the police that we didn't talk about our boyfriends."

"But you were lying, weren't you? You did discuss who your boyfriends were and where you were going on a date. Though it might be hard for you to imagine, Pauline, once upon a time, I was a teenager. My friends and I talked about our boyfriends all the time. I know things have changed over the years, but not that much. Young women of your age still like to discuss their new men friends, where they are going, etc."

Agnes took a sip of her coffee with her eyes still glued on Pauline.

It was a long shot. Agnes knew she had absolutely no reason to question the young woman. But, at the same time, when Alan mentioned how his short discussion with Pauline had turned out, she had a feeling the young woman knew more than she had actually divulged.

"This is your chance to put things right," Agnes prompted. "Janet was a young woman, just like you. She had her whole life ahead of her. But it was cut short because someone killed her."

Janet pulled off her apron and sat down in the chair facing Agnes.

"Okay, you're right, we did talk about our boyfriends," she said, quietly. "She met someone a few months ago. They dated a few times.

But I gather she wasn't very keen – something about him being too possessive. Anyway, she told him it was over and thought that would be the end of it. However, he didn't take it well and kept showing up wherever she went. In the end, she threatened to go to the police if he didn't leave her alone. She told me he was furious, but I understood he did stop following her. Though, to be honest, I think she was still a little nervous for a while afterwards."

"How long ago did she threaten to go to the police?" Agnes asked.

"About three weeks ago."

"I take it you know who the man is." Agnes raised her eyebrows.

Pauline looked down at the table. "Yes."

"Then why didn't you tell all this to the police?" Agnes asked. "This could be the person who killed your friend."

"I know I should have said something, but I wanted to stay out of it. I was afraid he might come after me… you know, to keep me quiet. Besides, the police have someone in custody now, don't they? So the man I'm talking about couldn't have been the murderer after all."

Agnes leaned forward in her chair. "Let me tell you something, Pauline. The man the police are holding is not guilty. I understand they are releasing him today. Therefore, the real murderer is still out there."

Alan had mumbled something about it that morning, before he left the hotel – though he could have changed his mind by the time he reached the station. She hadn't heard anything further, either from him, or from Larry's solicitor.

"How the hell do you know that?" Janet gasped. "Come to think of it, who are you? And how did you know the police spoke to me? Are you a police officer? Why are you talking to me?"

"Which question would you like me to answer first?" Agnes asked.

Pauline closed her eyes for a second and took a deep breath.

"The man who was obsessed with Janet works over there," she confessed, casting her eyes towards the Millennium Hotel. "I don't see him very often – he probably uses the staff entrance. However, come to think of it, I did see him today. I was out here clearing a table when I saw him using the front entrance."

She paused, giving Agnes a moment to recall that Peter had used the main entrance to the hotel a little earlier.

"Anyway," Pauline continued, "when the police arrested someone else working in the same hotel, I was relieved. I thought that perhaps I'd misjudged him – you know, got it all wrong. From that point, I really believed I didn't need to worry anymore. But now you're saying the police detained the wrong man." She shifted uneasily in her chair. "That means he could come looking for me, after all."

Agnes nodded. "Yes, he might, unless the police catch him first. So please, Pauline, will you give me the name of this man?"

"One more thing," Agnes said, once Pauline had given her a name. "Well, a couple of things, actually. Did you or Janet know Wendy Hamilton, the woman who was found stabbed in the Central Station, or Sue Matthews? She was attacked not far from here."

Pauline took a long, deep breath before answering. "Yes, Janet and I both knew Wendy and Sue."

Ten minutes later, Agnes was on her way back to the hotel.

Chapter Thirty-Eight

Agnes stood a few feet away from the hotel entrance to get her breath back before walking inside. Before leaving the café, it had crossed her mind to ring Alan. But, after looking at her watch, she had dismissed the idea. He would be arriving shortly, anyway. Not having heard anything to the contrary, she assumed he was free to pick her up before they headed off to view the apartment.

She took a deep breath and made her way into the hotel. While standing outside, she had decided to go up to her room and collect her jacket, then come back down to wait in the sitting room until Alan arrived. She would be able to see him walk into the hotel, due to the strategically placed mirrors. When Agnes had first seen them, she had been filled with dismay. Couldn't anyone walk around the ground floor without being watched? But since that first day, she had found them to be very helpful on many occasions.

The receptionist lifted her eyes from her computer and gave Agnes a friendly smile as she strode past the desk.

Ahead, the doors to leading into the lift were closed, and the display above them showed it was a few floors up. For a moment, luck appeared to be on her side. She didn't really want to get involved in a conversation with Brian at the moment. But then, as she drew nearer to the stairs, the doors of the lift slid open and three guests stepped out.

"Going up?" Brian gestured towards the empty lift.

"Er, yes, thank you," Agnes replied, not able to think of an excuse.

As she stepped into the lift, she caught a glimpse of Peter Moffat. He was standing at the far end of the reception area, by the corridor which led down to the kitchens and staff room. He appeared to be talking to someone, but unfortunately, the person he was speaking to was just out of her line of sight.

"So what have you been up to today?" Brian asked, as he pressed the button for the fourth floor. "Did you take the walk along the quayside you mentioned earlier?"

Agnes was about to lie and say that, yes, she had strolled along the quayside. But she suddenly thought better of it and told him the truth – well, perhaps not all of it. Who knows, he might have spotted her sitting outside the café, while he was ambling around the reception area, something both attendants often did when they weren't needed.

"I did think about going for a walk. However, when I caught the aroma of freshly brewed coffee coming from a café across the road, I changed my mind and decided to go there instead." She grinned. "Though I think I was lucky to get a seat. It was really very busy – obviously, it's a very popular place."

"Yes, I guess you were lucky," Brian replied. "It *is* very popular, especially being near the Millennium Bridge. Everyone hopes they'll be sitting there when it's raised." He paused. "Was it raised while you were at the café?"

"No, it wasn't – or if it was, then I missed it," Agnes replied. "But I don't think I would have missed something like that, do you?"

She wasn't sure whether Brian was making conversation, or she was being quizzed.

By now, they had reached her floor and Agnes was relieved when the doors slipped open and she was able to escape any further questioning. It had only taken them a few seconds to reach her floor. Yet it had seemed like an hour.

"Thank, you, Brian. I guess you'll be going off duty shortly. Enjoy the rest of the day."

The lift attendant looked at his watch. "Yes, another fifteen minutes and I'll be done for the day. I'm not sure who'll take over from me. It might be one of the porters." He reached out and pushed the button that would close the doors and send the lift down to the ground floor.

Now alone on the landing, Agnes slowly turned around and looked along the corridor. Only when she was sure there was no one else hovering around, did she hurry along to her room and slide the keycard into the lock. Once safely inside, she shut the door firmly and slid the chain into place. That done, she threw her bag onto the bed and walked over to the window to think through everything she had learned today.

Her conversation with Pauline had been most enlightening. Why had she waited so long before speaking to her? Had she known all this a few days ago, then maybe Sue wouldn't have been attacked. Thankfully, the young woman was making a good recovery.

Agnes sighed as she watched the ripples on the river sparkling in the afternoon sunshine as it flowed past beneath her window. If only life was so gentle. But then she recalled how, few months ago, there had been violent storms, so strong that they had caused the river to hurl itself against the walls of the quayside. At that point, she had been terrified the hotel was about to be flooded.

When she returned to the hotel after her enlightening conversation with Pauline, her first thought had been to apply a little more make-up, grab her jacket and wait for Alan downstairs in the sitting room. But now she wondered whether it might be best if she were to stay here. Or did she really mean it would be *safer* for her stay in her room? Now, she was starting to frighten herself.

The sitting room was a public room, for heaven's sake. Guests walked in and out all the time. Also, members of staff popped in all the time, making sure the guests had everything they wanted. No one was ever really alone in the public rooms. Surely no one would even think about attacking anyone down there. On the other hand, up here alone in her room, a member of staff could get hold of a master keycard and enter without too much bother. She doubted the chain, meant to stop intruders, would withstand pressure from someone determined to get in.

Get a grip, she told herself. This wasn't like her at all. All her life, Agnes had done her own thing; gone along with her own thoughts. Where would she be today if that hadn't been the case? Yet, after all she had been through since arriving at the hotel, was it any wonder that she was starting to be wary regarding her safety?

Making a decision, she grabbed her handbag and jacket and headed towards the door.

Chapter Thirty-Nine

Alan glanced at the clock on the wall behind the superintendent's desk. He would like to have left to pick up Agnes by now – especially as he wanted a few minutes to talk about the financial side of the apartment before they set off to view it. Yet Superintendent Blake was still droning on about Larry Parker's release.

"I ought to have been consulted before you made the decision."

"Yes, sir, sorry, sir," Alan mumbled. "Is that all, sir?"

"Yes, for the moment. But in future, I would prefer if you discussed it with me, before taking such action."

Once Alan escaped from the superintendent's office, he rushed off downstairs to speak to Andrews before setting off to the hotel.

"How did it go?" Andrews asked, as the DCI hurried through the door.

"Don't ask!" Alan pulled a face. "As you will gather, Blake isn't happy about Parker's release." He paused. "If you hear anything at all from our detectives while I'm away, I want you to contact me immediately."

Detectives Smithers and Jones had been sent out to keep an eye on Larry after he was released. Neither had been anywhere near the young man while he was in custody, so he wouldn't recognize them on sight. Also, they were very good at trailing a suspect without being noticed. One would lead, the other would follow, and then they would change places.

Andrews nodded. "By the way, I heard from Keith Nichols while you were upstairs. Sue Matthews has been discharged from the hospital. It seems she has recovered from the stab wound much quicker than first thought."

"That's good news," Alan replied. "Keith mentioned that she would be going home today if the doctors were satisfied everything was okay when they saw her this morning."

"Yes, and there's more. Keith's taking her out to dinner as soon as she has gained a little more strength."

Alan winked. "I think we both saw that coming, Andrews." He glanced at his watch. "Right, I'm off to pick up Agnes. But don't forget to call me if there is any news."

A couple of seconds later, he had swept out of the office and was heading along the corridor.

* * *

Agnes slowly made her way towards the stairs. However, as she was walking past the lift, the doors suddenly opened. She thought it rather strange that it had stopped on her floor, especially as there weren't any passengers on board. Nor was anyone standing here waiting for it.

"Going down?" The attendant stepped out of the lift.

Though she had heard those very words every day since she arrived at the hotel, they had never sounded so ominous.

"I thought I would take the stairs," she replied. "I don't think I'm getting enough exercise."

Agnes began to move off towards the staircase, but he was too quick for her. Grabbing her arm, he began to drag her into the lift. She tried to pull herself free from his grip. But it was no use, he was too strong for her.

"Let go of me! What do you think you're doing?" Agnes shrieked.

However, it was too late. The doors of the lift had already closed. The attendant pushed a key into the slot, which allowed members of staff to go to floors normally out of bounds to guests.

"Where the hell are you taking me?" Agnes yelled.

But when she saw that the lift was soaring up, bypassing any of the usual floor levels, she knew exactly where they were going. She had found herself in the hotel storage room once before. At that time, she had been drugged and dumped on a sofa. The man behind her kidnapping had planned to throw her off the roof once the hotel had been shut down for the night. Fortunately for her, on that occasion, she had awoken from her stupor earlier than her abductor had thought, which meant she had been able to raise the alarm before he had been able to kill her.

However, the burning question today was, would her luck hold out again?

Chapter Forty

After Larry Parker's release from custody, Detectives Smithers and Jones had followed him very closely. His first stop had been his home, where his parents had warmly welcomed him on the doorstep. Both detectives had wondered whether he might stay there for the rest of the day. However, a short while later, Larry left the house and caught a bus heading towards the city centre. Changing routes along the way, he eventually ended up on the quayside.

"I think we can guess where he's going to from here," Jones said, taking out his phone. "I'll report in."

Smithers nodded. "Yes, but we still need to keep an eye on him."

Once Jones had made his report, the detectives stepped out of the car and made their way past a coach parked outside the hotel. The passengers were making their way into the hotel, while the driver was unloading the luggage.

"Maybe I should wait out here," Smithers said. "Your clothes look a little more in keeping with the likes of this hotel. Besides, I went in there the last time. Someone on the desk might recognize me."

Jones laughed. "Okay, but keep your phone handy. Any problems and I'll give you a shout."

"Fine, but if you're going to shout, will I really need my phone?"

Smithers grinned. "Your holler carries for miles."

Joke over, Jones entered the hotel.

The reception was quite busy. At first, Jones couldn't see Larry, but after glancing around, he spotted him talking to one of the waiters near the sitting room.

The waiter shrugged his shoulders and shook his head. Whatever Larry had asked him, the man didn't know the answer. Or maybe he was reluctant to say anything at this point? As a detective, Jones had learned not to take anything at face value, but to always consider the opposite side of the coin.

Trailing Larry further across the reception area, the detective saw him stop again. This time, he had confronted a woman. Jones didn't fail to notice how surprised she looked to see him, or how quickly she composed herself and gave Larry a hug. To anyone else, the embrace would have seemed quite genuine. However, Jones could tell that her enthusiasm was faked, even though Larry appeared pleased enough to see her.

But then Larry's attention was drawn to the people gathering by the lift. Following his gaze, Jones saw that a group of people who had just checked into the hotel were waiting to go up to their rooms. One of the hotel porters, who had a trolley packed with luggage, had his finger permanently pressed on the button. But the dial above the doors showed that the lift still hadn't moved from the top of the building.

As he had expert knowledge of the hotel lift, Larry went to offer his help. He pressed his ear to the lift doors. Sometimes, if you listened hard enough, the soft hum of the lift machinery could be heard whirring into action. However, he stepped back in shock when he thought he heard the sound of someone in trouble. Turning to the crowd, he asked them to stay quiet for a few minutes, before listening again. There was no doubt about it. Someone was in distress. Even some of the people near to the door heard the screams echoing down the lift shaft.

Realizing something was up, Detective Jones hurried across and pushed his way through. "What's going on?"

"I don't know," Larry replied. "I think someone might be stuck in the lift. But it can't be a guest. The lift appears to be up in the storage area – out of bounds to the public. Therefore, it must be a member of staff, except..."

"Except what...?" Jones pressed.

"Members of staff aren't supposed to use this lift to visit the storage area during the day," Larry continued. "There's a goods lift at the back of the hotel, where supplies are unloaded and taken straight up to the storage rooms." Larry gestured towards the lift in front of them. "This one is only meant to be used when stocks to the bar or the restaurant are replenished and that is done late at night."

Jones nodded and then told everyone to be quiet, while he listened carefully. There was certainly someone in trouble up there. But he didn't believe they were simply trapped in the lift. There was definitely terror in the voice. He had been a detective long enough to know the difference. Pulling out his phone, he called Smithers. "We have a problem!"

"What's the quickest way up there?" Jones asked, once he knew his partner was on his way.

"Like I said, there's a lift at the back of the hotel," Larry replied.

"Okay, take us there," Jones said, as his partner charged towards them.

"But who are you?" Larry asked.

"The police," was the quick response.

Chapter Forty-One

"What do you plan to do with me?" Agnes screamed out, once the lift pulled to a halt and the doors had swept open.

She had a darn good idea what was going to happen, but she was trying to stall for time. Someone might just happen to come up here for something from the storeroom and see what was going on.

"Why couldn't you keep you bloody nose out of it?" he yelled. "You could have gone on living your life of luxury with everyone at your beck and call. You love that, don't you? Having people run around after you. But, no, you had to interfere in something that didn't concern you. You had to go poking around. I saw you talking with the woman at the café yesterday. I suppose she told you everything you wanted to hear." He paused for breath. "The police already had a suspect. They were happy, I was happy. Why couldn't you have left it at that?"

"Larry is innocent!" she screamed back at him. "I couldn't allow him to be sent to prison for murders he didn't commit."

"How did you know he was innocent? How did you know he didn't kill those women? Just because he acts like a nice guy and cozies up to the guests, doesn't mean he's some saint."

"But it was you, wasn't it, Brian? You killed those two women and then tried kill Sue."

"Yes, it was me. I admit it," he gloated. "Cool, eh?"

Agnes could hardly believe what she was hearing. There was nothing 'cool' about murder.

"Why? Why did you do it?"

"You know why I did it," he retorted. "I'm sure the lovely Pauline across the road will have told you – or, if she didn't, you'll have worked it out."

"You tell me. I'd like to hear it from you." Agnes was desperate to keep him talking.

Surely someone would call for the lift any minute now and it would go sailing down? But, come to think of it, why hadn't someone called for it already?

"Well now, let me see. Where shall I begin?" He tapped his chin with his forefinger.

He began by telling her about his short relationship with Janet and how she had ended it. Most of what he told her, she had already heard from Pauline earlier that day. Therefore, while he was talking, she took the opportunity to glance around the walls of the lift. There should be an emergency button somewhere. Most lifts had one. Just in case passengers got stuck between floors, due to some sort of failure. Usually it was located on the panel of buttons near the doors. However, Brian's arm was partly covering the panel, so she couldn't see all the buttons.

"Am I boring you," he asked.

He had noticed her eyes scanning the lift's interior.

"Not at all," she replied.

He stepped to one side. "If you're looking for this, I've already disabled it," he said, pointing towards the emergency button. "And just so you know, I have also locked the doors open. Meaning that even if someone downstairs calls for the lift, it won't work."

Agnes sighed in dismay. It appeared Brian had thought of everything. Why hadn't she waited in her room for Alan, instead of rushing off down to the sitting room? But then she recalled how she had met Brian by the lift on her floor. Had he been expecting her to leave her room? No, it was more likely he had planned to burst in on her. It seemed that whatever she had done, she would have been trapped.

"Now that's out of the way, shall I carry on?"

"Why not? It seems neither of us is going anywhere." She shrugged.

"Well, you're not, that's for sure," he replied.

"But why did you have to kill anyone?" Agnes asked, trying to put his last statement out of her mind. "For goodness' sake, just because a relationship ends, it doesn't mean that you have to kill your ex-girlfriend. You would have found someone else – life moves on."

"No one dumps me!" he shrieked. "I should have been the one to end the relationship, not her. The moment she did that to me, I knew she had to die."

By now, his face was bright red and eyes were almost bulging from their sockets. Agnes recalled that Brian had never been as friendly as Larry. Even when he had tried to sound pleasant, there had always been something about his manner which gave away the fact he was putting on an act. However, today she was seeing the true side of this young man, and it was frightening.

"But why did you have to kill Wendy Hamilton? What had she done?"

He lifted one shoulder. "She knew me, so why not? She could have pointed the finger at me." He took a deep breath. "Wendy and I went out together for a while, but when I realised she wasn't my type, I ended the relationship. How was I to know that she would meet up with Janet somewhere down the line?"

"You're saying, because she became friendly with Janet, she had to die?" Agnes couldn't believe what she was hearing.

"Yes. Of course she did. Don't you see? Once she heard about Janet, she would have spoken to the police. I couldn't have that."

Agnes stared at him. "But I don't understand. Janet was still alive when you stabbed Wendy. What if you'd had a change of heart and decided to forget the whole thing and get on with your life?"

"Why would I have done that?"

"I don't know." Agnes shook her head. "But say, for instance, that you met someone new at a club that same evening, you might have got together and started a whole new relationship."

"What is it with people like you?" He prodded his finger at Agnes. "I think you watch too many old movies. That sort of thing doesn't happen in real life."

"Doesn't it?" Agnes said, pushing his hand away. "It seems to work for a lot of people!"

Just then, a sound came from somewhere outside the lift. On one hand, Agnes hoped that someone might have come upstairs to the storeroom. Yet on the other, it would be best if no one ventured up here. She knew now that Brian wouldn't hesitate to kill anyone who got in his way.

Brian moved towards the doors and carefully glanced around but, as he didn't see anyone, he moved back into the lift.

"Come on, lady, we're wasting time. Let's get this over with."

Agnes shrank away from him as he stepped towards her.

"Wait! There are still a few things I would like to know," she insisted. "Did you kill the man who was later found in the River Tyne?"

"Short answer, yes," he snapped.

"Why? What had *he* done to you?"

"Nothing." He grinned. "But he was a friend of Wendy's and he happened to see me at the Central Station. I couldn't take the risk that he might have seen me stab Wendy, so he had to go. We had met once before. Next question!"

"He was a friend of Wendy?" Agnes said, slowly.

"Yes! Do I have to repeat everything I say?" Brian sighed. "Look, Alex lives abroad. She met him when she was on holiday one year and they kept in touch. He had come to England for a visit and I believe he was staying with her."

Agnes was still thinking through his last statement. The man lived abroad and was staying with Wendy. That was the reason no one had come forward to identify him. No one knew him!"

"Okay, can we get on with this?" Brian interrupted her thoughts.

"Did you know that Wendy was pregnant?"

That seemed to shake him for a moment.

"What? No, I didn't!" The words shot out of his mouth, when he recovered. "She told me that she didn't want to have sex until she was older. I guess the bitch lied to me. Another reason for me to kill her!"

"No, she didn't," Agnes replied. "Lie to you, that is. And even if she did, it is no reason for her to die."

"What the hell are you talking about…?" Brian broke off and thought for a moment. "Oh, I see, so she did it," he spluttered. "She went ahead and got pregnant for the couple who couldn't have a baby. She said she wanted to help and she needed the money." He looked back at Agnes. "Ah well, I guess the couple will have to find someone else now, won't they? Though I think they will find it difficult to find another virgin."

"You mean the couple particularly wanted a virgin to carry their child?"

"Yep!" Brian replied. "At least that's what Wendy told me – and before you ask, I have no idea why. That's why they were willing to pay so much money for her to carry it."

"Do you know why Wendy needed the money?" Agnes asked.

"She wanted to move abroad." He shrugged. "Maybe she planned to start a whole new life with Alex. But who the hell cares, anyway? They're both dead and gone now."

"How can you be so flippant about murdering these young people?"

He shook his head. "I have no problem with it. Actually, if you're interested, Pauline would have been next on my list, but then I saw her chatting to Sue. It struck me that she might have told Sue something incriminating. I couldn't allow her to pass on the information to anyone, especially the police, so I got to her first. Then I saw Pauline talking to you, so you definitely had to be next. But don't you worry – I *will* get around to Pauline once you are out of the way. Then no one will be any the wiser."

He took a step closer to Agnes. By now, she was pinned against the wall of the lift.

"Why did you have to put the blame on Larry?" Agnes gasped, trying to keep him talking. "What had *he* done to you?"

"Simple. I had to throw someone to the wolves. It didn't take me long to realise that Larry was the best option. Everyone loved Larry. He was their star player. But, with him out of the way, they would all look at me and I would get promoted to his job."

"How can you be so sure? Other members of staff would have applied for the job."

"Yes, but they wouldn't have got it."

"Why not? Someone might have been at the hotel longer than you."

"My aunt would have made sure the job went to me."

Agnes re-ran that last statement through her mind. Brian had an aunt working at the hotel?

"There now, I hope that makes you feel better." Brian said, calmly. "You can die happy, now that you know the truth."

"You won't get away with killing me. Once my body is found up here, they'll speak to every member of staff until they find the murderer."

"Who said anything about finding your body up here?"

He grinned at her puzzled expression.

"Why do you think we are still here in the lift? Once you are dead, I'll move the lift up a little further and drop your body down the lift shaft, where it will lie and rot." Brian laughed. "People will use this lift every day. Yet they'll never know that, beneath their feet, a previous guest is lying there rotting away and all because she couldn't mind her own damn business." He waved his arms in the air. "Except me, of course, I'll be doing a dance every time the lift reaches the ground floor."

He screwed up his eyes. "But this wasn't the place I had in mind. My first thoughts had been to kill you on the quayside, your favourite haunt and dump you in the river. But, with your friendship with the chief inspector, I couldn't risk hanging around. You had to die today, either in your room, or this lift. I guess you chose it to be this lift as you came to me."

"You're insane!" Agnes cried out.

"And you, lady, are dead."

Brian pulled a knife from his pocket and lurched forward. But before he could strike, he was grabbed and pulled away.

"Take your hands off me!" Brian yelled, as he fought to free himself from the grip of the two detectives. "I'll kill you all!"

But his protests were no good, as by now he had been handcuffed.

While this was going on, Larry squeezed past and put his arm around Agnes. "Are you okay?" he said.

She nodded. "I am now."

"I am arresting you for the murder of…"

"You've got nothing on me!" Brian screamed, as Detective Smithers continued reading him his rights. "I'll deny everything. It'll be my word against hers."

"I don't think so." Jones took out his mobile phone and switched on the recording he had made of Brian's confession.

"Now, Larry," said Smithers. "How do we get this lift back down to the ground floor?"

Chapter Forty-Two

Jones had called in to the station to inform them of the situation at the hotel, the moment he and Smithers had heard the voices coming from the lift. Andrews, who had taken the call, had immediately instructed uniformed officers to attend the scene, before calling his DCI with the news.

"I understand Jones recognised the voice to be that of Mrs Lockwood. But they are ready to pounce. Larry Parker is with them. Apparently, he showed them another route to where the lift was stationed. Uniform are already on their way," he had told his boss. "I'll be there ASAP."

By the time he received the call, Alan had almost reached the hotel; he could see it at the other end of the quayside. Another couple of minutes and he would be there. Nevertheless, he turned on the flashing blue lights and slammed his foot down hard on the accelerator.

A few seconds later, he pulled up outside the hotel. He took another call from his sergeant who by now was on his way, before hurrying inside to find a crowd gathered in front of the lift. Most were guests staying at the hotel, but there were also several members of staff hovering around. As he pushed his way through, Alan caught sight of Mr Jenkins with his ear pressed against the lift doors.

"Detective Chief Inspector Johnson," Alan said, showing his warrant card, even though he was aware the manager knew who he was. "We've had a report that there's a problem here."

"I don't know why you were called, Chief Inspector. There's absolutely nothing to worry about." The manager gestured towards the lift. "The lift has jammed up in the storage area."

"Oh, I see, so there's nothing for me to worry about," Alan retorted. "If that's the case, why have two of my detectives called in, saying they've arrested a member of your staff who's confessed to the murders of three people and the attempted murder of a fourth?"

"There has to be some mistake." Mr Jenkins looked round at the shocked faces surrounding him. "Perhaps we should discuss this in my office."

"There's no mistake," Alan replied. "And I think it might be best if we wait here to see who it is they've arrested."

Alan's eyes were glued on the lift doors as they slid open. Smithers and Jones were the first to emerge. They were almost blinded by the flashlight of a camera shooting photographs of the scene. Shielding their eyes, the detectives hauled their prisoner out of the lift and handed him over to the uniformed officers, who had arrived a few minutes earlier.

Agnes followed closely behind. She looked a little shaken, but she smiled when she saw Alan making his way over to her. Larry was by her side. He looked even more stunned than Agnes. The camera continued to flash. But now, the photographer was concentrating on Agnes.

Alan swung around to find Harold Armstrong behind him. "Give me that!" he yelled.

There was no way photos of Agnes were going to be splashed all over the news that evening. Not if he could help it.

"No!" Armstrong replied, pulling the camera close to his chest. "This is my job. I have every right to be here."

Andrews, who had just arrived on the scene, had heard every word. He took a step forward and bumped into Harold, knocking the camera from his hands.

"Oops, I'm so sorry," the sergeant said, picking up the camera. "But I know someone who could fix this. I'll take it to him this evening. You'll have it back tomorrow – he's brilliant at all this technical stuff."

"It's okay, I'll see to it." Harold held out his hand.

However, Andrews wasn't having any of that. "No. I wouldn't dream of it. Leave it with me." He cast his eyes on the camera. "Unless you have something on here that isn't legal – in which case, that would be another matter."

"Of course I haven't." Harold quickly withdrew his hand. "Thank you. I'll look forward to hearing from you."

The photographer gave Andrews a card showing where he could be reached, before shuffling off. A woman stepped out of the crowd and joined him before he reached the door.

"That was pretty swift thinking, Andrews." Alan sounded impressed.

"I think you already knew that I didn't like the man," the sergeant said, as he watched Armstrong leave the hotel. "I agree he has a job to do. Nevertheless, I still can't help wondering how he manages to appear at every crime scene at the same time as the police."

"Yes, we've discussed that before, Andrews. Have that camera checked out but at the same time, see what else you can dig up about him." He paused. "Also look into the background of his lady friend. Maybe she's getting the information as to where the crimes have taken place from someone at the station, before passing them on to Armstrong."

Andrews raised his eyebrows in disbelief.

"Come on, Andrews, how else would he get to the scene at the same time as the police?"

"But from whom? Who would do such a thing…?" Andrews closed his eyes for a moment as he thought back over the last couple of days.

"You don't mean Morris?"

"Morris?" Agnes interrupted, recalling the moment she had seen him talking to the woman on the quayside.

Alan nodded. "Yes, do you know something?"

She quickly told them what she had seen from her window. "But why would Morris pass on information to her? It doesn't make sense – unless she's blackmailing him. Yet, that doesn't make any sense, either. What could she have on him?"

"I don't know, Agnes, but we'll damn well find out." He looked at Andrews. "Not a word to anyone about this. You and I will speak to him together in private."

Just then, they were joined by Smithers and Jones.

"I have everything on my phone, sir," Jones said, tapping his pocket.

"I'm just thankful you both happened to be at the hotel." Agnes smiled at the two detectives.

"Yes, me too," Alan replied, thoughtfully. He realised they wouldn't have been there if he hadn't released Larry and then sent the two of them to follow him.

"We'll see you back at the station, sir," said Smithers.

Alan nodded.

"I'm surprised they want to hurry back to the station," Agnes said.

"Oh, I can assure you that they aren't going back to *work*." Alan laughed. "They'll be celebrating the closure of the case with the rest of their colleagues."

He glanced across at Larry. "Is he okay?"

"A bit in shock, I think."

"A little like Mr Jenkins," Alan said.

He pointed across to where the hotel manager was trying desperately to calm down the guests.

"Why don't you all go into the sitting room and enjoy a drink on the house?" they heard him say, as he wiped the back of his hand across his forehead. "The porters will have everything in your rooms by the time you go upstairs."

"Well, now that we have the real suspect in custody, perhaps we could enjoy a drink in the bar," Alan said, turning back to Agnes.

"Not so fast, Alan, there's someone else here at the hotel who I think you might like to have a quiet word with."

"Who? I thought Brian was working alone."

"He has an aunt who works here. I understand it was her who made sure he got the job in the first place and was even planning to get him promoted. I'm not saying that she was aware that he was the murderer, but it's possible it might have crossed her mind."

"Do you know who this person is?" Alan asked.

"Florence Telford, the staff supervisor."

"But I understood that she was helping you."

"I thought so too, at first," Agnes replied. "But there was something about her that made me think again. I now believe she was misleading me in order to help her nephew. When she said the head porter had been arguing with Larry at Christmas, I went along with it. I had no reason to doubt her word. Besides, I couldn't even check what she had said, because Peter, the head porter had since left the hotel after finding himself another job. However, earlier today, I learned that the argument hadn't been with Larry at all. It had been with Brian, and it had nothing to do with the staff outing that evening."

"Who did you hear that from?"

"Peter – I just happened to bump into him in the reception area. He had called in at the hotel to see a few old friends."

She omitted to mention how she had gone out of her way to 'bump into' him. She also refrained from mentioning how Pauline had misled the police. That could wait until another day. Actually, there were probably a few things, which could wait until another day. For the moment, she was just delighted that Larry had been proved innocent.

Alan nodded and turned to Andrews, who had been listening to the conversation. "Find Mrs Telford and take her in for questioning."

"Well, it's been quite a day," Agnes said, as the sergeant strode off to the staff supervisor's office, "and it's not over yet."

"I think you should take it easy for the rest of the day. We could have a drink in the bar and…" Alan began.

"Are you kidding me?" Agnes grinned. "Have you forgotten that we're due to meet the estate agent any minute now? We're going to view the apartment." She glanced at the clock behind the reception desk. "If you put your foot down, we should still get there in time. I told him to hang around for a little while in case you were tied up."

"About the apartment…" Alan began. "Can we have a quick word about that?"

But Agnes was already making her way towards the hotel entrance.

"Tell me about it on the way," she called out, as the doors slid open.

The End

About the Author

Eileen Thornton was born and brought up on Tyneside. She moved to London shortly after she was married, where she and her husband lived for twenty-five years. She now lives in Kelso in the Scottish Borders.

Her first published novel, The Trojan Project, is a suspenseful, intriguing thriller, shortly followed by a fun romance, Divorcees.Biz. A novel she hoped would show her readers that there was a lighter, more fun side to her personality.

Only Twelve Days came next. This is a charming love story set back in the late 1970's; a time before computers and mobile phones took over.

Eileen then decided to put together a collection of her short stories, previously published in UK magazines. This anthology is called A Surprise for Christine. The stories are all light-hearted and so easy to read.

In recent years, Eileen has turned to writing a series of cosy murder mysteries with Agnes Lockwood as the female amateur sleuth. Vengeance on Tyneside is the third in the series.

Other novels in the series;

Murder on Tyneside
Death on Tyneside

Eileen Thornton can be reached at:

http://www.eileenthornton.com/
http://www.lifeshard-winehelps.blogspot.com/
http://www.facebook.com/eileenthornton

Printed in Poland
by Amazon Fulfillment
Poland Sp. z o.o., Wrocław